Marjorie Wilenski was born 6 June 1889.

She attended the University of London just before World War I. She later married art critic and historian Reginald Wilenski, and the couple lived in St. John's Wood, London.

In 1939, just before the war that provided the setting for her one novel, *Table Two*, she was employed at a department store. The setting of the novel itself, which followed in 1942, strongly suggests she took on important war work in London during the conflict.

Marjorie Wilenski died 25 May 1965.

MARJORIE WILENSKI

TABLE TWO

With an introduction by
Elizabeth Crawford

DEAN STREET PRESS

A Furrowed Middlebrow Book
FM35

Published by Dean Street Press 2019

First published in 1942 by Faber & Faber

Cover by DSP

ISBN 978 1 913054 27 4

www.deanstreetpress.co.uk

INTRODUCTION

ELIZABETH BOWEN described *Table Two* as 'the most strik-
ing novel about women war workers that this war has, as far
as I know, produced' (*Tatler*, 25 Nov 1942). She particularly
commended it as a 'study of feminine psychology under wartime
Ministry conditions' and praised the 'subtle characterisation'
of its protagonists, women, of different ages and backgrounds,
who, during the autumn of 1940, work at Table Two in the
Translation Department of the 'Ministry of Foreign Intelligence'. Marjorie Wilenski surely had experience of women such
as these, relishing their interaction in this her only novel.

Marjorie Isola Harland (1889-1965) was born in Kensington,
London, the elder daughter of Wilson Harland, an engineer, and
his wife, Marie. Her younger sister, Eileen, was born in 1893.
Other details of Marjorie's life are infuriatingly sketchy. The
papers filed by both parents in a long-drawn-out case for judicial
separation suggest that in her early years Marjorie witnessed
many upsetting scenes in the family home, her mother citing
in lurid detail numerous instances of her husband's drunken
violence and swearing. By 1902 the couple had separated,
Wilson Harland returning to live with his mother in Brixton
while Marie retained custody of her daughters.

In 1907 the three were living at 37 Dorset Square, Maryle-
bone when Eileen died, aged only 14. The house is large and it
may be that Marie took in lodgers, although the female American singer and three Austrian businessmen staying there on the
night of the 1911 census are described as 'visitors' rather than
boarders. Nothing else is known of Marjorie's early years other
than that she was clearly well-schooled for she graduated from
Bedford College in 1911 with a 2nd class degree in history. Three
years later, on 5 August 1914, she married Reginald Howard
Wilenski (1887-1975) at Kensington Registry Office.

At this stage of his life Wilenski was something of a bohemian, having cut short his time at Oxford to try his luck as an
artist in Paris. Returning to London he maintained a Kensing-

ton studio until 1915 but finding that creating art did not pay instead turned his hand to art criticism, for which he became renowned. During the First World War he spent some time working in the intelligence department of the War Office and by September 1939 had again been recruited for war work, this time by the Ministry of Information. Marjorie, meanwhile, appears on the Register taken on 29 September 1939 as 'luggage buyer in a department store', a situation that would certainly have provided her with plenty of opportunity to observe her fellow workers. With a nod to her own experience, one of the occupants of Table Two, Mrs Just, had previously been 'an assistant-buyer in an Oxford Street store'.

In fact Marjorie's position in that department store might have been similar to that once held by 48-year-old Elsie Pearne, perhaps the novel's most intriguing character, dominating as she does Table Two with her bad temper and sharp tongue. She had once ruled over offices in Paris, Berlin, Barcelona, and Geneva but now, driven out of mainland Europe by war, was forced to accept work with lower status and pay. Like Elsie, four others of the group had worked all their lives to support themselves and now in 1940 faced worrying uncertainty as businesses closed or moved out of London, putting thousands out of work. No wonder Miss Purbeck, who had spent a lifetime in Italian pensions tending the demands of a series of old ladies, was so fearful of losing her position as a translator. Others at the Table are voluntary 'war workers', never before having undertaken paid work but prepared now to 'do their bit' for their country. Like them, the pretty heroine, Anne Shepley-Rice, had never expected to work, but orphaned and with the family money lost, is setting out, aged 22, to earn her own living. Luckily she had the contacts and an ability in Portuguese to ensure she landed on Table Two. For what the women have in common is a facility in at least one foreign language. For some, like Elsie, this had been earned through hard study; for others it is a by-product of an entirely different way of life. Aristocratic Hon. Cecilia Dunkerley had learned 'several uncommon and useful languages' when accompanying her diplomat father to the Balkans. The tension between the 'professional workers' and the volunteers is palpable, with, at its heart, the relationship between Elsie, soured by life's treatment, and Anne, on the brink of her new life and with romance blossoming. The author's description of Elsie's rented room in Brondesbury, which she had tried to make fashionable with a 'carefully thought out' colour scheme of yellow ochre and green, touches the heart. Hanging on the wall is a print of Titian's 'Young man with Gloves', a faint likeness of a long-lost, nebulous, romantic attachment; while in her Kensington room Anne is able to display a photograph of Sebastian, her childhood sweetheart.

We first meet Table Two at lunchtime on 2 September 1940 in the Ministry of Foreign Information, which Marjorie Wilenski places on the edge of Lincoln's Inn Fields, as Elsie and Anne watch an aerial dogfight high in the 'deep blue sky'. At this time 'no-one in London was then expecting air-raids' but five days later everything changed. On 7 September the women have their first experience of the Blitz, night-time bombing that was to dominate life through the autumn. They, like other Londoners, become used to sleeping in shelters and rising the next morning to 'gape and gaze at the great craters in the streets – [which] by Friday were just a familiar and tiresome obstruction to traffic; there were too many other things to think of . . .' But this cataclysm is merely a background to the bickering and jousting for position around Table Two when it is revealed that a new Deputy Language Supervisor will soon be required.

Table Two was published in the autumn of 1942 by Faber and Faber, the firm that since the 1920s had been Reginald Wilenski's publisher. It was widely reviewed and in addition we are blessed with a view of it in the hands of a reader. For in May 1943 a copy accompanied Barbara Pym as she waited in the queue for her Women's Royal Naval Service medical. She later wrote that 'I read my novel *Table Two* by Marjorie Wilenski (obviously about the Censorship)'. Alas, she offered no further comment.

Elizabeth Crawford

CHAPTER ONE
ELSIE WALKS DOWN KINGSWAY

THAT SUMMER was the finest summer that anyone could remember in England. The sun shone all day, day after day, and it seemed that there never would be rain. Everyone said all the time "What lovely weather, if only we were able to enjoy it." For in England everyone feels that they must "enjoy" a fine day because in ordinary summers more than one fine day at a time is so rare. But nobody was able to enjoy that wonderful series of fine days because it was the summer of 1940 and nearly everyone was working all day and often all night in offices or factories or A.F.S. or A.R.P., and there were no week-ends and no summer holidays. So in the daytime all the glorious sunshine was wasted and at night the rooms were stifling behind the blackout curtains.

It was still hot and fine on the morning of September 2nd when Elsie Pearne walked down Kingsway to the Ministry of Foreign Intelligence in Lincoln's Inn Fields. Elsie was a tall gaunt woman of forty-eight. She carried her head forward and her shoulders were rounded because she was always stooping to talk to people who were less tall than herself. She walked with a long ungainly rather mannish stride and there was something mannish in her clothes—the plain black coat and skirt, white blouse with collar and tie, and round felt hat. She had a long thin face, long thin nose and a long thin mouth with lips set in a straight line that turned down at the corners, and her eyes under wide brows were small. As she walked down Kingsway which the little trees, even in this wondrous weather, were still failing to make into a boulevard, she remembered that it was now just a year since she had begun to work in the Ministry. It's a lousy job, she said to herself, but at least I'm better at it than the others.

Elsie Pearne was not much loved at the Ministry of Foreign Intelligence. She was generally referred to as rude and difficult to get on with. Most people thought that her long mouth turned down simply from bad nature and ill-temper though there were some more kindly who guessed at disappointments and hard times, neither opinion being in fact quite right.

Elsie herself often pondered on her character and her past. Sometimes she decided that, as she phrased it, she had "got on well"; at other times she decided that she had all along been a victim of other people. The nature of the verdict depended on her mood at the time of the reviewing. But the memories reviewed were always the same—her childhood home in Kentish Town with her mother, the daughter of a chemist who had married a grocer, her schooldays, her first job where she had to pick up those hateful pins, her second job where she learned that a pretty face cannot only launch ships but sink them, her business life in Paris, Berlin and Barcelona and (especially on days when she felt lonely) Benno—Benito Braun with his dark eyes and olive skin and his bright blue suit.

Her childhood memories were chiefly about her mother and Aunt Min. Her mother was always complaining that she was a moody child and that her hair could not be coaxed into long curls to hang around her shoulders like the curls of Lily, the butcher's little girl next door. Aunt Min was a fitter at Bruce and Porter's; she was skinny and dried up and always wore black and when Elsie kissed her, as of course she always had to do, her cheek had a funny stuffy smell which Elsie detested. Aunt Min came to tea every Wednesday, which was early-closing day both at Bruce and Porter's and in the Pearne grocery, and they always had crab for tea and Elsie always had to wear her best shoes and her best hair ribbon and a clean pinafore. Once when Elsie had said something at the tea-table, Aunt Min said to her mother: "That child's head is too big for her body. It wouldn't surprise me if we hear one day that she's got water on the brain," Elsie worried for a long time about that water; she puzzled as to how it could have got into her brain; and in the end she comforted herself by supposing that everyone must have water on their brain and that that was where tears came from when you cried.

At school the teachers called Elsie a clever and industrious child. But the children called her cross and ugly and pushed her out of their games or made her the butt in them when they admitted her. In revenge Elsie called their games babyish and read in front of them large books that she got from the public library just opposite the school. And indeed it was a library book that she was reading one day near her tenth birthday as she was walking home from school when it was knocked roughly from her hands. Half a dozen of the children had surrounded her, jeering and laughing, while Lily of the long curls, the butcher's daughter, kicked the book into the gutter. Elsie made a dash to pick it up and as she bent down the children knocked off her hat, pulled off her hair ribbon and tugged at her hair. Raging and crying, Elsie hit out wildly all round and caught a boy a blow on the mouth which cut his lip; the boy hit back as hard as he could and when Elsie fell sprawling, he picked up her feet, dragged her by the heels along the pavement while her head bumped against the stones and the other children danced round and screamed. Then the children began to feel they had gone too far and ran away and left her sobbing.

Elsie watched them till they were out of sight, then she picked up her book and went limping home to clean herself as best she could; she was only half finished when her mother's shrill voice came up calling her down to tea, and with horror Elsie remembered that it was Wednesday and Aunt Min would be there and that she had no time to find a clean pinafore and that her best ribbon was lying forgotten in the gutter. She went in trembling; they were all at table, Father and Mother at the ends and Aunt Min in the middle. Mrs. Pearne was pouring out steaming black tea and did not look round at the forlorn little figure in stained blue serge with a large rent in one of her black woollen stockings and with her hair, still wet and muddy, hanging lankly on her shoulders. But Aunt Min, after coldly receiving Elsie's reluctant kiss, looked her up and down and said to her mother: "What a nice child that Lily next door has grown into. She's always so neat and clean and tidy!" Then Mrs. Pearne noticed Elsie's condition. "Whatever's the matter with you?" she said sharply.

"You look a sight! Where's your new hair ribbon? What have you done to your dress? What's that bruise on your forehead?" Elsie was too humiliated and shamed to tell the truth and began a faltering story about a fall on the way home from school. "And indeed I'm not surprised," said Aunt Min, "if you were wandering along with your nose in a book the way I saw you the other day—now Lily—"

But Elsie could bear no more praise of her tormentor; "I hate Lily," she shouted. "She's horrible! She's a little bitch!"

Her mother, furious at this display of vulgarity in the presence of her prim sister, shouted at her and scolded until her father said, "Oh! Leave the kid alone! Can't you see she's upset? And ten to one she doesn't know what the word means." And this saved her from a whipping but she was sent without her tea to bed.

The next day at school the children began to jeer at Elsie again. But this time she had a bag of pepper stolen from the grocer's shop which she threatened to throw at anyone who came near her, and by the look in her eye the children understood that she meant it; stopping at a safe distance, they stared in fright at Elsie who faced them, her eyes glittering, the bag of pepper ready in her hand. After that she always had some strange weapon in her pocket and the children soon gave up trying to torment her.

Her next memory was of her scholarship. She won it for the High School when she was thirteen. It made her rapturously happy; and at once she determined that later she would get a scholarship for Oxford too. But she had only been three months at the High School when her father died, and after the funeral her mother told her that she must leave school and start to earn her living. Aunt Min was there. "If you like I'll speak for her at Bruce and Porter's," she said. "They're always wanting juniors in the workroom." And her mother answered: "There, Elsie! What do you think of that! There's a grand chance for you! Thank your Auntie for being so good, and kind." "But—but— my scholarship!" stammered Elsie. "Oh we can't bother about that!" said Aunt Min sharply. "You've got to do something now to help your mother." "I want to stay at school," said Elsie defiantly. "I've won a scholarship. It doesn't cost anything for me to be there." "And I suppose your keep doesn't cost anything either and your clothes and all the rest of it," said her mother. Elsie's eyes brimmed with tears. The bottom had fallen out of her world. She put up a fight. But of course the grown-ups won. Three weeks later she was a junior at Bruce and Porter's.

The workroom there was underheated; it always smelt of sweat because the windows were rarely opened; and the floor was perpetually covered with pins. Elsie had to carry dresses ready for fitting backwards and forwards from the workroom to the showroom; she had to carry them with her arm held out stiffly at an uncomfortable angle so that they should not be crushed on the way and she had to do this up and down five flights of stairs which meant that her arms were always aching. But the physical pain was nothing compared with the humiliation of having to pick up pins; in any spare moment she was expected to pick up the pins that were scattered over the floor and stick them into the black velvet pincushion that the fitter wore on her wrist when she went down to try the gowns on the ladies; and every time Elsie knelt down she thought of her scholarship with rage. She had been there a month when one of the girls said to her: "Why do you mind picking up them pins so much? I never minded it when I was your age and had your job. I used to stick 'em in the pincushion so as to make B and P—you know, stands for Bruce and Porter—or to make a flower or something like that. W'y, it was one of my fav'rite jobs. Can't make you out. Don't you like it 'ere?" "*Like* it?" said Elsie passionately. "*Like* it! I *hate* it." And then suddenly she flung her handful of pins into the middle of the table, snatched her hat and coat from the wall, and ran down the stairs into the street.

There was another scene when she told her mother and Aunt Min that she was done with Bruce and Porters and that she was going to learn shorthand-typing. She had come to this decision in a teashop when she had overheard a phrase: "A girl can get anywhere nowadays if she has brains and good shorthand-typing." Her mother wept at her and Aunt Min stormed. But this time Elsie won the battle and in the end her mother and Aunt Min each put up half the money to pay for her course at Clark's College.

A year later with a shorthand speed of a hundred and thirty and a typing speed of ninety-five, Elsie was in the pool of typists at Harbord's, the American "canned meat" importers in the City.

She worked in that pool for eight years; the men used to telephone up and ask specially for her—"She's ugly and rude," they said to one another, "but she can read her short-hand and she always gets things right." The other girls in the pool called her "Old Crosspatch" or "Miss Perfection". But Elsie, as she put it, "kept herself to herself", and when they talked of their boys or gazed enraptured at picture-postcards of stars from Daly's or the Gaiety theatres, she would bend sideways across her typewriter and turn the pages of a book in French or German, for in those years she had learned both languages and also French and German shorthand in evening classes at the Polytechnic. The end came when the Chairman of Harbord's wanted a new private secretary. Elsie applied. So did a pretty girl with golden curls who had recently come and who reminded her of Lily, the butcher's daughter. And this second Lily was appointed. The rage that rose up in Elsie when she heard of this injustice, returned to her in after years whenever she saw Harbord's name. For years she would buy any sort of tinned thing rather than one with Harbord's name on the label. At the time she had gone straight to the room where the head of the pool had her office; she had found it empty; on the table there was her "dossier" lying open, with "Elsie Pearne" in large letters at the top. Elsie did not try to resist the temptation. She bent down and read: "Excellent technician but bad manner." She took a piece of paper, wrote her resignation on it, and walked out.

That was in 1915 and Elsie was twenty-four. The walls of London were covered with recruiting posters and the young men were pouring from shops and offices into the army and young women were wanted to replace them. So Elsie replaced a young man in Todd's Tours, the travel bureau. She had to write and read letters in French and German to allied and neutral countries, dull work, but she had found it exciting because it gave her dreams of places with strange names on the mysterious "continent", dreams which she decided she must somehow manage to make true. And indeed the dreams came true when the war ended and the young men came back to Todd's Tours and Elsie was told that she could have a post in a branch on the Continent or leave. One of the posts offered was in Paris. Elsie took it and she was there two years.

Paris in 1919-20. For Elsie the years were full of memories, but they were memories that she imagined she was trying to forget. They were memories that clung round Benno, Benito Braun, and on her good days she pushed them from her and took refuge in the Berlin memories which were better, because in Berlin she had had her first success, and it was of Berlin that she was thinking now as she strode down Kingsway to the Ministry.

Fourteen years. She had been thirty when she went there and forty-four when she left. For fourteen years she had been Fräulein Pearne of the M.A.Inc., a woman earning first three, then five, and towards the end, six hundred a year, Fräulein Pearne, a person to be reckoned with. In the 'twenties in Berlin there were scores of people who had sleepless nights when Fräulein Pearne had frowned. And in those years she had frowned often and scolded and as she phrased it, "put the fear of God into these Huns".

It had happened in this way. First an advertisement in the *Continental Daily Mail*: "International agency has vacancy for energetic woman in Berlin." Applicants were to communicate with an address in Paris. Benno had gone, Elsie was unhappy and wanted to leave Paris, so she replied. Her landlady said that it sounded most suspicions, it was probably White Slave Traffic or cocaine. But she was wrong. It was the M.A.Inc., the Merchandising Agency Incorporated, an American firm with offices in New York, Philadelphia, Chicago, Buenos Aires, Rio de Janeiro, London, Paris and Berlin. The M.A.Inc. was a boon and a blessing to buyers, especially to buyers of big firms. To the Berlin office buyers came from all over Europe and America. If they were buyers for small firms the M.A.Inc. gave them names and addresses of suppliers "up their street". If they were buyers for big firms they sent them to the same suppliers in an M.A.Inc. car and gave them luncheon and tickets for the theatre in the evening. When the buyer had gone the M.A.Inc. saw to it that the suppliers did their part and that the things were up to sample and punctually sent off. This last had been Elsie's function as Inspector of Suppliers. The American manager who engaged her in Paris had stared at her across an enormous desk while he methodically picked his teeth with a gold toothpick starting at one corner and working systematically all round— first the upper row and then the lower. Then he said: "We've got two posts vacant in Berlin. One's for a receptionist to spoon-feed the buyers and keep 'em sweet, and the other's for an inspector to ginger the suppliers and keep 'em on the run. I reckon you'd turn the buyers sour. But you might shape fine in keeping those darned suppliers at the double. Anyway I'm willing to try you. Pack your grip and report at our Berlin office in a week."

For fourteen years Elsie had kept those Berlin suppliers on the run. The work had suited her. Her label "Excellent technician but bad manner" was the label that the post required. The M.A.Inc.'s introductions were so important to the suppliers that they dared not complain that they were bullied by Fräulein Pearne, and indeed, being Germans, they were secretly impressed by her rough manners, and the ruder she was to them the more they fawned on her. Elsie had enjoyed those years of power; she never reflected that what really made the suppliers docile was the money that came to them through the M.A.Inc. In looking back on those years she told herself that her own force of character had been the reason of her success.

But things had changed when Adolf Hitler came to power. By 1935 after two years of Nazidom, the M.A.Inc.'s business had declined. Many of the suppliers were non-Aryans and their businesses were liquidated in favour of Partei nominees. Hundreds of foreign buyers for Jewish firms in North and South America, in London and Paris, who had come regularly once or twice a year, were now seen no more. The M.A.Inc., in desperation, appointed a German, a Partei member, as general manager of the Berlin branch. Between the new manager and Elsie there was a feud from the start—for he had heard her speak contemptuously of "those Nazi frauds". The clash came when he ordered that all staff members must give the Nazi salute to the portrait of Hitler in the hall. As far as foreign members were concerned, the order was in fact illegal; but many none the less obeyed. Elsie stalked past the picture daily without turning her head towards it till one day the porter stopped her and told her rudely to salute. Elsie answered: "You mind your own business," and slapped his face. An hour later a messenger brought her three months' salary in banknotes and a curt dismissal from the M.A.Inc.

Now at the corner of Portugal Street, Elsie had come to a shop which had written up outside: "Torch batteries in stock." She went in to buy one because the evenings were drawing in now and batteries were scarce as everyone used torches in the blackout and most of the shops were perpetually sold out. "Hear the guns last night?" said the man who served her. "We never do in London. We never hear anything but warnings," answered Elsie. "You're lucky," said the man. "The guns are chronic down my way. Round the Estuary they were blazing away all night. The last All Clear didn't sound till six o'clock." "I expect we shall get them some time," said Elsie, but she did not really expect it because no one in London was then expecting air-raids; everyone had expected them all the time at the beginning and then, when they were only in the outskirts, it seemed that in the centre of London they would never come at all.

Elsie bought two batteries and she would have liked to buy a big new torch but she did not do so because she could not afford it as her salary in the Ministry was barely a third of her salary in Berlin in the later years; for here, as she reflected with annoyance, she only ranked as a translator like the other translators in the Translation Department, and though of course she translated better than any of the others, no one considered her a person of importance.

She had in fact been falling from her Berlin eminence ever since that morning when she had left the M.A.Inc. She had learned enough of the Nazis to make her feel that it might be well to get out of Germany and she had gone at once to the Berlin office of Todd's Tours and asked them for a position somewhere else. They suggested Barcelona and she went there, glad to hear no more "heiling" of Hitler and glad also of the chance to see Spain and learn some Spanish.

That had been the first move down. The salary was four hundred and she was third in command of the office and she had hated Barcelona at first sight.

She remembered it now as a place where she had had to wait every night for her dinner till nine or ten o'clock and when it came she thought it oily and uneatable; a place where the men sat all day and all night in the café and where there was nothing of the German punctuality and order; a place that she dubbed "sexy" from the first evening when she watched with secret envy the countless couples of dark-skinned young men and girls under the trees in the Ramblas, strolling up and down. One night she had strayed by mistake into the Paralelo, the seamen's quarter by the port; it was a warm night and doors were left shamelessly open; as she hurried away in disgust, with beating heart and hot with shame, she hardly believed that what she had seen was real.

She was rescued from Barcelona by the Franco war. For Todd's Tours insisted that all the women must immediately leave. They sent Elsie to Geneva. But that was another move on the downward path. For when she got there she found that the only job they could give her was graded at three hundred. But she liked Geneva, where she arrived at sunset and thought the strawberry ice-cream peaks of Mont Blanc and the blue lake were as lovely as a coloured picture-postcard and where she found an English pension and where everything struck her as nice and tidy and clean. So she had stayed in Geneva till that August day a year ago, when in a train crowded with English people, she once more hurried across a frontier. This time she was making for home, and like everyone else in the train she was wondering whether she would get there in time before the war started.

The translator's post in the Ministry was undoubtedly a third move down. But after all, she reflected, there is a war on, and it is something to be a civil servant, if only a temporary one. And sooner or later someone would be bound to notice that she was so much better than the others and then. . . .

But now she had reached the Ministry doorstep and a young R.A.F. officer in his blue uniform had his hand upon the door. He stood back for her to pass and held the door open: "Thanks," she said and she said it disagreeably because he made her feel shy. She showed her pass and he showed his and they walked together to the lift. As the gates opened the young man again automatically stepped back. Funny, Elsie thought, he reminds me of Benno—it's his brown skin and dark eyes—and—of course—that blue suit—and his opening the door for me. Benno used to do polite things like that.

CHAPTER TWO
TABLE TWO ASSEMBLES

THE TRANSLATION DEPARTMENT of the Ministry of Foreign Intelligence made all the translations of the Ministry's foreign documents and letters. Everyone on the staff of the Department knew some foreign languages and most of them knew several and knew them very well. The Department worked in a large room on the first floor of the Ministry's new building in Lincoln's Inn Fields. The room had windows down both sides and it looked like a schoolroom because it had groups of flat-topped desks, set nine together on each side of a central gangway. At the head of each group of desks there was a larger desk. Each group of desks was used by nine translators known as a Table, and what looked like the teacher's desk at the top was used by the Language Supervisor.

At half-past eight on the morning of 2nd September 1940 the swing doors of the Department were pushed open and Mrs.

Doweson came into the room. Mrs. Doweson was the first to arrive that morning as every other. She was a very old woman who looked at least eighty. She would not tell anyone just how old she was but it was known that she had great-grandchildren as well as grandchildren. Her husband had been killed in the Boer War, her two sons had been killed in the last war and one of her grandsons had already been killed in this war. She did not try to hide her age by a younger way of dressing; she wore an old-fashioned cloth coat and a very long full skirt which came down to her ankles, and boots which reached the bottom of her skirt and were big and sturdy, and a flat shapeless hat stuck firmly on to a small bun of white hair.

Her face had a sweet and mild expression but she was nevertheless a tough old woman, tenacious and formidable. This could be seen from the way she walked, stumping along with firm and purposeful steps, although she was hung about with burdens almost like a soldier on the march. She carried on her shoulders a service gas mask and a tin hat and on her hips swung a rolled up mackintosh and a haversack with a thermos flask sticking out and all sorts of odd nobbly bundles inside. In one hand she carried a big leather handbag and in the other an umbrella because although it had not rained for days she had seen so many wet English summers that she just could not believe any morning that it would not rain before she left the Department at five o'clock in the evening. Fine or wet she always walked all the way to the office from Manchester Square where she lived; and wet or fine she always walked back in the evening. The last winter had been one of weeks of snow and frost, hard and bitter as the summer was hot and fine, but Mrs. Doweson had walked through the snow and slush and mud as steadily as through the heat and dust. Of course she had learned to walk like this when she was a young woman and there were no motor-cars and women always walked great distances to get to where they wanted to go, and wore long heavy skirts to walk in because that was the fashion; and somehow she had skipped the time in between and had not grown soft getting used to motor-cars and the like.

On this fine morning the sun was streaming into the Translation Department when Mrs. Doweson came through the swing doors which flapped behind her. She took off all her bundles and laid them on the desk, and she was glad that she was the first to arrive and that no one else was in the room; for now she had a chance to do what she always came so early to do—to open all the windows as wide as they would go. She did this now with gusto. As she opened window after window, the wind which began with a gentle breeze, blew more and more strongly through the room, lifting up all the papers which lay on the desks and driving them on to the floor where they fluttered about in confusion.

Just as Mrs. Doweson had finished opening the last window a young woman pushed against the swing doors which were blown against her by the force of the wind from within. The young woman pushed harder and the door gave and the extra draught made a great whirlwind through the room. Mrs. Doweson sat down quietly at her desk. But the newcomer ran quickly across the room and tried to catch a vase of flowers on one of the bigger desks which was just being blown over by the wind; it fell before she got there and all the water spread over the desk and dripped down to the floor.

The young woman's name was Mrs. Just. She was Deputy Language Supervisor and someday she hoped she would become Supervisor. She was the daughter of a hairdresser who had married a French girl and before joining the Ministry, she had been an assistant-buyer in an Oxford Street store. She was about thirty-five, she dressed well and she had a good figure but she was by no means pretty; in fact she would have been a very plain young woman if she had not been so clever. Her face was really not at all pretty but it was a very long time since anyone but herself had seen it as Nature made it and she herself only looked at it long enough to put it to rights. She knew just what to do to improve it and put the right coloured paint in the right places and had her hair very neat and shining and cut in the right shape.

But as she ran across the room now to pick up the fallen flowers, the wind was blowing her hair out of place and her face was an unbecoming red because she was so angry with Mrs. Doweson for opening all the windows. She wanted to pick up the papers and mop up the wet mess and shut the windows all at the same time. She jumped at the papers and put weights on them to keep them from blowing away again and she flapped at the spilt water with blotting paper and dragged open a drawer to find a duster to soak it up and she shut all the windows down one side of the room with just the same bang that Mrs. Doweson made when she opened them. And all the time she was looking angrily at Mrs. Doweson and Mrs, Doweson was trying to look as if she was suffocating and could not breathe without great pain now that so many of the windows were closed. When Mrs. Just began to shut the windows on the other side Mrs. Doweson got up and began pulling down the blinds on the side where Mrs. Just had already shut the windows. That was the side where the sun was streaming in and Mrs, Doweson pulled down the blinds to show how much she was suffering from the heat.

And now the stage was set for a wrangle. But no wrangle came because Mrs. Doweson, though a stout old fighter was also a stout old aristocrat and too proud to wrangle and Mrs. Just who had always worked with other people and had always got on with them, had done so because she had found out at the age of sixteen that one never gets anywhere if one quarrels with the people one works with every day. So after shutting a few more windows, she left the last four open and turned to Mrs. Doweson and said, "Good morning", and then, "I'm afraid the others will want the blinds up but we'll just leave them and let them settle it themselves." She smiled quite nicely as she said this and old Mrs. Doweson smiled back and asked if she had heard from her husband. Mrs. Just's face lit up. "Yes," she said. "I heard from him only this morning—of course it doesn't say much—it's only the usual Prisoner-of-War postcard. But he's quite well and had all his parcels."

"I'm so glad," said old Mrs. Doweson. "It's a bad show and we're not through yet."

"I'm afraid that is true," said Mrs. Just and she smoothed down her hair and went over to her desk and she and Mrs. Doweson chatted amiably for a few minutes more.

Then Elsie Pearne came in and that was the end of amiable chatter and peace. She came through the swing doors and glared at once at the four end windows which were still open for these windows were just behind her own place at Table Two. Striding over to her desk, she slammed down her attaché-case and her gas mask and her bag and pulled off her hat and gloves, looking angrier each second. Then she went to the windows and banged them to. Her face was quite white and her small eyes were glittering. She knew it was Mrs. Doweson who had opened the windows and when she had finished shutting them she swung round and glared angrily down at her from her great height, with her head thrust forward and her chin sticking out. "If you think I'm going to get lumbago just because you're a fresh-air fiend, you've got another think coming," she shouted, and then she noticed the blinds which were pulled down and strode across the room. "And if you think I'm going to go blind working in the dark, you've another think coming there too," she added in the same loud angry voice and noisily jerked up the blinds. When she had finished doing this she went over to her desk and sat down and began ostentatiously to arrange it for work, while Mrs. Doweson and Mrs. Just smiled meaningly at each other in silence and exchanged little nods and shrugs.

The swing doors now began to open and shut every minute because it was nearly nine o'clock and all the translators were arriving. Miss Saltman, the Language Supervisor of Table Two, was one of those who came in now. She was bustling and hurrying because she was later than she had meant to be. She always was later than she had meant to be and she was always bustling and hurrying and losing things and forgetting things and going back to fetch them. But as she had Mrs. Just to put everything straight for her and to find everything that was lost, she got on very well and all the higher powers at the Ministry thought she was exceedingly efficient. She was about fifty and was plain and didn't do anything about it. She was the daughter of a Harley

Street specialist who had left her a comfortable income and her hobby was painting. Every year she exhibited in the Royal Academy the small landscapes she painted in the South of France and in Spain and Italy and the other pleasant places where she spent most of her time. In the summer of 1939, she was in a more fortunate position than those who had to earn their living and stay in whatever job they were in already, and she was able to go to the Ministry and volunteer for service if war came. She knew three languages extremely well, and she was on the spot, and directly the war started she was appointed head of Table Two. The appointment could not be called unfortunate; all her table liked her and said that though she was always fussing and never knew where anything was, and they were sure that Mrs. Just did most of her work for her, she wasn't really a bad supervisor and one knew where one was with her because she never got a "down" on people and because she was always amiable and very polite.

When she came in now, Mrs. Just stood up and took her hat and gas mask from her and hung them up and picked up her gloves and newspaper which she had dropped and found her glasses for her and got her settled down at her desk. Miss Saltman promptly lost the most important paper on her desk and Mrs. Just was in the process of finding it for her again when they were interrupted by a hand which thrust at them a large bunch of roses and by a voice which babbled:

"Couldn't resist them. A man was selling them just near the bus stop and I jumped off and wasted my fare, threepence it was and I always think it's a ridiculous amount for such a short distance really but the roses were so lovely and the man looked so tired and thin and with everything so bad people don't buy flowers as much as they used to do and do you know he reminded me of a man who used to sell flowers in Vienna just near the office where I was—" Miss Saltman held up a warning hand and the voice broke off. "Oh! Am I making too much noise?" said Mrs. Jolly, its owner, giggling a little and shaking her golden curls.

"A little too much," said Miss Saltman. "Thank you so much for the roses. They're really lovely." She laid a finger to her lips as Mrs. Jolly began to talk again. "Past nine o'clock and time to begin work. Run along now and do at least look as if you were going to start."

Mrs. Jolly trotted off obediently. She was about fifty, short and fat and she had her hair dyed bright gold and wore it in little fluffy curls all over her head and she had a rather pink face which was almost always flushed because she was almost always excited and hot with the exertion of talking so much. She wore dresses which fitted her tightly and the general effect that she made was that she was bursting—talk bursting out of her lips and her body bursting out of her clothes.

When she reached her desk she sat down and opened it and turned to Elsie Pearne. "How time does fly!" she said loudly. "Here we are nearly at the end of the summer though really with all the—" She stopped short and put her hand over her mouth as a loud "Hush!" came from the left-hand side of the room. This side belonged to Table One. For some reason which everyone had forgotten, there was a permanent feud between Table One and Table Two and nobody at one table ever spoke to anyone at the other table, unless she could think of something disagreeable to say.

With her hand still over her mouth, Mrs. Jolly turned round and stared angrily at Table One where all the translators were pretending to be already hard at work in order to set an example to Table Two. Then she flounced back into her seat. "Well, really," she said indignantly, "considering that it's only—"

"Oh! Do be quiet, Mrs. Jolly, and let me get on with my work," said Elsie, twisting round in her seat so that her back was turned on her talkative neighbour. Mrs. Jolly stopped talking but she could not be quiet and her jaws moved up and down as she continued the conversation to herself. Everyone was always telling her to be quiet and she would stop talking for a moment and try to remember that she talked too much. And then some exciting thought would come into her head and she had to say it out aloud and then she was off again and could not stop till she was pulled up again. She was a nuisance but she was very generous and good-natured and kind and every day she came with little presents of sweets or fruit or flowers for the people she worked with. Everyone liked her but everyone liked her best when she was talking to someone else and leaving her in peace.

"How very kind of Mrs. Jolly!" said Miss Saltman, and like everyone who has just been given flowers she put the roses up to her face and smelt them several times to show how much she liked them; she then handed them to Mrs. Just who said she would get some water for them. Before getting up Mrs. Just laid the papers she had been sorting on the far side of the desk where she hoped Miss Saltman could not reach them. But by the time she came back with the roses in a vase, Miss Saltman had taken up the papers and already she had lost the most important which had slipped out and now lay in the waste-paper basket while she turned the other papers over and over trying to find it.

Mrs. Just put the roses on the desk and gently took the papers from Miss Saltman's hand and put them into order again and found the one which was lost. Then she put them one by one before Miss Saltman and suggested what she would do with each one. Most of the papers were the documents to be translated and Miss Saltman had to divide them among the translators but, as she was always forgetting which translator knew which language, it was Mrs. Just who had to allocate them and to tell the translator when the document was long and difficult that Miss Saltman had particularly asked her to do it. So now Mrs. Just went down to Elsie and said, "Miss Saltman says there are two things here and will you say which you would rather do. There's a short German paper which they want translated very exactly, as literally as possible, and a very long Spanish, of which they want a good clear précis."

"I'll take the Spanish," Elsie said coldly. "It's more likely to be interesting and there aren't many people here who make a clear précis. Let Mrs. Jolly do the German. She's a fancy for short things."

"Well, of all the rude people!" said Mrs. Jolly. "There is really no need to keep hinting in that way. I know—" But Miss Saltman was shaking a warning finger at her again and Mrs. Jolly's protest sank to a mutter as she began reluctantly to read the

German script, while Elsie, taking up the Spanish text and moving as far away from Mrs. Jolly as possible, began rapidly to work.

As Elsie sat there engrossed in her translation, her left elbow on the table and her left hand supporting her tilted head, she was seen to her best advantage. For the hard lines of her mouth were now in shadow and the light played on her high broad brow and the finely shaped crown of her head and seen thus it was Elsie's intelligence that seemed to dominate and Elsie's ill-humour that receded into shade.

All the translators had by now taken their places at Table Two. At the left-hand top corner of the table sat Miss Purbeck, round-faced, flabby and colourless. She was a spinster in late middle-age, of the type that can be found in any boarding house in England or the parts of the continent frequented by the English and indeed she had spent practically all her life in these surroundings. As a young woman she went out to Italy as companion to an old lady and lived with her for some years in a pension in Florence. When that old lady died she became the slave of a series of old ladies in a series of pensions, varying the monotony by occasional periods when she acted as English "Miss" to spoiled Italian children or barely kept herself alive by giving English lessons. She was badly educated and stupid and had been so knocked about by her old ladies that she had almost lost her wits but she was amiable and good-tempered. She was one of those people who take a real pleasure in death and all its accompaniments and in bad news and disaster of any sort. She never allowed any expression of optimism to go unchallenged in her presence and she was able instantly to put her finger on the weak spot in good news of any kind. She was thoroughly enjoying the war.

She sat nearly facing Elsie and was quite as willing to be friendly with her as with anyone else. But Elsie's habit of referring to Miss Purbeck, publicly and in her hearing, as "that nitwit" had not been conducive to friendship.

Next to Miss Purbeck sat Miss Younge, a plain skinny woman of about thirty, with small greenish eyes and a dingy completion. She had never been known to wear anything but the same dark blue dress, summer or winter, and it never looked very clean or very dirty; a cigarette seemed to be permanently glued to her lips and she had very large feet and wore brown shoes with rubber soles on which she crept silently about the room, managing thus to overhear a good deal that was not intended for her ears. For ten years Miss Younge had taught commercial subjects in schools in Germany and France and she knew French and German thoroughly. She was an inverted snob and she had muddle-headed ideas on Socialism and the like, which she frequently tried to express to her colleagues but was usually cut short by Elsie who was irritated by her confused loquacity. This was a perpetual source of grievance to Miss Younge who believed that she and Elsie were natural allies and should have stood together. But Elsie thought her a fool and would have none of her.

On Elsie's left-hand side was a vacant seat soon to be occupied by a new translator and next to her on her right sat the talkative Mrs. Jolly.

These four women, Elsie, Mrs. Jolly, Miss Younge and Miss Purbeck, unlike though they were in character and appearance, had one thing in common; they were all professional workers. They had all worked all their lives for their livings and were solely dependent on their exertions for their livelihood. This was not true of the other women at the table.

Of these, Mrs. Doweson sat at the end facing Miss Saltman's table. On her left was the Hon. Cecilia Dunkerley. Miss Dunkerley, hard as she worked, was undeniably an amateur for when she joined the Ministry staff she found herself in an office for the first time in her life. She was a middle-aged faded aristocratic-looking woman, daughter of a highly placed diplomatic official, and had spent much of her life in the Balkans where she had learned several uncommon and useful languages. For patriotic reasons she had felt it her duty to put these languages at the disposal of the Ministry where they were badly needed. She was hard-working and supremely conscientious but she hated the place; she disliked the office routine and the petty hardships of uncomfortable travelling and dingy lunches and found little in common with most of her colleagues who took these things as a matter of course. The buns and bags of sweets, which they ate all the time and offered to each other, caused her to shudder inwardly and she had to invent an almost permanent toothache in order to refuse them tactfully. In return for the hospitality which was pressed on her, she occasionally brought large boxes of very good and expensive chocolates and handed them over for distribution round the table. She also very frequently handed round her own box of expensive Turkish cigarettes, but while everyone accepted the chocolates, few would take the cigarettes and for this she was very sorry, for she detested the smell of the cheap Virginian tobacco that her colleagues all seemed to prefer.

Miss Dunkerley was the one person with whom Elsie had never managed to quarrel. She looked upon Elsie as a tiresome ill-bred person who probably didn't wash often enough and she treated her as if she were not there. In fact Miss Dunkerley seldom talked to the others. She had come to the Ministry to work and work she did in every moment of her working hours, only occasionally exchanging a few words with Mrs. Doweson who seemed to her the one link with reality in this unpleasant world of Milk Bars and Tube trains, toffee and Goldflakes.

Next to Miss Dunkerley, between her and Miss Younge, sat Miss Jones and her place at the table was appropriate for she came between the two groups of professional workers and amateurs. Daughter of a clergyman, she had spent many years in Switzerland, where she had supplemented a small private income by giving lessons at an expensive finishing school for girls. She was plump, prim, kindly and efficient and everyone but Elsie liked her mildly and she mildly liked everyone but Elsie whom she snubbed for her rudeness and ill-manners. Elsie in return called her old Smugface and took care that she heard it.

The ninth seat at the table on Mrs. Doweson's right belonged to Miss Whyter, known generally as Bobbie, which she said was her Christian name and which was the only name to which she would answer; if she were addressed as "Miss Whyter" she looked vague and began to giggle, pretending not to understand; no one knew why, but then no one could ever explain Bobbie. She was a curious-looking little woman, aged about fifty, daughter of an archaeologist, with whom she lived and to whom she referred as "Daddy". She was very small and elected to dress herself like a child of eight. Like a child Bobbie was always eating and there were some who said that they also found something child-like in her intellect. In her travels with her father she had acquired several rare languages; so rare indeed were they that material for translation seldom came to the Ministry and Miss Saltman was hard put to it to find enough for her to do and was glad to lend her whenever possible to the Library.

Everyone now had settled down to work. The hands of the big clocks that hung down from the ceiling at each end of the room jerked from minute to minute about an inch at a time and made a little click as they hit the next minute and there was hardly any other sound to be heard but the rustle of papers and the scratching of pens and a steady mutter from Mrs. Jolly as her jaws moved up and down like the jaws of a puppet doll when someone is pulling the strings. Most of the women were smoking and the sun shone in through the windows on to the cloud of blue cigarette smoke that hung around their heads and on to the roses and made their scent spread over the desks. It was very pleasant looking down the room for there were flowers on nearly every desk and it was like a garden in the sunlight.

But when the clocks jerked to 10.45 everyone looked up at the same time and someone said "Coffee!" Bobbie jumped up from her seat at the corner and burrowed into a secret hiding-place under her desk and brought out a huge white enamel jug and started to go off with it to buy from a teashop, in the street outside, the coffee and buns and biscuits for which everyone was so eagerly waiting. She looked an odd little figure, carrying the huge white jug, and wearing a green dress over a white blouse like a child's gymnasium costume which came down straight from her shoulders to a little above her knees. It was just a kind of tube and hung quite straight down and did not cover her knees which were very thin and knobbly. On her legs she wore long black woollen stockings and her shoes were flat-heeled and strapped over the ankles like the shoes small children wear. Her hair was reddish, streaked with grey and was cut very short and she had a small green cap on the back of her head and as she ran towards the swing doors she chewed a large sweet which made a bulge in the side of her thin cheek.

Before the clock had jerked round to eleven Bobbie came back with the big white jug full of steaming hot coffee and her pockets full of buns and biscuits and sweets. Everyone from Table Two came up to her with mugs and cups in bright colours which they had bought from Woolworth's and Bobbie divided up the coffee, and they all began to sip and eat and talk about guns and sirens, because those who lived on the outskirts of London heard the barrage every night while those who lived in the centre still slept quietly; for though the sirens sounded often in London, both by day and by night, there had not yet been any raids on the capital. "I don't believe they will ever get through," said Mrs. Just, and "Now, as usual, Wailing Willie will tune up!" said Mrs. Jolly, and they both of them raised their mugs and were going to take the first sip of the luscious hot coffee, when the sirens began to wail. There was a chorus of "Damn's" and "Blast's" and moans and groans and most of the women burned their mouths trying to swallow the hot coffee as fast as they could. Most, but not all, for some sternly pushed aside their cups and rose eagerly to their feet. These were the Wardens; they wore green armlets marked W and a whistle on a white cord hung around their necks. They quickly slung their service gas masks on their shoulders and they seized their whistles and each blew three shrill and deafening blasts. Mrs. Doweson was one of them and she blew the shrillest and most deafening blasts a few inches from Elsie's ear. She blew so loudly and so long that she could not hear what Elsie was saying to her but she could tell from her angry grimaces that it was nothing that she wanted to hear. Then the wardens began to shout "All Down! All Down!" and to pull the blinds and curtains over the windows which were supposed to keep out the broken glass if the windows were smashed during a raid.

One or two women stood up slowly and began to form a line down the centre of the room but the others were still trying to drink their coffee and eat their buns and biscuits as they groped about under their desks for books and cushions and their gas masks which were always getting lost. "Hurry up!" shouted the wardens and "Put out your cigarettes!"

"No, Mrs. Jolly," shouted Mrs. Doweson, "you may *not* take your coffee downstairs. I've told you that before." Mrs. Jolly muttered and looked round for something to put on the mug to keep the coffee warm while she was away and as there was nothing that would do properly she used a dictionary which at once overbalanced with the mug. She screamed and turned back and tried to mop up the spilt coffee with blotting paper and was holding up the whole table while Mrs. Doweson stood and scolded her fiercely and tried to get them all on the move. "Take your places in the line, at once," she cried. "We are supposed to clear this room and be downstairs in four minutes and two have already gone." Then Mrs. Doweson caught sight of Miss Saltman, also in trouble with her papers and her gas mask and her coffee, and she stumped round the table towards her. "Now, Miss Saltman," she said sternly. "Hurry up please; we can't all wait about for you." During a raid the wardens were the most important people in the building no matter what rank they held in the Ministry. Quite junior people were able to tell quite important people what they were or were not to do and the important people obeyed them in much the same spirit as the lord of the manor submits to the jurisdiction of the village black-smith who is captain of the cricket team. The wardens enjoyed these moments very much and the others endured them with good temper as one of the necessary evils of the war.

By the end of another minute the room was in semi-dark-ness and everyone was filing out through the swing doors to the shouts of "Hurry up, please" and "No smoking, *please*" from the wardens. When the wardens had been appointed they had been told that one of their duties was to prevent and avert panic but most of them would have welcomed a touch of panic if it had made their charges less lethargic; many of them secretly hoped for a bomb—just a little, quite harmless bomb—to make the people a little less slow. And this morning everyone was particularly slow, Mrs. Doweson went down the passage to the top of the staircase and stood watching them go down. They shuffled along the passage towards her and they stopped to speak to their friends and when she scolded them they shuffled on again and dropped things and stopped to pick them up and shuffled on again and dawdled, but at last they all reached the head of the stairs. Then they shuffled down, eight steps down to the landing, then round the corner and eight steps down and round the corner again and eight steps down and round again, till at last the tops of their heads disappeared from her sight. Then a group of women with F.A.P. armlets, the First Aid Party, clutching their boxes of bandages and drugs, went down and round and down out of sight; and after them came the men stretcher bearers with their green metal stretchers each with a hard little cushion tied on, manoeuvring skilfully round the staircase bends. Then they too disappeared and after them the junior wardens went down and down. And at last Mrs. Doweson was left quite alone. The old lady gave one look round, up, down, behind and right and left. Then snorting like a war-horse she too went stumping down.

CHAPTER THREE
ANNE ARRIVES

WHEN THE SIRENS sounded the door of the Ministry had been closed and locked and six members of the recently formed Home Guard, armed with fixed bayonets, had taken up their stand in the hall. Other Guards went to points controlling passages and other positions where an entrance might be forced, for at this time there was much talk of invasion and German parachutists were expected to drop at any moment from the sky, however clear it might be.

In these early days of air-raids, all the traffic stopped when the sirens sounded. Outside the Ministry the street was as quiet as a street in some country village and what made it look more like a village street was a row of horses and carts standing along one side by the pavement, with the horses unharnessed and tied to the backs of the carts and the drivers standing about in groups and chatting, just as if they were all waiting for the market to end. The few other people who were about were either hurrying to their destinations or walking deliberately slowly to show that they were enjoying the sunshine and were not afraid.

In the small street which runs along the back of the Ministry, a young girl in a blue frock was hurrying, almost running, partly because she was a little afraid and partly because she feared she would be late for her appointment and she had lost her way. A few yards ahead of her, a small camouflaged motor-car was drawn up by the curb and in it sat a very small spectacled young soldier with a rifle over his knees. He was a very inexperienced young soldier, not entirely certain how his rifle worked; he was trying to get certain as the girl in the blue frock passed the car and stopped short because the rifle had gone off and the bullet had knocked pieces from the wall of the building beside her. The girl turned round and looked crossly at the young soldier who was tumbling out of the car. "Do you know you almost shot me?" she said severely to the embarrassed boy. "I'm sorry, Miss," he stammered, "but you see it was this way—" "You ought to be more careful," said the girl. "But I've no time to argue now. I'm late as it is. Do you know the Ministry of Foreign Intelligence?" The boy pointed with a trembling hand to a small door in front of them. "Here, Miss," he said and turned to look for traces of the bullet. The girl pointed to the wall. "It went in there," she said and then added with a smile, "I hope you won't get court-martialled," and pushed open the small door and went inside.

The girl now found herself in a narrow passage which smelt of coal; as she went on coal dust crunched beneath her shoes; she was clearly on her way to a boiler-room or some place of that kind. But on her left she saw a small stone staircase and she ran quickly up the stairs. Soon she came to a landing with a swing door on the right; she went through the door and was almost struck in the face by a revolver held by a Home Guard officer who was waving it to explain some point in an argument that he was carrying on with three other Home Guards. One of them glanced at her and said mechanically, "All down, please," and made to continue his discussion. But the officer with the revolver noticed that she was a very pretty girl in a blue dress with a ridiculous little hat set jauntily on the side of her head. "Now where have you sprung from?" he asked in a chatty voice, "I've got an appointment," replied the girl, "and I've just come up the stairs from the street door." The Home Guards stared at one another with stupefaction. "Good God!" said one, "the coal-room door's open!" and rushing out of the room, followed by the others, he hurried down the stairs up which the girl had just come.

This girl, whose name was Anne Shepley-Rice, was the new member of the Translation Department whose chair awaited her at Table Two. She was now alone in a small room which she decided must be the Guard Room of the Ministry's section of the Home Guards, for it was hung round with their duty rotas and similar documents. After a minute she went out on the landing and looked down on the Home Guards clattering on the stairs below. Then she heard light footsteps above her and a child in a brown overall with M.F.I. on the shoulder, came bounding down the stairs two at a time. When she reached the landing Anne said quickly, "I want the Translation Department, please." "Next floor, straight on down the passage. Can't stop. I'm a fire-fighter," said the child and went on leaping down the stairs.

Anne followed the child's directions and hurrying up the stairs walked quickly along the passage till she reached some swing doors with "Translation Department" on a board outside. She went in. In the semi-darkness of the empty room, she could see the rows of desks on each of which stood a cup or mug of coffee and on the floor she saw the pool of coffee from the mug which Mrs. Jolly's dictionary had overbalanced. Suddenly a warden pounced on her from the gloom. "You must not dawdle here," she said fiercely. "Hurry up, please, everyone else is downstairs already."

"But I want the Translation Department," said Anne. "M4," said the warden sternly, "and you ought to have known it. Go down at once, please," and she pointed towards the stairs with a commanding gesture. Wondering why she ought to have known M4 and what on earth it meant, Anne set off down the passage, found the main staircase and went down. When she reached the basement she found a maze of long dark passages, She chose one at random and plodded along stolidly, for by now she was rather tired; other passages crossed hers from time to time and at each corner stood a warden who reproached her for being late or slow. To each of them Anne said politely, "M4, please," and was told "straight on," or "right", or "left". And at last she did indeed see a huge notice "M4" over the door of an enormous cellar into which she was pushed by the warden on guard outside.

The bright lights were dazzling after the dark passages and Anne stood at the door blinking and looked round the shelter. The white-washed stone walls were covered with notices, "M4", and "To the Stairs" with arrows pointing in various directions, and "No Smoking"; the floor was stone and the ceiling white-washed brick. The place was filled with women, rows and rows of them, most of them squeezed on the benches made of cement which filled the centre and a few luckier ones on deckchairs and canvas garden seats which stood round the sides and which were all labelled in huge letters with their owners' names. Nearly everyone was talking and a buzz of conversation rose and echoed from the stone walls and floor; and nearly everyone was knitting. Here and there were one or two who read or wrote letters or polished their nails; a bridge party sat with a newspaper over the players' knees to serve as table and some played draughts and chess.

Anne squeezed herself on to the corner of a very cold and hard cement bench and began to wish that her linen skirt did not feel so thin and that she had brought a cushion like most of the other people on the benches. She pondered how long she would have to stay in the shelter; she was certainly going to be late for her appointment and only hoped that the air-raid warning would be accepted as an excuse; there seemed to be nothing to do but to wait as patiently as she could.

Just behind her some people were talking; she could hear every word but she could not understand very much because most of the talk was in mysterious initials. She recognized the B.B.C. and after a while guessed who was the P.M. and what was the F.O. and M.F.I. and even the M.O.I. but was floored by the P.C.B. and the P.C. and M.E.W. and the B.O.T. A girl on her left was saying, "Of course, Jean's mad to be an L.S. but I'd be quite satisfied to be a D.L.S." The other answered, "I'm earmarked for a D.D.," and then they both laughed; and while Anne was wondering what the joke was, she heard a squeaky voice behind her say angrily, "What are you doing here? You don't belong to us." Anne turned round and saw Bobbie, sitting in her child's dress on the bench behind with an apple in one hand and a currant bun in the other and staring at her as she bit first into the apple and then into the bun.

"What are you doing here?" said Bobbie again and stood up. "I shall go and tell the Shelter Marshal that you don't belong here." But Mrs. Just who was sitting next to her said, "Shut up, Bobbie, and don't fuss," and pulled her back into her seat by tugging at her dress.

"But perhaps she's a German spy," said Bobbie, indistinctly, because her mouth was full of bun and apple.

Anne turned and smiled at her. "I'm not a spy," she said. "I'm new. I've only just arrived and I came down here because I was told to." And she looked at Bobbie and thought that she didn't really seem quite all there and she looked at Mrs. Just and noticed her well-fitting clothes and her trim hair and thought she looked sensible and nice. And then Mrs. Just said, "M.H.I.?" and Anne looked puzzled and said, "I'm sorry but I don't know!"

"There! I told you she's a spy," said Bobbie, jumping to her feet again but Mrs. Just pulled her down again and went on and explained. "M.H.I. and M.F.I. are both in this building you know and I thought perhaps you had got into this shelter by mistake." And then Anne said, "I'm in M.F.I.," very pleased to be able to be technical at last and then Mrs. Just said "T.S.?" and Anne was stumped again. But she answered, "I understand I'm to do translations. I know some French and Portuguese."

"Then you are T.S.," said Bobbie and Mrs. Just said, "I believe you are coming to our table. Aren't you Miss Shepley-Rice?" And when Anne said "Yes" Mrs. Just said "How do you do?" and shook hands with her and explained that she was the Deputy Language Supervisor. Ah! thought Anne, that's a D.L.S., as she shook hands with Mrs. Just who was telling her that she would introduce her to Miss Saltman, the L.S., who was over there playing chess with Miss Jones. So Anne went across with Mrs. Just who was just going to introduce her when Miss Saltman caught her elbow in the board and sent the chessmen rolling on the floor. Anne rescued a knight and three pawns and Miss Saltman thanked her and shook hands while Miss Jones tried to set the fallen pieces in the spaces where they belonged. Anne talked a little with Miss Saltman till Miss Jones said firmly, "Your move I believe," and Miss Saltman smiled and turned back to her game; Anne felt quite at home with her and liked her at once; Miss Jones, she thought, was surely a schoolmistress, she looked so prim and proper and Anne began to wonder how she was going to get on with all these different types.

Anne herself was the daughter of a naval officer who had distinguished himself in the last war and died soon after his retirement. Her childhood had been spent with her mother in a pleasant old manor house at Chewston Parva in Somerset. She went to school at Barkham Abbey and in the holidays she rode and swam and played tennis—happy and comfortable days that went on till she was nineteen and had just left school. That was three years ago. She had gone that year to Portugal to stay with a rich aunt and when she came back everything began to be different. Her mother was ill for one thing and something had gone wrong with their money. The family solicitor was often at the house explaining that these dividends had been "passed" and those must be written off and talking about the "crisis" and advising them to sell the manor house. After Munich there were lots of London people who began to think that Somerset would be a nice safe area to be in if war came. And one day the solicitor came down with an offer which he insisted they should accept and the manor house was sold and they had moved to a small house at the other end of the village. It was quite sweet, Anne thought, with an old walled garden but dreadfully poky after the manor house with its large rooms and broad staircase and the huge garden and the tennis courts. Just when the war started, her mother's illness became more serious and soon Anne could do nothing but keep her company and nurse her till, in the early summer of the next year, she died. Then there had been more long interviews with the family solicitor from which Anne learned that she must face up to life with a hundred and fifty a year and no prospect of more till dividends began to blossom again which might be next year or might be never but would certainly not be this year nor any year till the war was over and done with. Anne's grandmother had begged her to come and live with her; the old lady was rich enough to go on living in her own home in Bath; she was nice too, and Anne was fond of her. But Anne wanted to be independent and there was a war on and she wanted to be in it. So the solicitor spoke to someone in the War Office who spoke to someone in the W.T.I.D. who spoke to someone in the M.F.I. and Anne had been summoned for an interview with Colonel Hilles, the D.D.—the Deputy Director.

The interview had been, Anne thought, a success. When she got over her first terrors she decided that the Colonel was an old pet. He had asked her a great many questions to which she had been able to reply promptly and, she hoped, intelligently and when she had summoned up courage to tell the Colonel that she was hoping to make a career for herself and what were her prospects in the M.F.I., his eyes had twinkled a little and he had considered and then replied: "H'mm! You might do well as a Deputy Language Supervisor." And then he had talked about her father and her mother and she had found that he knew her family quite well.

That had sounded promising and Anne had gone away in high spirits which gradually turned to deep depression as the weeks went by and she heard nothing at all from the M.F.I. But during that time, though of course she did not know it, important and mysterious departments were occupying themselves with her affairs, "checking up" on her history. And finally when all her statements had been proved and all her circumstances found to be blameless, she received a telegram one Friday morning, telling her to report for work at the M.F.I. at 11.15 a.m. on the following Monday.

Anne wondered now, as she went back to the vacant seat on the hard bench, whether she was going to make a success of it. She felt a little bewildered but all the same, rather important. She was proud to be starting on real war-work but rather nervous at beginning her first job. It was jolly lucky she had worked hard in Estoril and learned the language or she would never have got it. As she looked round the shelter everyone looked older than she was and they all looked experienced and assured even though some of them were rather comic. From where she was sitting, she could see Miss Purbeck and Mrs. Jolly, two old funnies, she thought them, with their heads together over a bag of sweets, like two greedy old babies. Mrs. Jolly was talking and shaking her yellow curls and prodding Miss Purbeck's fat arm to make her listen and Miss Purbeck was yawning in her face. And near them was the rather grand-looking woman with a beautiful pearl necklace, who, Mrs. Just had whispered to her as they came back together, was the Hon. Cecilia Dunkerley, Lord Clannicombe's daughter; she was sitting alone and knitting a khaki scarf and Anne did not think that she was a very expert knitter or that she liked knitting very much; she had a kind of disagreeable-duty-must-be-done expression and she sat very upright on the hard cement bench with her skirts bunched together and her feet tucked up with only the toes touching the ground and, Anne reflected, she's afraid of beetles and I bet there *are* beetles—and bugs too—on this floor. Miss Dunkerley had found herself a kind of alcove and Elsie Pearne was in the corresponding alcove a few feet away. Soon Anne was looking curiously at Elsie and thinking she was perhaps the most interesting one of them all; she has a clever face, she thought, and a lovely forehead and brow but there's something twisted and queer there; she'll look like Punch when she's very old for her long nose will come down and her long chin will go up until they meet. And Anne was still wondering what this strange tall woman would be like when the All Clear sounded and everyone stood up with a great clattering of feet and Mrs. Doweson's voice rang out with stern instructions: "All upstairs, please; two at a time; quietly, please; don't forget your gas masks!"

"Oo-oo, left mine behind!" cried Bobbie when they were already half-way down the passage and she turned back and began struggling against the crowd pushing its way towards the lifts and staircase.

Anne went up with the others and rather breathless after the long climb, followed them into the Translation Room. Most of them made at once for their deserted cups of coffee, now tepid or quite cold, which all the same, they drank, grumbling and cursing Hitler, to the last drop.

As the others settled down in their places Anne saw that Mrs. Just was signalling to her to come to the top desk. When she got there Miss Saltman said, "I suppose you've been already to the E.O.?" "I'm awfully sorry," said Anne. "Er—that's the er—er—?" "The Establishment Officer," explained Mrs. Just. "You've got to get your papers before you start work. Miss Younge will take you to his office."

So with Miss Younge, Anne now started off once more down the passages, round corners and up and down stairs. As Miss Younge padded along beside her on her large feet in their crêpe-soled shoes, Anne squinted at her sideways; not quite so old as some of the others, but she must be over thirty—quite old, she thought, as is the way with young persons of Anne's age. On the stairs they met Bobbie who grinned widely at them and held up her gas mask. "Found it," she squeaked. "Such a job," and scampered off. Anne looked at Miss Younge who shrugged her shoulders. "This place is full of freaks," she said. "It's the languages. We're supposed to be able to translate from thirty-nine. And funny languages seem only to be known by funny people when they have to be British as well."

"It all seems to be most exciting," said Anne. "It's not. It's lousy," said Miss Younge. "Here's the E.O.'s office," and left her at the door.

When Anne came out she was laden. For joining the staff of the Ministry was a complicated business and she only hoped she would remember even half the rules and regulations of which she had been told. She had a huge box containing the test of these rules under her arm; she had also been given a pass and a locker key and a clean towel and a piece of nasty-smelling soap and a lot of pamphlets and several lectures on the confidential nature of the work she was about to undertake and many warnings of the D.O.R.A. penalties she would incur if she betrayed official secrets or committed any of an enormous list of possible offences. She had signed her name to a terrifying document in which she declared that she quite understood all this—and she only hoped she did—she had been interviewed by so many people that altogether she felt completely shattered. But it was rather grand all the same to be a full-blown, if temporary, Civil Servant entrusted with secret documents which it was an awful crime to lose or talk about. As she walked back to the Translation Department, she thought about these documents and resolved that never, never, never would she allow herself for an instant to be careless or forgetful while they were in her possession.

Anne found that her place at the table was next to Elsie Pearne. Mrs. Just took her over and introduced her and she also introduced Mrs. Jolly, who sat on Elsie's right. Mrs. Jolly jumped to her feet, shook hands and started babbling at once. "Oh! Miss Shepley-Rice, I am pleased to meet you. I do hope you'll be happy here with us. We're a funny lot, you'll find but not so bad when you get used to us and we do try to be as nice to each other as we can because as I always say we're only alive once and it's up to us—"

"Shut up!" said Elsie Pearne with a venomous glare.

Mrs. Jolly stopped talking and stared with her mouth still open but before she could start again Mrs. Just introduced Anne to the other people sitting near and then gave her what she described as an easy Portuguese translation to start with and left Anne to settle down to her first official piece of work.

While Anne was engrossed with her translation, Elsie looked at her a good deal and thought her a nice little thing and very attractive and pretty. The child had a really lovely complexion and such pretty bright blue eyes and curly fair hair and a pretty blue dress. Elsie was specially fond of blue; it always reminded her of Benno; when she had known him she was not so very much older than this girl—in Paris, in the spring. She has a nice friendly way with her, shy but not frightened, like a puppy or a kitten. How very different from all these disagreeable old hags at the table; it was to be hoped they wouldn't get hold of her, spoil her, make her like themselves, set her against Elsie and get her on their side. . . .

The Portuguese document seemed to Anne not an easy but a formidable affair. But in half an hour she had made a pretty good rough draft of the translation and now, as she was ready to make the fair copy, she began to refill her fountain pen from a bottle of ink which stood on her desk. But the ink was a murky bluish liquid and her pen refused to write and after a few words gave out again.

"Here, have some of mine," said Elsie gruffly. "Don't use that awful stuff. Some government contractor must have made his fortune adding water and the Lord knows what to have made that ghastly mixture." She pushed a bottle of ink over to Anne, who refilled her pen and thanked her with her prettiest smile.

"Don't mention it," said Elsie. "I say, what time are you going out to lunch?"

"Miss Saltman told me to go at half-past-one."

"Same time as I go. I can put you on to the only decent place round here if you'll swear not to tell any of the others. I don't want it to be crowded out with the M.F.I. lot. At present none of them know it. Care to come with me?"

Anne said that that was really awfully kind of her and thought that though she looked so cross, this Miss Pearne was really rather attractive—or interesting anyhow—a rough diamond or something of that sort. And when one-thirty came, they went out together for the luncheon hour.

CHAPTER FOUR
ELSIE AND ANNE

ELSIE TOOK ANNE to a small teashop in a turning near Fleet Street. It was like all the teashops of this kind that women like and men hate. It had small rickety tables and they gave you a lot of courses for a small sum and when you looked at the menu you thought you must have eaten a lot but you felt almost as hungry as before.

They sat down at one of the tiny tables and gave their orders to the waitress who was one of those who wear a smock overall and never call the customers. "Madam" to show they are not really waitresses by birth. And Anne, who had been to teashops of this kind in the country, looked about her and was surprised to find they existed in London, especially in the City, where she had expected everything to be very big and magnificent and business-like.

"And now tell me all about yourself," said Elsie when the waitress had left them. "What did you do before you came here?"

"Nothing, I'm afraid," replied Anne rather apologetically. "At least I mean I was always doing something and it seemed quite interesting at the time but I've never really done anything properly—every day regularly you know and all that."

"Is this your first job then?"

"Yes," said Anne. "I'm afraid it is."

"Of course you're only a baby. It can't be long since you left school."

"Oh, I'm not so young as all that!" said Anne. "I'm twenty-two. I was at Barkham Abbey till I was eighteen. I wanted to go to Oxford but things went wrong at home and my mother fell ill and I had to nurse her instead."

"Oxford!" said Elsie. "I wanted to go to Oxford too but I've had to earn my living since I was fourteen and I've been working ever since."

"Of course it must be much more interesting to be always working," Anne said politely. "I'm thrilled to be beginning. But it all seems terribly difficult and responsible and important."

"Oh, I don't call this work responsible and important," said Elsie. "It's just translating and if you know the language you can do it and that's just that. I'm used to work that was really responsible and important."

"I'm sure you are," said Anne. "I thought at once when I saw you that you looked kind of interesting and clever." Elsie looked up sharply. Was the child serious or was she pulling her leg? Had they got at her already? But Anne was saying, "I suppose you know a lot of languages," and Elsie replied mechanically, "French, German and Spanish are my best." "And you have been in France and Germany and Spain?" Elsie nodded. "Do tell me about them. I've only been to Portugal and France but I've always wanted to go to Berlin and Madrid." "I know them well—and Paris too," said Elsie. "I've had real jobs in all of them. I had a very big job in Berlin. And I earned a big salary too—not a miserable pittance like they give you here. I was head of a big office—and weren't they all frightened of me! My word! Those were the days!"

"And why did you leave?" said Anne politely. "Because the dirty Nazi manager was jealous of me! And the other men in the office were jealous of me too and spread lies about me. Men are all like that. When you're my age you'll have found out all about it. I could tell you some things that would surprise you! But now it's your turn. Tell me all about yourself. I suppose with those curls and those blue eyes there's a boy friend isn't there?"

"No," said Anne. "I do wish they'd hurry up with that coffee. It's ten past two already." "There's lots of time," said Elsie, "We don't want to go back to that old hen-coop before we need." "I rather want to get back," Anne answered. "You see it's all new to me and they all seem awfully nice." "They all seem nice at first," said Elsie. "But they're a sly lot and always waiting to do you down. I don't have much truck with them. I keep myself to myself. It's much better, you know. If the truth were known they're a bit frightened of me." She spoke complacently. "You've got to be on the look-out always or people take advantage of you. Better to hit them first before they hit you." "Oh, do you think so?" said Anne. "I never thought of that. I mean why should they hit you at all?" "Because they're stupid and stupid people always hate people with brains. Now take old Fusspot—" "Fusspot!" said Anne; "which one is that?" "That's my name for Saltman. I've got names for all of them." "Have you?" said Anne laughing. "We used to have nicknames for everyone at school but I thought you'd all be much too serious for that sort of thing in a Government office. Do tell me what they are." "All right, and then we can use them when we are together." Elsie felt a little glow of contentment as she said this. "This is what I call them and you'll see what good names they are when you get to know them better. Bobbie Whyter is the Village Idiot, and Younge, you know, the one in the dark blue dress with the big feet, she's the Mutt—and Mrs. Jolly, that's the fat one who dyes her hair yellow and is always talking, she's the Gasbag and as I've said, Saltman is old Fusspot and old fat Purbeck, who has always been a companion to old ladies, is the Nit-Wit and Jones is old Smugface and the Hon. Cecilia is my Lady Haw-Haw and old Mrs. Doweson is the Fresh-Air-Fiend."

Anne was much amused with this catalogue and said in answer: "They're marvellous names. Lady Haw-Haw is just perfect. I think she's rather terrifying though as a matter of fact she was quite nice to me when I was putting on my hat before we came out, and said she had known some of my family who have a place in Devonshire not far from the Clannicombes' place. And old Mrs. What's-her-name came up and said she had hunted with my granny. It's funny, isn't it, how small the world is."

"A small world but a beastly one," said Elsie. "I think hunting's cruel."

"I think I do too, really," said Anne, "when I think about it in cold blood—but I just can't help enjoying it. And somehow it seems part of country life. And I adore that. I've only been a few days in London and I'm homesick already for country noises—the cocks crowing and the hens clucking and the birds—and my dogs barking and scampering towards me and all the country smells. There's nothing to smell here but petrol fumes and nothing to hear but—"

"But that!" said Elsie as the sirens began to wail. "Oh, isn't that sickening!" said Anne. "And now I suppose we must rush back."

"Not at all," answered Elsie. "We'll pay our bills and go for a stroll in the sunshine. It's my afternoon off and I'm going home now. But I'll leave you at the Ministry when the All Clear sounds. If you go in now you will only be sent down to that revolting shelter. Yesterday we were bundled down four times. Perfectly idiotic! There's supposed to be a war on and we're supposed to be doing urgent work and they send us down to do nothing for hours at a time. Just because we're women we're supposed to be so fragile that we can't carry on during a warning. And there's never a raid anyhow. They're always turned back as soon as they've got to the suburbs—Croydon and round about there."

They paid and went out of the teashop and walked along slowly, enjoying the unaccustomed quiet, their footsteps echoing on the empty pavement. Opposite the Law Courts they crossed the road, casually without having to wait or run or dodge the traffic. They passed a warden who looked at them fiercely from under his tin hat. "He looks very cross," said Anne. "Perhaps we're supposed to take cover."

"We are *supposed* to," said Elsie. "But this is a democratic country. We are *supposed* to but we are not *compelled* to. We do as we like, thank God." "But they'll make us go down at the Ministry," said Anne. "They'll make you go down if you go in. But if you don't go in they can't make you do anything about it. As a matter of fact, as the doors are locked during an air-raid and you have to ring to be let in, it's easier as well as more pleasant to stay out. You'll see for yourself. We're just coming to the shop." They were turning into Lincoln's Inn Fields and as they rounded the corner of the block, they saw, outside the Ministry, about a hundred of the staff, sitting on the piles of sandbags which protected the pavement lights, basking in the sun, talking, smoking and eating sandwiches out of paper bags and drinking milk through straws from bottles. "There you are!" said Elsie, "Isn't it grotesque. Outside they're all defying the air-raid and inside they're all made to huddle in a basement as if they were afraid."

But now everyone was looking up at the deep blue sky. Far away tiny dots made trails of white smoke into patterns on the blue, "See the dog-fight?" said one girl excitedly. "Look! Look! I'm sure we've got one!" One dot sank rapidly leaving a vertical trail to mark its fall. "It must be over Southend," said one. "Oh, miles nearer!" said another and a third said, "My brother who's in the Air Force says we can't judge the distance. They've been attacking our aerodromes, he says, for the last fortnight, at Northolt, Kenley, Croydon and places like that and they've jolly well paid for it too! He says we brought down two hundred and forty-five Jerries in two days, the week before last."

Elsie and Anne stood gazing skywards with the others. The trails of smoke grew fainter and melted into the sky and the fight seemed to be over. A few minutes later the All Clear sounded and they, like all the others, felt quite disappointed.

All the M.F.I. staff now began to crowd to the doorway. "I must leave you, my dear," said Elsie to Anne, "Be good when you go home to-night."

"Oh, perhaps you can help me!" said Anne. "I shall have to go to Bond Street. Is it best to go by bus or Tube?"

"Bond Street?" said Elsie. "Does that mean that you're living in Mayfair?"

"Oh no!" answered Anne. "I've only been staying there for a few nights and I've got to go and fetch my luggage. I'm moving into my new flat just off Cromwell Road to-night. But my grandmother always stays at Farland's Hotel in Dover Street when she's up in town—she has always gone there all her life—I don't believe she has ever stayed at any other hotel in London—and she stood me a week-end there till I could get into my flat. Of course I couldn't afford to stay there on my own, it is much too expensive although it is a quiet old-fashioned-looking place, but it's very comfortable and nice."

"Farland's Hotel! That's a proper sort of grandmother to have!"

"She's a darling," said Anne. "But do tell me how I get to Bond Street from here." Elsie told her. She told her all the route in detail and as she told her she held her hand. Anne felt a little embarrassed: "Thank you so much, Miss Pearne," she said at the end, withdrawing her hand. "I'll try and remember all those bus numbers, I'll have to make a note of them when I get in." And Elsie said with one of her rare smiles, "We'll meet to-morrow, then. We're going to be friends I hope. It would be nice if you called me Elsie—or just Pearne." Anne smiled back at her. "Goodbye, Elsie," she said. "And thank you for taking me to that nice place for lunch. And oh!—to-morrow, please, my name is Anne."

The Ministry staff were still filing through the doorway and Anne now took her place in the queue. It took a long time for everyone to get in for each one had to show a pass which was carefully examined as the holder went through. Just inside stood Mrs. Doweson, wearing her warden's armlet. She was very angry and scolded them as they came in. "You'll stand outside there once too often. What would you have done if a bomb had fallen near? Rushed to this door in a panic, I suppose." "Oh no we shouldn't!" said one of the girls pertly. "We'd have fallen on our tummies to escape the blast like we've been taught—or something of that kind. Anyhow there aren't going to be any bombs on London. The R.A.F. won't let them come. Why you could see our Spitfires just now chasing Jerry away. It was a lovely fight!" "Don't talk nonsense," said Mrs. Doweson. "London may be bombed at any hour and you won't find it anything to laugh at."

*   *   *   *   *

Elsie had enjoyed her lunch with Anne and the chance to chatter with someone with such an entirely different point of view and she was still thinking about her when the bus reached the Kilburn High Road and her own stopping-place near Hengistbury Crescent, Brondesbury, where she had a furnished room. She got off the bus and walked the few steps to the turning which led up from the noisy High Road to the more genteel Crescent. At the corner stood a hawker with a barrow full of flowers. She passed him and then turned back and bought a bunch of blue scabious which caught her eye. She seldom bought flowers for her room because she was so little in it, it didn't seem worth while; but she liked the scabious, they were the colour of Anne's dress and the blue of which she was so fond. Elsie felt happy and elated this evening, a rare mood for her. Always she had faced the world courageously but never gaily. Latterly even her courage had been giving way and she had been subject to moods of depression and despair, when her brain, usually so clear, grew clouded and confused and she could no longer quite distinguish between what was real and what she had imagined. Her age, she supposed. But this afternoon, as she walked up the hill with her big ungainly strides, she forgot for once her misgivings and her gloomy fears. It was a lovely day; the sky was so clear and blue and the sun shone hotly on the monotonous row of red brick villas and turned the red to an ugly dirty crimson. But she did not think the villas ugly; she had always when in England lived in red brick or yellow brick houses and never thought of them as ugly or pretty; they were "nice comfortable digs" or otherwise. She walked now up the short pink tiled path through the tiny front garden; and as she put her key into the front door she thought with satisfaction that these were comfortable digs, clean, quiet and respectable; if she had had a rich grandmother perhaps she too would have been staying in a Bond Street hotel; fancy that kid doing that! Elsie had never in the whole of her life stayed in a hotel—not a real hotel that is—not even when she had been abroad earning really good money had she ever aspired to anything more than a cheap pension and indeed it would never have occurred to her to waste her money in such an absurd fashion when, if you knew the ropes, you could so easily find comfortable rooms.

This time she had been very lucky. She liked very much her room on the first floor and thought so this afternoon as she opened its door and observed with pleasure its spotlessly clean and tidy appearance from the shining well-polished green linoleum, which covered the floor, to the white stiffly starched lace curtains, which hung over the windows. It was an up-to-date little room too—and not so little either—with a divan bed so that she could make it into a sitting-room if she ever had visitors (ladies, of course, for the landlady would not have tolerated gentlemen in an upstairs room) and a dressing-table in imitation mahogany with a circular unframed mirror, quite in the modern style, which the landlady had bought specially for her when she first took the room. The colour scheme too had been carefully thought out. The hearth rug, the cushion in the little tub-shaped armchair by the fireplace and the curtain covering the recess where she hung her clothes—all were the same shade of yellow ochre with a matching modernistic design; the fire-screen and the lampshade were of yellow parchment smartly hand-painted with green and blue zig-zags and shafts of lightning and a fringed satin table-runner running diagonally across the green serge tablecloth picked up once more the same note of yellow ochre colour; matching the green tablecloth was a large painted deal chest of drawers across one corner and a small bookcase next the fireplace, as well as one or two other odd bits of furniture—and the lino was green to match these. It was a pity that the divan cover was royal blue and did not match anything else; but Elsie meant to buy one for herself one day soon; it would always come in useful and she liked to have a few things of her own—such as the cigarette box, matchstand and ash-tray and the parrot bookends all to match in pink alabaster which she had brought back from Berlin and which now stood carefully arranged on the yellow satin table-runner. All the books in the bookcase were hers too, dictionaries and textbooks in several languages, a few yellow-back foreign novels which she had bought for reading practice, a few Everyman classics and a number of rather ponderous volumes on economics which she had acquired at one time when she was studying that subject in a Home University Correspondence course. The picture over the fireplace was hers too—Titian's "Young Man with a Glove" in a Louvre coloured print that she had bought long ago in Paris because he was like Benno. For many years he had been put away at the bottom of her trunk but now he hung in the place of honour looking out at the landlady's "Summer's Glory" on the opposite wall which he had supplanted. On the top of the bookcase stood other treasures, a framed picture-postcard of a matador administering the *coup de grâce* to a bull and a little cast of the Egyptian princess with the towering head-dress from Berlin, one on each side of a leather travelling clock.

Elsie took off her hat and gloves and wondered where she could put the bunch of scabious that she had just bought. She bought flowers so seldom that she had nothing suitable, no tall vase, nothing but a squat pottery bowl that had once contained a fern. She opened the door at one end of the room and went into her kitchenette, switching on the light as she did so, for it was little more than an enlarged cupboard really and had no outside window; but it was big enough for her requirements because the landlady cooked and brought up her evening meal and she only used it to prepare her breakfast on the gas ring which stood on the tiny table next the little sink—where she was able to wash her stockings and other "smalls"; there was still room left for a chair and some shelves and altogether it was a very useful little place and one of the many assets of her present digs because she could shut its door on any kind of untidiness and have her bed-sitting-room kept tidy and nice as she liked it to be. She could still find no vase for her flowers so finally she washed out a milk bottle; that would have to do for the present; when her landlady brought up her supper Elsie would borrow a vase from her till she could buy one for herself; she polished the bottle and carefully dried it underneath so that it would not mark the furniture and then moving away the clock, put the flowers in its place between the little Princess and the matador.

When she had done that Elsie changed her office clothes for a loose and cooler dress and then made herself some tea and pulled the armchair up to the open window and sat down with a book. But very soon the book dropped on to her lap and she began to think about Anne. She's a nice kid! I like her, she thought, and I believe she likes me. But what a baby for twenty-two! I was keeping myself and helping Mother when I was her age and Aunt Min was nagging at me all the time because I didn't give Mother more. I used to save a bit even then—two bob, I remember every week, into the Post Office and then for a time I gave up pudding for lunch and made it four bob till I got a rise. I bet young Anne has never thought of saving a penny in all her life! She doesn't need to, I suppose; she knows she'll be all right; that's what it is; she feels secure. She just takes it for granted that she's all right; money to her and the people like her is something which is there in the background and they don't really think about it at all—not like I do—and Younge and Purbeck and people like us. We really have to think about it all the time—do this because it saves a shilling or two, go without that because though it's only a few pence every day it's something at the end of the week. Everything we do, we think of in terms of what it costs us. And it isn't quite a question of being rich or poor—the men I knew in Berlin and Paris, the manufacturers and the rest of them, lots of them were rich enough but money was just as important to them as it is to me; everything they did they thought of in terms of money—not so much what a thing would cost but how it would help them to make more money. They spent their money and they let their wives spend it but they did it in a way so that people could see them spending it; they wanted everyone to know they were rich; they were always ready enough to tell you how much they spent—they wanted you to know it.

Now Anne and her lot aren't like that. They don't want to *look* rich; they don't talk about money and what they spend and what things cost; they take money for granted. They don't *worry* about it—that's the point. They have nothing in the world to worry about, they are perfectly secure. It's interesting to meet people who are so different from the ordinary everyday people one generally meets. I wish I could have got Anne to talk more about her house and the dogs and the way she lived but she rather shut me up—thought I was inquisitive, I suppose. But I'm really interested. I've never met anyone like Anne and the Haw-Haw lot before—not to talk to, that is. And the Haw-Haws are much too grand to talk to me. They don't talk much about themselves anyhow—not like Younge and Purbeck who are ready enough to tell me everything about themselves if I was ass enough to listen. What bores they are! Really I hate that lot more than the Haw-Haws, they're so damned rude. The Haw-Haws plot against me just as much but they're a bit politer about it! But Anne's not going to join in the plots against me. She belongs to the Haw-Haw crowd but she's quite different. But they're after her, trying to get her away from me. She told me so herself, as soon as they saw she was coming out to lunch with me they were after her—couldn't let her put her hat on without trying to stop her. Old cats! I can just hear my lady talking about the Devonshire Shepley-Rices! That's the way she always talks of people. My mother was one of the Clapham Smiths; I'm going to say that right out to her one of these days. See how she takes it. Let her see what a fool I think her. And now they're trying to get hold of Anne. Why can't they leave her alone? They've got everything. They'll talk about me, make up lies about me, all of them, Younge and her lot as well as the Haw-Haws. They're all alike. But they shan't get Anne. She's my friend; I'm going to watch them and keep them away from her. They shan't get her.

CHAPTER FIVE
SEBASTIAN, ANNE AND MARY

WHEN ANNE came out of the Ministry that evening she was very tired after her first day's work and so many new experiences and so much tramping along passages and up and down stairs. She walked slowly across the square and stood for a moment to look with pleasure at the beds of dahlias. But even as she responded to the colours—the deep reds and lemon yellows with the background of grand old houses glimpsed between big trees, she remembered half unconsciously that dahlias mean the latter part of summer and that it was a pity that the end of this wonderful summer should be so soon at hand.

Remembering Miss. Pearne's instructions, she found her way easily down Kingsway to the corner of Holborn and on to the bus that would take her to Farland's Hotel. She sat down in one of the double seats near the front and just after the bus had started a young Flight-Lieutenant dropped heavily into the seat beside her. Out of the corner of her eye Anne looked at him and her heart gave a funny little jump and she felt happy, so happy that she seemed to be floating right up in the air.

"Well, Anne," he said, "are you going to cut me?" He was panting a little and Anne thought he must have been running for this bus, as she said aloud, "Seb! Oh Seb! Where do you come from? What are you doing here?"

"Chasing after you. I saw you come out of the Ministry but I got jammed in a cluster of ancient females in the doorway and by the time I got free you were half-way across the square. I had to sprint for it to catch you on this thing." Anne was back on earth now though she was miraculously sitting beside Seb, in London, on a bus. It was miraculous and lovely but she must get away at once. "It's marvellous to see you," she said, "but I'm afraid it's only going to be a glimpse. I'm getting off at Bond Street."

"Oh! Let's get down now," he said, "and take a taxi and go somewhere where we can talk. I want to hear all about you. Come on, it's going to stop at the next corner." He got up to make room for her to pass him. She was shattered. She did not know what she could do. She wanted terribly just to give way; but if she did, it would be nice now and awful afterwards. It was so long since she had seen him and she had got used to it and it hadn't been so bad; now, unless she left him at once it would all begin again. But the bus had stopped and the conductor was shouting, "Come along please," and mechanically Anne went out and Sebastian came after her and he took her elbow as they stood together on the curb. Anne made a feeble little gesture as if to shake off his arm but already he had signed to a taxi. "No, Seb," she said. "I can't go anywhere. I'm too filthy." But Seb just laughed at her. "You noodle," he said, "the taxi's ticking, get in. You look sweet."

Seb was Sebastian Kimble and he and Anne had known each other almost all their lives. He was the only son of Sir Henry Kimble who owned most of the village of Chewston Parva and the land around and farmed some of the land himself and who would have been a much richer man if he had not been rather a bad farmer and such a good landlord. The gardens of the Kimble mansion and those of Anne's home, the Manor House, had run side by side. Seb and Anne had played together as children, Anne, an obedient little slave, following Seb into whatever mischief he planned. Seb went to Charterhouse and came home in the holidays and Anne was always there, always ready to do whatever he wanted, always jolly and good-tempered. Seb went to Oxford and Anne was still there when he came down for the vacs, as interested as ever in him and all that concerned him, but, though as ready as ever to be the good companion, she had become a little reserved and on her guard with him, a little afraid of letting herself think too much of his dark hair and olive skin and his white teeth and his jolly laugh which seemed to come out at the very moment he was talking as though he were so pleased with everything that he wanted both to say so and to laugh with pleasure and did not know which he wanted to do first and so laugh and speech came tumbling out together in a kind of race. Then Seb finally came down from Oxford and there had been a summer together when Anne knew that she was dreadfully in love with him. But she never knew how much or how little Seb cared. He had known her so long that he seemed, as it were, to take her for granted. That was partly why she had been so glad of her aunt's invitation to go to Estoril and partly why she had stayed there so long and tried to bury her thoughts in Portuguese grammar and idioms. When she came back Seb had gone into the Air Force. And she had not seen him in the dreary year when she nursed her mother or in the last few months when she was staying with her grandmother at Bath.

Seb told the driver to go to Oddenino's because it was so hot and he thought it would be nice to drink a cocktail on the porch there which is the nearest thing to a café terrace that London can provide. In the taxi they fired questions at one another. Anne told him that she had been some days in London but nobody knew it or where she was working as she had told no one except Granny and Granny was sworn to secrecy. Seb confessed that he knew it all already because he had been down yesterday to Bath "to have a peep at her" and found her gone and her grandmother had sworn him to secrecy and had then told him where she was working. Anne said it was perfectly disgraceful of Granny but how was everything and how were the dogs? And Seb said, "I saw Micky and threw stones for him till my arm ached and Sam put his nose on my knee and told me all about it and I saw Sally who is terribly proud of her puppies which are really too comic for words." And Anne said, "Yes, Heaven only knows what they'll look like. She got out somehow. We suspect the Vicar's dachshund. But it might have been the gardener's cairn." And then Seb told her how he had "crocked" himself in France ("entirely my own fault, I was doing a fool's trick") and how he had been two months in hospital and Anne was careful not to confess that she knew it already as she had made her grandmother write to Sir Henry Kimble and find out. And just before they arrived at Oddenino's, Seb told her that he was now seconded to the Ministry till he was well enough to fly again and as Anne did not know that, but had imagined that he had just called at the Ministry that day, she was thinking wildly, while Seb paid the taxi, that if he was going to be always in the Ministry it would certainly be simply hellish—but heavenly as well.

By the time they were seated on steel chairs before a glass-topped table, drinking cocktails at Oddenino's, Anne had made up her mind, or thought that she had made up her mind what she must do. She looked straight at Seb and said with a little air of determination and defiance, "Seb, I think it would be best if we don't speak at all in the Ministry." "Why?" he said. "Are you ashamed to know me?" "Don't pretend to be silly," she went on. "You must see what I mean. You're sort of a high official and I'm just a translator among a lot of others. And the others will get jealous and think things." Seb roared with laughter. "You are a scream, Anne! Fancy anyone thinking things about you. Even with a sinister-looking card like me!" "Oh Seb!" Anne said. "Do be serious. You must see really what I mean. All the old creatures at my table would say I was trying to pull strings or something. There are one or two of them who sort of know people and would understand. There's an old woman called Mrs. Doweson who says she used to hunt with Granny, and one of the others knows the Devonshire crowd, but most of them couldn't have met anybody and that sort are always terribly inquisitive and horrid. Of course they don't mean to be. I went out to lunch with one of them to-day. She wanted to be nice to me because I was new—I could see that. But she just did nothing but ask personal questions and say horrid things about the others all the time. I can't think what she'd say about me if a higher power like you came in and said 'Hallo, Anne!'."

"All right then," said Seb. "I'll say 'Good morning, Miss Shepley-Rice!'"

"No, Seb. You mustn't say anything at all."

"Then I'll come in and jerk my thumb," said Seb. "And that'll mean 'meet at the Waldorf for luncheon'. How will that do?"

But Anne was not to be put off and she stuck to her guns— and in the end it was agreed that Seb would not speak to her at all in the Ministry but would communicate if he wanted to by sending a note by a girl messenger. That, thought Anne, is the first round won. But she knew that the second round was to come. And it came at once, for Seb said, "Anyway we can make up for it outside. Where, by the way, are you living? Your grandmother told me you were in the Ministry but she did not give me your address."

Anne told him she had been at Farland's Hotel but was leaving to-night. Then she said: "I've got a sort of flatlet. You remember our old parlourmaid Agnes? She's married and living here and lets rooms. So I've fixed up there."

"That sounds a good scheme," he answered. "Near the Ministry?"

Anne stared hard in front of her. "I made Granny swear", she said, "that she wouldn't give the address to anyone."

Seb looked at her in blank amazement. There was something here that he could not understand. Why on earth should Anne refuse him her address? Was she being coy? But Anne was not a fool like that. It seemed to him just "crackers". He felt suddenly constrained with this girl whom he had always thought jolly easy to get on with; he felt anger rising against her and fearing that he might say something that would offend her, he said nothing but signed to the waiter for two more drinks. Anne took out her compact and began to powder her nose looking over the mirror at Seb as she did so. He looked sulky and cross, she thought, but nicer than ever with his brown eyes and dark skin and lovely white teeth. The drinks came and Seb said rather pompously, "Well, I'm still waiting to hear why you think it necessary to refuse me your address."

Anne shut her compact and put it in her bag. "Oh, Seb," she said. "Don't you see everything's different now. When Mummy died her pension ended. Something happened too to her other money. It appears to have been all in things that didn't pay any more when the war started. Even before the war when there were scares, it got much smaller. So I haven't a bean now except what I earn—or very little. Of course Granny has been awfully kind and wanted me to live with her. But I made up my mind to earn my living and war work gave me an excuse to get away without hurting her feelings."

"Yes, I understand all that. But why this mystery about your address? Are you secretly married or something like that?"

"No. Nothing like that. You're as bad as Miss Pearne. And awfully difficult to explain to. The thing is that I'm sort of beginning a new life. And I'm not keeping up with anyone of the old life—even people like you that I've always known. I've got to forget them all and start everything afresh. I've got to stand on my own feet and make my own career."

"Oh fiddlesticks!" Seb interjected. "I thought you had more sense. You seem to have changed completely. You're talking like someone in Bernard Shaw."

"No. No. No," said Anne and to her utter horror she began to feel that she would like to cry. "I've not gone all modern or any rot like that. But you've been away so long and you don't know what I've had to go through. It's all been so hateful that I've *had* to change or I should never have got through. You see when I came back from Portugal I was still Miss Shepley-Rice of the Manor House. Then Mummy had to sell it and that was an awful wrench. And what made it worse was that while we were at Ivy Cottage and I was nursing Mummy, the perfectly dreadful people who took the Manor House were pulling it about and spoiling it—sticking in dozens of bathrooms and building on a hideous garage and making a swimming-pool in the orchard and turning the whole place into a bear garden with crowds of howling people from London with enormous cars. It was simply beastly."

Seb said, "It's no use being sentimental about that sort of thing. People always alter a house when they buy it—and the Manor House *was* rather short of bathrooms—old houses always are." But Anne went on:

"Oh, it wasn't only the things they did to the house. It was just that they were such perfectly frightful people. There was a hard-faced daughter who simply stank of money, with eyes that glittered like diamonds—dreadful creature—horribly well-dressed and dashing, making everyone decent look dowdy and poverty-stricken—which I suppose we were. But anyway, I made up my mind to keep my end up, and when Mummy died I just took a sponge and washed Chewston from the slate. I just can't bear to think of it being polluted by a vulgar vamp like Mary Shephard."

"Mary Shephard!" said Seb beginning to laugh. "Daughter of the Canned Foods Shephards! Yes, I knew that they had got the Manor House."

"Yes," said Anne. "Tins! Sir 'Arry and Lady Shephard and Mary the Vamp."

Seb's laugh came tumbling with his speech. Here was something that seemed to him an excellent joke. "Mary the Vamp," he said between the ripples, "I know her quite well. I met her once when I was home on leave and she turned up as a V.A.D. or something up in Norfolk and used to come to the hospital. Terrifically made up. But I rather liked her. She was such a scream."

Anne saw her chance and took it. "I'm sorry, Seb," she said with theatrical coldness. "I don't admire your taste. And now I must be going. Thanks for the cocktails. As the vamps say, 'I'll be seeing you. Cheerio, old bean'." And before Seb realized she was really going, she had gone.

Sebastian jumped to his feet; but before he had time to pay the waiter and to run after her, he saw Anne drive away in a taxi that she had picked up from the refuge in the centre of Piccadilly Circus. Now why on earth did she rush off like that, thought Sebastian—and he hadn't her address or even her telephone number and could only communicate with her by sending a silly note by a girl messenger. He ordered another drink and sat down again at the table, feeling cross and offended and wondering why Anne was no longer the docile little girl that she used to be. If I annoyed her by something I said, why on earth didn't she say so, he asked himself. In the old days she would have had it out with me there and then—had a flaming row which would have been all over in a few minutes and we'd have been better friends than ever. Now she's all high horse and offended dignity! I can't make her out—she's changed a lot. She's much more beautiful of course—really lovely—and she has the most perfect figure. Of course there's some other man. Anyone who's as attractive as that is bound to have crowds of men after her. I don't mind crowds so much; there's safety in numbers—point is whether there's one that matters—there must be—that's why she wouldn't give me her address.

Sebastian continued to brood on this idea and the more he thought about it the less he liked it. He'd always taken for granted that he would marry Anne, ever since he was old enough to think about marriage. If it hadn't been for the war perhaps they would have been married now. But then there always had been the war—or rather the expectation of the war. During all his time at Oxford he had been waiting for this war and so had all the other men. And when he came down, war seemed practically inevitable. With a faint hope that an enormous increase of recruits might frighten off the Germans, he, like many other men of his age, had joined the R.A.F. And he had gone on waiting and it had seemed useless to make plans.

And now we were in the middle of the war and some day it would end. And what then—assuming of course that he was still alive? Even if the old men made a mess of things as they had done twenty-five years ago, there'd still be an interval of peace, he supposed, when one could get on with one's own life.

He loved Anne and she was the sort of woman he wanted to marry and he could give her the sort of life that she liked. At least he had supposed so and he had supposed that Anne would like him too—but he wasn't quite so sure of it now as he had been.

He went back through their conversation to try and find whether he could have said something to offend her—to make her run away suddenly like that. Did I hurt her feelings because I laughed when she was telling me about the way the Shephards have spoilt the Manor House? I oughtn't to have laughed just then but really I didn't think she would have taken their efforts so much to heart. Besides I *wasn't* laughing at that. I was laughing at Mary. Nobody can help laughing at her, I don't see why Anne doesn't see how funny she is—she's a perfect scream! He grinned to himself as he remembered the last time he had met her, two days ago.

He was coming back to the Ministry after lunch. As his taxi rounded the comer of Grover Street, a large car, driven by a young woman, came round the corner very fast and well on the wrong side. To avoid a collision the taxi-driver had to pull hard on his wheel and drive almost on to the pavement. The two cars stopped and the taxi-driver climbed down and went over and told the young woman just what he thought of her and what he thought of her was not at all flattering and required the use of strong language. Sebastian really quite agreed with him and thought the young woman deserved all she got and he did not hurry as he walked over, fumbling in his pocket for the fare. But as he got nearer he saw that he knew her—it was Mary Shephard—and as soon as she recognised him, she jumped out of her car with a squeal of delight, clutched his arm and begged him to "do something about this dreadful man".

"Thank goodness you were there, Seb," she said when the driver had been pacified with a large tip. "He was really quite nasty, wasn't he?" She released Seb's arm and took her compact from her trouser pocket. Seb looked at her and thought she was surely an eyeful in those singular clothes! She certainly lightened the dreariness of Grover Street.

Mary Shephard was an extremely pretty young woman with big baby blue eyes; she was very carefully and elaborately made up and was wearing a uniform of dark blue jacket and slacks with red facings and a comic but smart little cap of military style. The general effect was highly decorative and completely theatrical.

"I never saw such disgraceful driving," said Sebastian. "What on earth are you doing here? Are you a Waaf or a Waac or something?"

"Heaven forbid!" said Mary. "I am—or was until this morning—in the W.V.A.—I joined them last Monday but there was a spot of trouble yesterday about my not turning up in time. I'm supposed to drive a tiresome old colonel about; a frightfully dull old man—and really quite disagreeable about my driving said it was dangerous—and I didn't see the fun of carting him about and getting up at some godless hour to do it! The uniform was my own idea. Rather smart, don't you think? You see everyone's wearing one nowadays."

"I see," said Seb. "Do you know I rather think there'll be more trouble if you don't move your car. You seem to be quite unpopular with that van driver." The car was still standing out in the road, completely blocking the path of a delivery van whose driver was hooting angrily. "Oh, what a nuisance," said Mary calmly. "Do you think he's really in a hurry or only impatient. I suppose I'll have to move the thing. But *don't* go away, Seb, It's ages since I've seen you and I've so much to talk about."

"Don't be too long then. I must get back to the office." He followed her up to the car and gave her such assistance as he could as with horrid screechings of the gears and convulsive jerks, she finally manoeuvred the car into the curb. Its tail stuck a yard out into the road but she sighed with relief and got out her mirror and comb and signed to Seb to get into the seat beside her.

"Only two minutes, then; I'm one of the world's workers, you know," he said. "Darling Seb! It's so lovely to see you again. I've only just heard that you were in this Ministry place. Wasn't it lucky that we saw each other; I wondered if we would." She drew herself a new mouth in lipstick and then put away her tools in her pocket and squeezed his arm affectionately. He looked round at her and smiled. A bit of a boob, he thought, but amazingly pretty and good fun. "Now tell me all your news," she cooed, "and just what you've been doing since we last met." He told her his news and she told him hers and then he had to leave her. "But we must meet again," she said and made him promise to go with her to a party and made him write down the date so that he should not forget.

As he sat on the terrace at Oddenino's he remembered this promise which he had completely forgotten till that moment. He took out his diary and saw that the date of the party was the following Saturday. He would ring up Mary and make some excuse to get out of it—but there was plenty of time yet.

How Seb has changed, thought Anne, as the taxi took her from Piccadilly to Farland's Hotel where she picked up her luggage and then went straight on to Cromwell Road to her new flat. In the old days he would have seen through Mary Shephard at once—now he finds her amusing! Well, if that's the sort of amusement he wants. . . . She was not going to see more of him than she could help, she had made up her mind to that, but before she had time to make any more plans the taxi had stopped and Agnes was on the doorstep welcoming her in and it was a little like coming home from school for the holidays when Agnes had always been waiting for her at the door.

Joe Barnes, Agnes's husband, brought in the luggage and then they all went upstairs to Anne's little flat. When the door was opened Anne gave a cry of pleasure; since she had engaged it three days ago it had been redecorated and now it was all clean and shining and full of flowers. "I'm so glad you like it, Miss Anne," said Agnes with a beaming face. "When the tenant moved out, we thought it didn't look as nice for you as it should, so Joe did it up for you himself. The flowers came from your grandma this morning and she sent you some nice fruit too."

"It's lovely, Agnes, thank you so much. And now I must unpack," said Anne.

"I'll do that for you, Miss Anne, as soon as I've given you your dinner. There's a nice bit of chicken all ready and I'd like you to have it at once."

While she ate her dinner Anne looked round her room with delight. Like most small rooms which have been contrived out of big rooms, it was too high for its size and the long window from floor to ceiling was wrongly placed and quite out of proportion; but the clean paper and paint made it look very attractive and the furniture was plain and of good quality and the curtains and covers, gay and fresh. Anne's own pictures were already hanging on the wall—a reproduction of St. Ursula's bedroom with her little dog at the foot of the bed, a couple of water-colours of her old home and several framed enlargements of dogs and horses, one of which included a very good photograph of Sebastian holding up a puppy to the camera. On the mantelpiece in silver frames were photographs of her father in naval uniform and her mother as a young woman in Court dress and another of her in later life as Anne remembered her, and everywhere were vases of the flowers her grandmother had sent her.

As soon as she had finished dinner Agnes came up to unpack for her. "Agnes, you mustn't spoil me," protested Anne, curling herself up in the armchair and lighting a cigarette. "You know I'm a working woman now." "Yes, Miss Anne, of course," said Agnes, smiling faintly. "You packed this case yourself, I can see!" she added, pulling out a mass of crumpled garments. "I'll take these away and press them for you to-morrow, I hope Joe hung the pictures right for you. That's a good photo of Master Seb. How is he, Miss Anne? Have you heard lately? I suppose he's in the army now?"

"In the R.A.F.," said Anne. "How do you like living in London?"

"Well I do and I don't," said Agnes, "London's not so bad but I hope we aren't going to get any of these air raids though I think we're safer right in London, than outside."

"I'm sure we are; I don't think they'll ever be able to get through," said Anne confidently. "They never seem to be able to get past Croydon. Agnes, do you remember . . ." and the two of them began to talk about old times till the unpacking was finished and Anne's room was tidy for her again and ready for her to go to bed.

She went to bed early but certain that she would never sleep, her head was so full of the impressions of the day, her new flat and her new job and all the crowd of strange faces and the funny old thing she had lunched with—whom, by the way, she must remember to call "Elsie" to-morrow—and Seb turning up like that and Seb in the Ministry—she would be certain to be always running into him and something would have to be done about that—but before she could decide what was to be done, she was asleep.

CHAPTER SIX
A NEW DEPUTY REQUIRED

THE NEXT MORNING Miss Saltman received a shock. Mrs. Just was going to leave her; she was handing in her resignation that very day because she had been offered a job in another Ministry at nearly twice the salary she was receiving here. "I suppose you must take it?" said Miss Saltman sadly. "I'm afraid so," said Mrs. Just, smiling very cheerfully. "It's a much better job—and I shall be glad of the extra money so that I can send more parcels to my husband. I had another card from him only this morning begging me for cigarettes and food."

"Yes, of course you must take it," said Miss Saltman and gave herself up to dismal visions of life without Mrs. Just. She saw in imagination the hideous confusion of her desk—trays full of translations all made by the wrong translators because she could never remember who was best at which language—memos multiplying themselves by every post because she would never have time to answer them—mountains of forms to fill up and returns to be completed—and no Mrs. Just by her side to deal with each problem as it arose and solve it for her quickly and quietly with no fuss. Never, never, never, thought Miss Saltman, would she find such a competent assistant as Mrs. Just. She sighed heavily and her gaze fell on two forms which lay before her on her desk and she took them up and began to read them. "Translators, Duty Returns of (Daily and Weekly; units and half units)", was the title of one and the other was headed: "Translations; Received and Despatched. Daily (Totals) and Weekly (Averages)." They were good examples of what she had to cope with, she thought, and mechanically she passed them over to Mrs. Just saying impatiently, "What on earth do these mean? How can a translator be half a unit? Either she's here or she isn't!" Mrs. Just took the forms and glanced at them and as soon as she read through the instructions, she understood what they meant. But she was too tactful to let Miss Saltman see that she understood them so quickly and she pretended that she had to read the forms over several times before she said slowly, "I think I see what it means—a unit is a whole day and half a unit is—" "I see," said Miss Saltman interrupting, "but what I don't see is how on earth I can find anyone to take your place."

"What about Mrs. Doweson?" said Mrs. Just.

"She's too old. I shouldn't like to ask her to run about and do things for me like you do."

"Miss Jones?"

"She's efficient certainly—but a bit of a prig. She's been setting a good example to schoolgirls for so long that she's hardly human."

Mrs. Just laughed. "What about Younge, then?"

"She'd preach socialism at me all day and cover my desk with cigarette ash. I couldn't stand it. I'm afraid it will have to be Miss Pearne."

"Miss Pearne! The sinister Elsie!" said Mrs. Just, surprised. "Do you really mean it? The others all hate her."

"Yes, I know she's not very popular; she's rather disagreeable but she's really intelligent and she really knows her languages and I must have someone who can cope with forms and all these tiresome things." Miss Saltman seized a neat pile of papers and looked at them with disgust and threw them back on the desk in confusion before Mrs. Just had had time to rescue them out of her grasp. "Of course, I know you don't like her," continued Miss Saltman, "but I've decided to try her and if the others don't like it they must lump it—there's a war on. I've just made up my mind what I shall do. When you go away for your long weekend I shall try out Miss Pearne—have her up here and let her work beside me." She spoke with great decision. She had suddenly made up her mind and she did not intend to be persuaded into altering it.

"I think that's a splendid idea," said Mrs. Just. She did not think so really. She thought, well, it's her funeral. It's no good my saying anything, she won't listen to me, she only thinks I'm prejudiced. I shan't be here for the dust-up. Let her find out for herself.

"Yes," said Miss Saltman. "I shall try her out that week-end and if it's a success, I shall recommend her to the D.D. Anyway, thank heaven, I shall have you for another month."

Miss Saltman said no more for Miss Younge was at her elbow. Late as usual, Miss Younge had padded in even more silently than usual in her rubber-soled shoes and was signing the attendance book as unobtrusively as she could.

Miss Younge walked away thoughtfully, turning over in her mind the words she had just overheard. "I'll recommend her to the D.D. Anyway, thank heaven I shall have you for another month." That meant that Mrs Just was leaving! There would be a new deputy—someone had already been selected.

Someone had already been selected. Could it be herself? Surely she was just the right person; she had had the right experience. In her last job in the school of commerce at Rouen, she had deputized for the principal when he was away ill that time and on the form, when she had applied for this job in the Ministry, she had described herself as Deputy-Principal. And she had been so useful to Miss Saltman; she'd done a lot of filing and then she had had that splendid idea of cutting up those out-of-date forms into scribbling pads for the others to use because the Stationery Department would never let them have any rough paper. And what would the stationery cupboard look like if she didn't keep it tidy? And who else ever thought of collecting the dirty towels and dusters at the end of the week and seeing that the right number was given out on Monday morning?

Miss Younge went through all the miscellaneous odd jobs that she had done in the last ten months. For she was one of those people who prefer to do any work except the work they are paid to do and she was always looking for something which gave her a chance to look busy and avoid translating which very much bored her; and she particularly liked jobs which kept her in the neighbourhood of Miss Saltman's desk where she could pick up a little information and where she liked to think she was a sort of Deputy-Deputy.

So now Miss Younge thought she was the obvious person to replace Mrs. Just. At first she thought she would keep the whole story as a secret but she was so excited that when she went back to the table she couldn't help telling the others what she had overheard. She stood with her hand on the back of a chair and looked round triumphantly. "Well, chaps," she said importantly. "I can tell you a real piece of news. Mrs. Just is leaving in a month and Miss Saltman is recommending someone to the D.D."

"*What's* that?" "*Mrs. Just leaving?*" "How do you know?" They all spoke at once. Miss Younge smiled complacently, "I slipped up quietly to sign the book and they didn't notice I was there and I managed to hear what they were saying."

The whole table now had a new burning topic for conversation to displace coffee, the tiresome habits of air raid wardens, and even the question of whether the windows should be open or shut. The post of Deputy Language Supervisor was coveted for, though the increase of salary was small, it meant escape from the rank and file and was supposed to be a stepping stone to the post of Language Supervisor. The work also was more interesting and the deputy sat at Miss Saltman's desk and looked important and was able to see and hear most of what was going on.

"I don't know who they will give it to," said Miss Younge. "But I know who ought to get it and that is someone who can make herself generally useful and above all, someone who *needs* the extra money."

"I don't agree with you," said Elsie Pearne. "There's a war on. They ought to give it to the person with the best translator qualifications. This is a translation department. Promotion ought to go to someone who knows her languages and is a good translator and has *done* translation for the last year. Some people seem to think that anything and everything is more important than translating in this place!"

"That's a nasty one for you and me, Younge!" squeaked Bobbie, putting three bulls-eyes stuck together into her mouth and passing the bag round the table. "I've not had any Hindustani to do for the last ten days."

"They'll probably choose Bobbie," said Elsie. "She's good at fetching coffee and she's always eating and they say that an army marches on its stomach."

But now old Mrs. Doweson was saying in her deep rich voice. "I think that authority in this place as in others should go to people with experience of the world and *tact*."

"That's just what I think," broke in Mrs. Jolly. "It ought to be someone who's been about and travelled and someone who's nice and friendly with everyone, not someone who's sarcastic or anything like that—" And Elsie riposted, "Someone strong and silent like Mrs. Jolly."

Everyone laughed at this home thrust but everyone thought that she hoped that the job, at any rate, would not go to that odious Miss Pearne. It was true that she was clever and she talked good sense—she often said exactly the right thing—but almost always in the wrong way.

And soon they all fell silent as each one, pretending to be engrossed in her work, counted up her qualifications and thought that they were just what were required for the post of Deputy.

Even Miss Purbeck stopped thinking of a delightful horror she had found in the newspaper that morning, and in the intervals of her struggle with a list of Italian rolling-stock, she cast her mind back to her old ladies and the life they had led her. If anyone knows about the need for tact, I do, she thought, and how to look bright and cheerful no matter what they say or do to you. I've had plenty of experience of the world and goodness knows I've travelled! And I'm fond of eating though I think that was one of Miss Pearne's sarcastic jokes—I can't see what that's got to do with being a Deputy—and no one wants the money more than I do. She went on pondering on the qualifications as enumerated by her colleagues and she seemed plainly to possess each one.

A good influence, thought Miss Jones, that's what is wanted here as everywhere else. And that, she knew she had always been able to exert; her late headmistress, dear woman, had always given her credit for her good influence on the dear girls under her care. No doubt, Miss Saltman had noticed how she always tried to be an inspiration to the rest of the Table and for that reason had selected her as Deputy. Well, if she were chosen, she would not fail to do her duty.

Of course, there is no doubt who ought to be chosen, thought the Hon. Cecilia Dunkerley, taking a brief moment's rest from her work to consider her own suitability for this post. Authority should be given to those best fitted by birth and heredity to exercise it properly. The difficulty was that she did not in the least want to be Deputy. The extra money and privileges meant nothing to her and she was satisfied that the work she was now doing was of more use to her country than the work she would do as Deputy. What she would have really liked would be for them to offer her the job in recognition of her right to it by reason of her superior claims of rank and for her to be able to refuse it. Yes, she would certainly refuse it. But would she be justified in refusing— after all, rank had its duties as well as its privileges. A difficult question! She must not waste time thinking about it now.

Promotion usually goes by seniority, thought Mrs. Doweson, and I'm senior in every way; I joined the Ministry a week before any of them, even Miss Saltman herself. But I'm too old. I don't want the job; promotion ought really to go to one of the younger ones—to encourage them. If I'm asked I shall say that.

Miss Pearne said they'll probably choose me, thought Bobbie, and she's sure to be right because she's ever so clever though I didn't understand what she meant about my stomach and I didn't think it a bit nice to talk about it before everybody like that. I'm afraid Miss Saltman wouldn't let me eat sweets if I sat up at her desk, I mean it would be a bit awkward if one of the big pots came up to the desk when I was in charge and I had a lump of toffee in my mouth. But I could eat plenty to make up at other times and it would be an awful lark to be Deputy.

Anne's clear young voice broke the silence. "I'm not perfectly sure what a Deputy *is*," she said shyly to Elsie. "But I rather think it's what I'm going to be. When Colonel Hilles interviewed me for this job, he said I might become a Deputy."

Every head jerked up. Everyone stared at Anne. Elsie looked as surprised as the others and did not answer immediately. Anne felt herself growing red. Had she said something terrible? Why were they all looking at her so indignantly? What on earth was the matter?

"I think you must have misunderstood him," said Miss Dunkerley, smiling at Anne to reassure her. "Miss Shepley-Rice is quite new and would be very likely to make a mistake of that kind," she said to the rest of the table.

"Of course," said Anne, who by now was scarlet to the ears. "Of course I've made a mistake. I didn't really understand what he said. Of course he meant something else and I've got it all wrong."

No further comment was made. Anne was too new to office life to realize the enormity of her crime but she saw that she had made a serious gaffe. With burning ears and hot face she bent low over her desk and hoped that by humility she might at last persuade her colleagues to forgive her.

At eleven o'clock Bobbie fetched the coffee as usual and they all stood round in groups, drinking, and munching buns and talking again about the enthralling subject of who was to be the new Deputy. Anne stood next to Elsie, sharing with her a bag of biscuits which Bobbie had fetched them.

They were both silent, Anne, because she was still feeling rather embarrassed by the thought of the howler she had made, and Elsie, because she was still pondering on her chance of becoming Deputy. Behind them Miss Younge was holding forth in her favourite soap-box manner to a little circle which stood round her. As she grew more excited she raised her voice and Anne heard her say. "That's just the sort of thing they do here. It's going to be another piece of jobbery. We're going to have one of the pin-money girls as Deputy—and a schoolgirl at that!" Someone hushed her loudly and pointed at Anne, who blushed once more and moved away out of earshot, fearing that by her unhappy remark she had made an enemy of Miss Younge.

Miss Younge indeed had taken a dislike to Anne from the first moment of her arrival. There were two reasons for this. In the first place she was jealous because Elsie was so clearly interested in this new girl and had never taken any notice of Miss Younge—indeed had always been rude and hostile to her. Miss Younge believed herself to be clever and knew herself to be poor. Elsie she thought, came into the same category. There they were, two of them alike, both clever and poor and she thought they should stand shoulder to shoulder against the rich and stupid. The second reason why Miss Younge disliked Anne was because Miss Younge was 'class-conscious' and was always glorying in her humble birth and her poverty and was always certain that people like Anne and the Hon. Cecilia despised her for these very reasons.

There was an air raid warning that afternoon, and down in the shelter Anne rubbed against a dirty wall and soiled her dress. "You've dirtied your pretty dress," said Mrs. Jolly. Anne glanced down and said indifferently, "What a bore! But it's quite an old one and I'm so tired of it. I wish I could afford a new one."

"Some people have to go on wearing their clothes whether they're tired of them or not because they haven't the money to buy new ones," said Miss Younge.

"Well, I *said* I couldn't afford a new dress," said Anne, very meekly because she felt she had once again somehow said the wrong thing in Miss Younge's hearing.

"Yes, but you don't mean it the way I mean it," replied Miss Younge aggressively. "You can afford it if you really want to while some people couldn't afford a new dress not if they lost the only one they'd got—"

"Some people," interrupted Elsie, "some people could afford plenty of new clothes if they didn't spend all their money on cigarettes!" And she continued in an audible aside to Anne. "They might even afford a clothes brush to brush the ash off the clothes they've got!"

Miss Younge opened her mouth to reply angrily and then looked at the derisive grin on Elsie's face and thought better of it. She turned round haughtily and stood up and walked away pretending that someone was calling her from the other side of the shelter.

"Elsie!" said Anne, giggling, "you really are naughty!"

"Serve her right," said Elsie. "Teach her to leave you alone. I heard what she said about you at coffee this morning. And anyhow it's true; it makes me sick to see her clothes all grey with ash like that. And what's more we've got rid of her. But what she said—or was trying to say—was rather interesting. I could see what she meant."

"I couldn't," said Anne, "What did she mean? You either can or can't afford a new dress."

"I think the point is that you each mean something different by the word afford. You mean, I fancy, that you think you oughtn't to buy one—it would be extravagant or inconvenient at the moment. But if you really wanted a dress you could raise the money at once. If you haven't got it handy, I bet you've got relations who'd give it you in a moment if you asked for it. (Quite true, thought Anne. Of course, Granny would send it by return.) And if you were ill or lost your job you've got people behind you who will look after you. And by the time you're too old to work any more someone will have died and left you enough money to live on. I know I'm right from the things I've heard from you and the people like you."

"Yes, I think you are right," said Anne. "But the people Miss Younge was talking of—surely they've got relations who would help them in any difficulty?"

"The people Younge was talking of have no one to help them. The relations they have are so poor that they've pretty certainly got to help to keep them. They've got to depend on *themselves* and *only* themselves. They have to put away a bit each week out of their miserable screw in case they get ill or lose their job—and an accident, bad health, a spell of unemployment can eat up in a very short time what it's taken half a lifetime to save. They have to dye their hair and look young somehow (Mrs. Jolly, who was so interested in listening that for once she was not talking, smoothed her golden curls a little self-consciously), they've got to look young somehow because they daren't look old or they'd lose their jobs—and a woman who looks over fifty has a tough time getting a new job. And when they're too old and can't hang on any longer they've nothing behind them but the few pounds they've saved—if they've been lucky. A career", she went on, her voice growing more and more bitter, "a career sounds grand when you're a girl just starting but by the time you're a middle-aged spinster it has lost most of its glamour!"

The All Clear sounded. Miss Purbeck shivered a little as she stood up to follow the others out of the shelter. Unpleasant as Pearne was, she always hit the nail on the head, she thought. Funny, that was just how things had happened with her. Twenty years it had taken her to save that hundred pounds and nearly all of it went in her journey home from Italy at the beginning of the war and the weeks that had passed till she found employment again. She was fifty-two, she had nineteen pounds in the bank and how long would it take her to find work again at her age once the war was over!

Anne had been out to lunch with Elsie that day. At one o'clock that day and every day that week they went off together. It was always Elsie who suggested it and Anne always agreed because it seemed the natural thing to do as they sat next each other and went at the same time, and also because it was a kind of armour against Seb. Each day Anne half hoped and half feared that she would find Seb on the pavement waiting with a taxi ready to take her to some real restaurant to lunch and each day she tried to persuade herself as she walked away with Elsie to the teashop that she was terribly glad that he had not been there.

And each day as they walked to the tea shop, Elsie put more into this casual friendship, reflecting that it was, after all, a bargain on both sides, for if the carrying off of Anne each day was a feather in her cap against the others, it was also something worth while for Anne, who was a sweet kid and all that and had met posh people but had never, it was clear, had much to do with anyone with brains. Anne was nothing but a baby, an absolute innocent who didn't know her way about at all and there were lots of dangers against which she could warn the child. And each day, as Elsie sat opposite Anne in the teashop, she thought how

pretty she was and she warmed at the thought that Anne was
there with her because she liked her better than the others and
had chosen Elsie and not any of the others to be her friend.

But to Anne, Elsie was just one of her colleagues and she was
still not quite sure whether she liked her or not, though she was
beginning to make up her mind about the others. Anne was sure
now that she disliked Miss Younge who was a nuisance with
her everlasting wrangling about nothing at all. Mrs. Jolly was
a nice old thing and easy to get on with; like Mrs. Just she had
worked in offices all her life and knew that you just had to like
your colleagues—or at least make the best of them. Miss Jones,
Anne thought, was kind but dull, and Miss Purbeck was just a
nonentity; she had been so knocked about by her old ladies that
she had no character or opinions of her own, nothing but her
ghoulish interest in death and disaster. Miss Dunkerley was
kind too but Anne was getting a little tired of being asked about
distant relatives whose names she could hardly remember—and
it bored the others and gave Miss Younge a chance to mutter
remarks about "snobs". Old Mrs. Doweson was one of the people
whom Anne was sure she liked. At their first meeting Anne had
thought her a most alarming old woman, but she soon changed
her mind. One evening they went out of the building and walked
towards the Tube. At the station Mrs. Doweson shook her head.
"I always walk home," she said. "After that odiously stuffy place
one wants some fresh air."

"I go in the same direction. May I walk a little with you?" said
Anne who felt suddenly ashamed of her laziness in face of the
older woman's energy. "I shall enjoy your company. I'm always
flattered when young people talk to me," said Mrs. Doweson,
and they set off together at a brisk pace.

After that they had begun to walk away together most
evenings. Anne chattered and told Mrs. Doweson all about her
old home and the dogs and found to her great delight that she
liked dogs too and had the same habit as Anne of stopping to
talk to every dog she met in the street. And Anne found that Mrs.
Doweson knew Seb and she liked to lead her on to talk of him
in a casual way. And she did not mind really that the old lady

suspected her secret though, of course, Anne was *very* careful not to give herself away! Mrs. Doweson talked to her of her own youth and told her amusing stories of the London world that she had known so well in the far-off 'nineties and of the days of King Edward. Soon they got to know each other quite well and a friendship grew up between the old woman and the young girl. But, indeed, she did not seem an old woman at all. She liked the company of young people and made them talk and listened to what they said and never snubbed them for their absurd enthusiasms and ideas. She was interested in everyone round her and everything that was going on in the world; she was interested in everything but herself and so her mind always remained young and lively.

All through the week the Table chattered and wondered about the new Deputy. Miss Younge hovered perpetually round the desk and strained her ears but she could hear nothing. Mrs. Jolly tried to pump Mrs. Just. "So you've heard I'm leaving, have you? I wonder who told you that?" said Mrs, Just and looked at Miss Younge. "Sorry I can't tell you anything. You'll all know when the time comes!" And that was all anyone was able to discover.

But on Friday, while Mrs. Just was out at lunch, Miss Saltman beckoned to Elsie to come up to the desk. Elsie stood up slowly and strode across the room. As Miss Saltman watched her coming and looked at her face, sullen and unsmiling as usual, she began to feel doubtful. But it was too late to change her mind now. "Miss Pearne," she said; "Mrs, Just goes away for her long weekend next week or perhaps it's the week after, I forget now. And I should like you to take her place and see how you get on. It's some time ahead, so I don't think I should say anything about it to the others till the time comes."

Elsie smiled with delight and triumph and for once she spoke good-temperedly and naturally like anyone else. "Of course I shall be very glad to help you, Miss Saltman—and I shan't mention it of course till the time comes. I'll get Mrs. Just to show me how she does things then I shan't have to bother you with questions."

"That's a good idea. Arrange it between you." Miss Saltman turned again to her own work and Elsie went back to the table, still smiling radiantly. All the afternoon she was smiling and good-tempered and the others stared and nudged each other in surprise at such an unusual state of affairs.

CHAPTER SEVEN
THINGS LOOK WELL FOR ELSIE

ELSIE WENT OFF to Surrey to spend the Friday night and the next day with her Aunt Min, for Saturday was her holiday, her day off instead of Sunday which was a working day in the Ministry. The weather was so fine and sunny it would be rather nice to spend a few hours in the country even in the rather boring and depressing company of Aunt Min. And it was a long time since she had last visited her aunt. The old lady would be delighted to see her—and still more delighted, thought Elsie grinning sourly, to see the two pounds which she was bringing her, the monthly allowance which for many years now she had regularly given her to supplement her pension.

Her working days over, Aunt Min lived in two rooms that she rented in a small villa in the outskirts of Guildford, the town where she and her sister had been born and to which, when she had to give up work, they had returned to end their days. She lived alone now for her sister Mrs. Pearne, Elsie's mother, was dead.

As Elsie strode briskly up the road from the station that evening, she saw her aunt waiting for her at the garden gate, no longer the Aunt Min of her childhood, prosperous and upright, but a bent shrunken little old woman of nearly eighty, who fussed around her with excited affectionate twitterings while

Elsie bent down and gave her a perfunctory kiss and followed her into the stuffy little sitting-room so overcrowded with large pieces of old-fashioned furniture that it was almost impossible to move. While the old woman made tea Elsie looked about her and thought that though she hated the furniture because it had come from her aunt's old home in London and reminded her of the miserable years she had spent there as a young girl, at the same time it gave her a feeling of satisfaction because after all she had escaped from the home she so much disliked and had gone out into the world and made good. I've done pretty well for myself, she thought, no doubt about that. I've had my ups and downs, of course, more downs than ups, lately, but that was only to be expected, all those war scares and then the war, nothing to do with me really, just bad luck. But my luck has changed I'm sure. I'm going to get Just's job; that's a start and it may lead to something. Why, Saltman herself might resign, or even get the sack—after all she's jolly inefficient and she'd have been found out long ago if she hadn't had Just to cover it up, to do everything for her. Of course I'll do what I can for Saltman but I don't know that I'll go as far as Just does. I'm not sure that it's fair to other people who really are competent. They'd have an eye-opener upstairs if they knew some of the idiotic things that Saltman does and Just puts right for her!

Aunt Min noticed at once that she was looking well. "Better than I've seen you for some time. How are things at the office?" she asked handing Elsie a cup of strong sweet tea.

"Not too bad," replied Elsie. "I'm liking it much better than I did at first," And then she told her aunt about a new friend she had made. "Real posh and ever such a nice kid. Makes me die of laughing the things she says sometimes." She related all that she had gleaned of Anne's life, the rich grandmother and the big country house and the horses and the hunting and the dogs. "Nice if they asked you down there for the holidays," said her aunt. "Perhaps they will," said Elsie. "You never know!" And she was getting on well at the office, she told her aunt, and was expecting to be promoted quite soon now.

"More money?" asked her aunt at once. "A bit more," said Elsie, "but nothing to speak of." There was a moment's silence. Aunt Min began to clear away the table and Elsie rose to help her. "Even a bit more is a help nowadays," said the old woman. "Things are going up so, it's a job to manage." "Well, I'm afraid I can't give you any more at present," said Elsie rather sharply. "It's a job to manage for all of us nowadays." Her aunt broke into hasty apologies. Elsie was a good girl to her and she hadn't meant to hint at anything, only there it was, it *was* a job to manage and only yesterday her neighbour had said to her—and she chattered on in her thin old-woman's voice while Elsie lighted a cigarette and leaned back in the armchair looking dreamily out of the window at the darkening garden.

Her aunt was right; it was a job to manage, and Aunt Min's weekly ten shillings was a far bigger strain on Elsie's resources now than when she had first begun to give it to her. Long ago, when Elsie was a child, after her father had died, Aunt Min had helped to pay for Elsie's training and had taken Elsie and her mother to live with her. As soon as Elsie began to earn she contributed to the cost of the household and later, in her prosperous days in Berlin, she had made her mother a good allowance. After Mrs. Pearne died Elsie helped Aunt Min, not out of affection but because it was the right and proper thing to do. While she was abroad and earning a good salary it had been no great effort; she was making good money and was able to save and hardly missed Aunt Min's allowance. It was very different nowadays. The salary she earned at the Ministry was very small compared with her salary in Berlin and even in the succeeding years when she had been less prosperous. But she had a tiny income of her own—some twenty pounds a year, the interest on her savings—which nearly covered Aunt Min's allowance, and after all, she reflected, the old woman was nearly eighty and couldn't live for ever! And there was nothing to be done about it. Aunt Min had nothing to live on but an annuity of twelve pounds a year and her old age pension and if Elsie didn't help her she would practically starve. And she was a damn sight luckier than Elsie, who would have no niece to help her in her old age—who would have nothing but her miserable twenty pounds a year and her old age pension.

Cheerful prospect! She always thought about it when she came to see Aunt Min. But to-night she put her gloomy thoughts aside; perhaps something might turn up, anyhow it was a lovely evening and good to be out of stuffy London with its dusty hot pavements. She let her aunt babble on about air raids and how dear the things were in the shops and she pretended to listen and now and then made a comment; and after the curtains were drawn they went out together into the garden for a few minutes and looked at the starry sky and the young moon and the people from upstairs came down with their dog and Aunt Min proudly introduced her clever niece who had such an important job in a government office in London but found time all the same to come and visit her poor old auntie.

Elsie found that the nights were noisier down there in the country than they were in London. People had told her that; outside London, the barrage was very heavy, and she found it quite difficult to sleep. "It's been like that now for some time, something terrible!" complained her aunt at breakfast the next morning. "Well, it keeps them away from us," said Elsie laughing, "and I expect you're used to it by now. Of course in London we never hear the guns; we have lots of warnings but we're so used to them now that we hardly take any notice."

"Touch wood," said Aunt Min. "I only hope those devils never do get through to you. They've done a lot of damage in Portsmouth, so one of the neighbours was telling me. Her daughter. . . ." She chattered on and Elsie sat lazily enjoying her brief holiday in the sunshine and fresh air. The country is very nice in the summer time, she thought, though I wouldn't much care to be here in the winter; I wonder how Aunt Min can stick it. Of course some people do like it always. Anne loves it summer and winter, she told me so. I wonder what she's doing now. Elsie glanced at her wrist watch. Just going out to lunch, I suppose. I wonder who with? And her face darkened.

Her aunt noticed that at once. They were sitting just outside the kitchen door and Aunt Min was busy shelling peas for their dinner. She dropped her hands in her lap and looked anxiously at Elsie who was staring sullenly down at the bottom of the garden. What could she have said to annoy her touchy and irritable niece—she was only saying that the butcher kept the best meat for those who had the most money. I suppose she takes that as a hint that I want her to give me more, thought Aunt Min. Goodness knows I do, but I'm not going to say so. I don't want her to get into one of her tempers; she can be so nasty when she feels like it. Aloud she said: "I've got such a nice tin of crab for tea, Elsie. I've had it saved ever since the beginning of the war, waiting for a nice treat and I think we'll open it to-day. I know you're fond of crab, always were when you were quite a kiddie. Remember, we always used to have it for tea on Wednesdays when I used to come to tea with you before your poor dad died?" Elsie yawned and smiled rather absent-mindedly. "Thanks," she said graciously, "that will be a treat. Mrs. Evans, my landlady, never gives me anything like that! What shall we do this afternoon? Would you like to go to a flick?"

The sun was low in the sky when she packed her case that evening and got ready to go back to London. "I must hurry," she said. "It's later than I thought. That clock right?" and she checked her wrist watch with a clock in an elaborately carved wooden case that stood on the mantelpiece. "Never loses a moment," said her aunt. "Remember when you brought that home? Your mother could hardly take her eyes off you!" Elsie smiled complacently and she was still smiling as she took leave of her aunt and hurried off to the station. She well remembered that day; she was home from Berlin on holiday, just before her mother died; it was her first visit home since she left England and she came to show herself off, to show how prosperous she was and how well she was doing and she had bought herself new clothes, an expensive fur coat, good shoes, new luggage, everything that was calculated to impress but was good buying all the same because it would last and would always be useful. For ten days she had peacocked about the house and bragged of her successes and enjoyed her triumph. Aunt Min had jeered at Elsie's ambitions when she was an unhappy frustrated child; now she had to accept her success and to admire the outward signs of her prosperity. She had been a fitter all her life and she knew quality in clothes when she saw it. She took Elsie's fur coat to the window and blew into the fur and even unpicked a little of the lining to look at the back of the skins; and she pinched the cloth of Elsie's skirts between her dry old fingers and looked closely at the silk of her blouses and grudgingly had to admit that everything was of the best that could be bought.

Those were the days, thought Elsie as she sat on the platform at Guildford and waited for the train. I haven't had much real luck since I left Berlin. But I believe my luck has changed.

It was quite dark now and still there was no sign of the train. She peered at her wrist watch by the light of a darkened lamp; the train was nearly forty minutes late. This was tiresome, she wanted to get home and go to bed early and be early at the office in the morning.

She was just walking down the platform to ask someone what could have happened when the train came in and she climbed thankfully into an empty carriage. After an unusually long wait at the platform, they moved out, only to stop again when they were hardly outside the town. When at last the train moved on again, it barely crawled and then it stopped again and then crawled on a little and stopped and then crawled on and stopped and crawled. Elsie fell asleep. When she wakened up the train was standing still and she could hear loud gunfire. She felt that she had been asleep for a long time but she had forgotten to wind her watch and it had stopped. She peered out through a crack of the blind. There's a funny glow in the sky over there. I suppose it's the moon rising or setting or something— looks more as if there was a house on fire. I wonder where on earth we are; we seem miles from London still. I believe it's an air raid. She went out in the corridor. A Canadian officer and an elderly man were standing talking at the far end and she went towards them. "Do you know if there has been an accident?"

she asked them. "This train is hours late already and we don't seem to be near London." "I'm afraid there has been a little trouble further down the line, Madam," said the elderly man. "But there is nothing to be nervous about. We're quite safe here." "I am not at all nervous, thank you," said Elsie rather coldly. "But I'm very tired and I want to get home. If you ask me, I believe the Germans have got through to London. The noise gets louder and louder as we get nearer in and I believe we're running into an air raid." The officer smiled at her. "I guess you're right. But I should hardly call this pace running."

Chapter Eight
SEBASTIAN AND MARY AT A PARTY

THAT FIRST night raid on London took most people by surprise. Of course there was no excuse for this. There had been plenty of official warnings. All through the summer, in every street, workmen had been building shelters while the passers-by looked on with amused eyes and said to each other that these shelters would probably never be used; the A.R.P. people went on with their practices and perfected their organization as they had been doing since the first days of the war while the outsider wondered if it were really necessary to have quite so many men "standing by"; the wail of the siren had been heard often enough, but day after day the sky over Central London remained clear and safe and Londoners went calmly about their business and did not believe in bombs till the first one fell.

That night, Sebastian Kimble, who believed in bombs on London as little as anyone else, was at a party with Mary Shephard.

It was the party to which she had asked him when they sat together in her car in Grover Street. The date then had seemed such a long way ahead that he had vaguely promised to go, and at once had forgotten all about it. Then Anne had talked to him of Mary on the terrace of Oddenino's and he had taken out his diary afterwards and looked up the date and thought that he must do something about it and had forgotten it again. But one didn't escape Mary so easily. The day of the party she telephoned him at the Ministry. As he picked up the receiver and heard her telling him that they were absolutely counting on him and that he was to meet her at the Dorchester at eight and they were driving out to the Andersons—at that moment his chief appeared at his elbow and Seb said, "All right, I'll be there," and hooked up the receiver as quickly as he could. That was the quickest way of ending the conversation. As the taxi took him to the Dorchester he was still undecided whether he wanted to go to a party at all but he meant to rely on the inspiration of the moment for some way of escape from the Dorchester if the rest of the programme seemed too unalluring.

Mary put down the receiver when she heard the click at the other end. Rather abrupt he had been but she supposed there had been someone else in the office. Now what was she going to wear? These uniforms that the men all wore now were one of the ways in which the war complicated your life; before the war you could be certain that a man would be your black and white background. Mary's eyes were baby blue and she was fond of emphasizing that colour in her clothes. But you couldn't do that when the man was wearing air force blue—the two shades clashed most horribly. Mary saw life as a series of pictures, in which she was the central figure; how she looked in those pictures was more important to her than anything else in the world, it was really the only thing that mattered. It was seeing herself in a picture that made her first decide to marry Sebastian. He fitted so well into those pictures, he was so tall and dark and tanned and he was just the right height and the right figure and the right type to throw up her fairness and her elegance. One day she had seen in a mirror the reflection of herself walking beside him and it had struck her at once how well they would look walking down from the altar and from that day she had decided to marry him. It would be a most suitable marriage too—Sebastian, son of Sir Henry Kimble and Mary, daughter of Sir John Shephard. Father would like it and would certainly cough up very handsomely, he could afford to now, he was making simply packets with all these government contracts. Sebastian wasn't so badly off himself, nothing of course compared to herself and he never seemed to have much ready cash—but there was land and a big house, estates and all that sort of thing—it wouldn't look as if all the money were on one side—Father would like that better, he didn't approve of penniless young men. And, of course, she was madly in love with Sebastian too, he was so charming, so much nicer than any of the men in Father's set, or Joan Anderson's set or, indeed, any of the sets she moved in. He was really county, of course, much better family than her own but that didn't matter because she had the money to make up for that.

She took out her mirror and looked at her hair; she would like to have it set; Mondays and Thursdays were her days; every third day she had it done, that was Jules's hard and fast rule, unless you had it done twice a week he wouldn't take you on, but if you wanted it done oftener, it was almost impossible to get an appointment. Jules was a marvellous *coiffeur*, not another in London like him, but he was a brute, you dare not be a second late yourself but he would keep you waiting half an hour if he felt like it. But what could you do? It was such an awful risk going to anyone else, especially now with this wretched war on; you might easily get someone who didn't know the job and have your hair absolutely ruined. This war was awful! They had no right to take hairdressers for the army. Suppose they took Jules! What on earth would she do?

But Jules was still there when she reached Maddox Street that morning. He was a soft plump elderly man with a soft plump hairless face. He looked soft, but Mary never found him soft, he was the hardest man she had ever had anything to do with. He was the only man on earth who had the whiphand of her and he knew his power and enjoyed using it. For ten minutes he made her coax and crawl and cringe and then he condescended to try and "fit her in for a quick set" if she waited till he was free. Mary, who had been prepared to wait hours if necessary, joyfully settled down for a morning of setting, manicure and facial.

The manicure girl was very tiresome that morning. Mary had to have the polish taken twice off her nails before she was satisfied. Mary was very proud of her nails. She wore them very long; they protruded quite half an inch beyond the end of her fingertips where they came to a point. They were the shape of an almond and about the same size. Of course she couldn't use her fingers at all, but then, of course, she never had to. She had broken the tip off one nail and she was frightfully upset about it. The colour of her nails was difficult. Pale colours were supposed to be the fashion in wartime and at first time she had quite a pale pink tint put on. But this morning, somehow, it looked dreadfully insipid and she had it taken off at once and tried a rust that the girl recommended. That looked very dowdy and she remembered now that she had decided to wear a sort of pinky mauve dress that evening. So, finally, she had a deep blood red that was almost purple. She wasn't even sure if she liked that, but she had to leave it. With two applications of polish each time, that had made six altogether, and it took some time. The girl who did her had been a bit off-hand the last time Mary had changed her mind—it was Saturday and long past one when they had finished and the girl obviously wanted to get away—Mary remembered that when she tipped her; the working classes were so selfish, always thinking of their own pleasures and Mary often found them rude and ungrateful. She suddenly thought of that dreadful taxi man on the day she had met Seb in Grover Street and she giggled at the thought of his purple angry face.

When Seb arrived at the Dorchester there was Mary waiting for him with three other girls and two young subalterns. "Darling Seb," she cried, and she floated towards him. "It's lovely of you to come." She squeezed his arm a little and drew him towards the others. "This is Seb Kimble—Pamela, Daphne and Jennifer, Captain Short and Freddie Standish. Freddie, get Sebastian a drink." One of the young men put a glass into Seb's hand, Seb emptied it and then fetched himself another drink and drank that and felt better and began to look round at the rest of the party. All three girls were like Mary, platinum blondes. Like her, they wore their hair in long curls reaching to their shoulders and their eyelashes were long and mascaraed and their eyebrows had been plucked clean and replaced by long painted lines and their faces were painted all over in much the same way, so that all four looked alike and as if they had been turned out of one mould. They all had slim well-shaped legs veiled by the sheerest of stockings and slim attractive bodies, and all wore very smart clothes and very short skirts.

They were all talking very loudly and at the same time and presently Seb gathered the subject of their conversation. They were, it appeared, a man short, and what was worse, a car short.

"We must find another man from somewhere, quickly, someone who has got a car and some petrol to make it go," said the girl whose young man had not turned up.

"We'll have to hurry up," said Mary, glancing at the little diamond-set watch on her wrist. "Can't you think of someone, Seb?"

"Well, as a matter of fact, I can," said Seb. "There's a man I know over there. I'll ask him if you like." There was a chorus of approving shrieks and Seb crossed over to where a young man was sitting alone at the bar and staring rather moodily in front of him.

He turned round with pleasure on his face when Sebastian spoke to him. They were old friends and had been at Oxford together.

"Doing anything to-night, Denis?" said Sebastian as he took a seat beside him and signalled to the barman. They ordered drinks and Sebastian delivered the invitation. "Can I come in these clothes?" said the young man whose surname was O'Connor and who was a journalist on the staff of a Dublin paper. "Of course—it's just a few people collected for drinks and a dance— at a house just out of London. You've got your car here?"

"Such as it is, it's outside," replied O'Connor. "and I can just manage the petrol. What will you drink?" They ordered another round but before they had time to drink it, Mary came over to them and met O'Connor and fluttered her eyelashes at him and then made them join the rest of the party.

They had a few more drinks and then Mary decided it was time to go on to the Andersons. Jennifer, she said, was to go with O'Connor in his small two-seater, while the others all crowded into the big chauffeur-driven Bentley which awaited Mary at the door. Captain Short was exiled to the seat beside the driver, Seb and Freddie Standish sat in the back seat, and the girls nestled down all round them in a scented tangle of slim legs and flowing silvery locks of hair. Seb put one arm round Daphne and one round Mary—no, it was Pam, no it wasn't, it was Mary all right—and they set off on their journey. He felt extremely hungry and hoped that dinner would form some part of the evening's entertainment, but he did not allow himself to hope too much for he had learned already that exquisitely slim young women like these around him, took little practical interest in food and were always ready to miss a meal for the sake of a pound or two lost in weight.

Their destination was a village about twenty miles to the north of London and they reached it about nine. The house where the party was given stood on the outskirts of the village and it was possible to locate it from quite a long way off by the noise which came through the windows, blacked-out and muffled though they were.

Nothing much could be seen of the house in the darkness except that it seemed large. It was, it appeared, the house to which the Andersons had evacuated themselves on account of possible air raids, but only Joan Anderson would be there to-night, her father and mother being away, most fortunately, said Mary, because they were frightfully dull and stuffy. Joan Anderson, who was waiting anxiously for them, looked very much like the four young women she was greeting so enthusiastically and also very like the dozen or so young women who had already arrived and were dancing with young men in uniform. Their hair varied from silvery gold to reddish gold; their eyes varied in colour and there was some difference in their features and the shape of their bodies, but their hairdressers and dress-makers and beauty specialists had so improved upon nature that the differences were almost obscured and they all conformed to the best Hollywood model. Joan, Sebastian learned, was one of Mary's oldest friends; like all the other young women, she dreamed of a career on the films and occasionally she got within sight of a part in the crowd; her parents appeared to be rich and to have a well-stocked wine cellar and that was all Sebastian ever discovered about her.

The party soon got going and Sebastian had soon drunk enough to be oblivious to everything but the necessity of enjoying it. And he was enjoying it. It was so long since he had been to a party that it seemed a new and delightful pleasure; the girls were pretty even if they all looked alike, and they all danced well and were gay and noisy and ready for any sort of fun that came their way.

Sebastian hugged them all impartially and danced vigorously to the very loud and efficient radiogram and had a lot more drinks. Everybody had a lot more drinks and there was a good deal of noise and a good many glasses were broken and then there came a big crash when three of the young men happened to sit at the same time on the edge of a table which gave way.

Luckily, as Joan said, it didn't really matter because the Andersons had taken the house furnished and no one probably would ever notice it. They had to stop dancing while two disapproving and sulky-looking maidservants swept up the mess; Sebastian and O'Connor escaped into the garden leaving their partners peering into mirrors and repairing the cracks in their make-up.

O'Connor was glad to be out of the stuffy noisy house; he was bored with this party and wondered how long Sebastian meant to stay and whether he himself would be able to get away. They walked together up and down the lawn and he talked volubly, glad of a more intelligent listener than Jennifer, in whose company he had had to spend most of the evening. Sebastian interrupted him suddenly. "Did you ever think of getting married, Denis?" he asked. "Married?" said O'Connor vaguely. He had been telling Seb a most interesting invasion-rumour story to which Seb appeared now to have been giving very little attention. "Married," he repeated rather sulkily. "No, I can't say that I ever did—not very seriously. For one thing my job's not very suitable for a married man—always on the move and generally in the direction of any spot of trouble that seems to be blowing up. Well, if you are married—" O'Connor stopped; he saw clearly that Seb was not interested in marriage as an abstract proposition or marriage as it affected O'Connor, but marriage as it affected Seb himself. So old Seb had fallen for someone, thought O'Connor, and supposed it must be Mary Shephard. "Of course it all depends on the woman," he went on aloud; "I suppose if I met someone whom I liked so much that I was ready to chuck my job for her and settle down at home—"

"I've never had to face that problem; I'd be only too glad to settle down. As for looking for a spot of trouble it seems to me that we've had the trouble looking for us ever since I can remember." They had reached the far end of the garden and now they turned and walked back towards the house. The sky was clear and full of stars and a young moon hung low over the trees. "Gunfire!" said O'Connor. "Can you hear it? You mean you've been waiting for this war?"

"Ever since I left school. And while I've been waiting it hasn't seemed worth settling down, getting interested in anything, or anybody for that matter—and then having to chuck up everything just as you are getting interested and having to go into the army."

"But you don't think the moment has come to settle down *now*, do you?" asked O'Connor. "The war certainly doesn't look like stopping just now."

"No, it doesn't, but it will sooner or later—it can't last for ever. And I feel much more settled and far easier in mind than I did in 1938 for example, when I was waiting for it to start; it's come now and some day it will end and if I haven't been killed by then, I shall have a chance to live my own life as I want to live it and not as someone else wants me to live it."

"How do you want to live it?" asked O'Connor. He was staring out towards the south-east where there was a faint red glow in the sky.

"As far away as possible from any of your spots of trouble," said Sebastian. "They just bore me and interfere with my plans. I want to live peaceably in the country, on my own land, or rather my father's land till he dies, when it will be mine. There's plenty for me to do. My father's getting old—health's not very good; he'd be glad if I took over the management of the estate. Or course money's the real trouble, our land is not very productive, we haven't got a coal mine underneath, we don't own any flourishing seaside towns, it's just plain honest-to-God agricultural land and what with taxes and death duties—my father inherited from his father only twelve years ago and we've hardly yet recovered from that—" They were near the house now. The door opened and a splash of light showed on the lawn and disappeared again immediately. They heard a man's voice raised in expostulation, angry and barely respectful and a girl's voice, petulant and complaining. Two girls were coming to meet them, Mary and the dumb little Jennifer. "Silly old fool, that butler," grumbled Mary, "fussing about the blackout all the time. Aren't you coming in, Seb? We've started dancing again." She hooked her arm through Seb's and led him towards the house. Jennifer, who was much younger than any of the others and barely out of the school-room, looked wistfully at O'Connor and wished he would take some notice of her. "Like to dance?" was all he said when they were back in the house, and then they were on the floor and O'Connor was looking over her head and watching Mary and Seb all the time. Mary was certainly attractive and deliciously pretty with her shining silvery hair and pale blue eyes and scarlet mouth. But her hands were claw-like with their long red nails and her face was ill-tempered for all its prettiness, drawn into pettish lines even now when it lay against Sebastian's brown face. . . And I seem to find the happiness I seek, when we're out together dancing.

They all danced. "Cheek to cheek." Sebastian gathered Mary more closely into his arms and whispered into her ear and she gave a little gratified smile. "I'm in heaven! I'm in heaven!" moaned the radiogram. "Isn't this a *lovely* tune?" gurgled Jennifer. "You know I *do* think the old tunes are nicest. I was still at school when 'Top Hat' was on, and one holiday I went seven times to see it. . . ." Jennifer chattered on and O'Connor thought, I don't like these people, they're bogus all through, bogus film stars, bogus society girls with bogus complexions and bogus manners—everything's phoney and the Shephard girl is the phoniest of the lot. I'm sorry Seb's going to marry her. There are the guns again. I'm going to get away from here and see what's happening,

"There's a big show on, I believe," said O'Connor to Sebastian over the heads of the girls they were dancing with, "I'm going to have a look-see. You can't see anything from here, the house is down in a hollow but I believe you could from the top of that field opposite."

"All right, I'll come with you. Give me a call," said Seb. He danced with Mary next. "Isn't it damned hot," she complained. "Let's go outside. It's a glorious night. No, not out there," she said as Seb turned obediently to the door which led to the garden. "There's that mouldy old dragon out there to see we don't smoke. Let's go the other way." They walked on down the road into the shadow of a wood. As they moved further from the house the noise and laughter and music died away and the sound of the guns from the direction of London became louder. Mary shivered.

"Cold, Mary?" said Sebastian and put his arm round her. She nestled up against him. "No, not cold a bit, but those guns are so depressing. Let's be rustic and sit on that stile over there." They crossed the road and walked slowly under the shadow of the trees to a path which ran through the wood and was closed by a stile where it joined the road.

Seb lifted Mary on the topmost rail and stood beside her; obviously she expected him to kiss her; well, he would in a moment, she was eminently kissable, but just now he wanted to finish his cigarette more than anything else.

He had just ground its butt into the soft earth with his heel when he heard footsteps running down the path behind them through the wood. Seb stepped forward and almost collided with O'Connor, hurrying towards him. "Just going up to the house to look for you, Seb," he said panting. "There's the biggest fire you ever saw over there." He waved his hand towards the hill down which he just come. "I'm going to look at it. Coming too?"

"A fire? Where?" said Mary. She jumped down from the stile and stood powdering her face by the dim light of the setting moon. "I'm not going to look at it. Whatever do you want to go for?" She spoke pettishly and, turning her back on Seb, began to walk back in the direction of the house.

"It's an enormous fire," said O'Connor, "and there's an extraordinary show going on—there's certainly a big raid over London. You can see the shells bursting and the searchlights." Seb began at once to think of Anne. Where was she? Was she safe? Would she be frightened? "I've never seen a really big fire," he said aloud. "I wonder if it's far away. Where is it, do you think?"

"It can't be far away. You can see the glow quite distinctly." They caught up Mary and walked one on each side of her back to the house.

"You aren't coming with us, Miss Shephard?" said O'Connor when they reached the front door. "No, of course not!" she snapped. "I'm not such a fool. Don't be long, Seb." She went into the house and the door slammed behind her.

The two young men walked back down the drive to the line of cars.

"Where's the fire?" said O'Connor to a chauffeur who came out from the kitchen quarters at the sound of their footsteps. "I don't know, sir, exactly. They're saying half London's afire. Jerry's over here in his hundreds—it's a bad business. Be careful of your lights, sir, if you're going out." He helped O'Connor get out his car and guided them into the dark tree-shaded lane and they crept along through the darkness till they came out on the London road lying clear before them in the starlight. O'Connor put his foot down. The road wound up an incline and round a bend at the top and as they followed it, they saw the dull glow of the fire on the horizon. Searchlights were sweeping over the sky, converging and then separating again, giant white fingers, feeling their way delicately, hunting for the enemy who twisted and turned to avoid them. From here they heard the thud and bark of the guns clearly and distinctly and saw the shells bursting and dissolving.

"A big show," said O'Connor soberly. "They've got to London all right."

"Go on further," said Seb, "Let's find out what's happening. That fire can't be far away."

They drove on a few miles and the glow seemed to grow brighter. "It's over there!" said Seb excitedly. "Behind that hill. Take the first cross road on the left." After another mile or so they came to a small side road and O'Connor turned up it. They were facing south-eastwards now and the fire was almost in front of them. The whole sky above it was red and its glow was reflected on the great clouds of smoke which rose up and rolled slowly towards them. The narrow road twisted continually and always the fire seemed to be round the next bend.

"It's further away than I thought," said O'Connor after a while. "I've no notion where we are but we're nearly into London." They were off the main road and fields lay all around them, but ahead, outlined against the fire, they could see factory chimneys and houses. The road climbed another small hill. When they came out on the top the whole arc of the sky was exposed before them. The searchlights seemed all to be converged on one point and in the light a German plane could be seen, struggling to escape. "Look! Look!" cried Sebastian. "They've got that chap!"

O'Connor looked, and as he looked, the front wheel slid gently off the road and the car came quietly to rest in the ditch. "Damnation," he said changing into reverse and accelerating violently. That was clearly of no use and Sebastian, who was uncomfortably near a prickly hedge, climbed out at the back. O'Connor followed him and they made ineffectual attempts to push or pull the car out of the ditch.

"No good," said O'Connor at last. "We'll have to get a tow. What's the time?"

Sebastian yawned. The effects of the drinks had passed off and he felt extremely sleepy. He struck a match and looked at his watch. "Nearly four. It will soon be light. It doesn't look as if much came down this road, though, even in daylight."

"Afraid there isn't much chance of getting back to that party," said O'Connor.

"I don't mind," said Sebastian. "It was pretty dull. I'll phone Mary in the morning and explain that we had a breakdown. One of us had better walk back to the main road and try and stop a lorry."

"I think the show's nearly over now." In the last half hour the guns had become noticeably quieter and they could no longer hear the throb of enemy planes, but the fire burned redder than ever, waxing and waning. "What fools we were, that fire is nowhere near," said O'Connor staring over in its direction. "It's in the East End of London, it must be in the docks. I heard they'd started some trouble there in that raid in the afternoon—they've come back to finish the job. I believe we passed a farm about a mile behind. I'm going to walk back to it—-they're probably awake by now. You stay here in case anything comes along."

O'Connor went off down the lane and Sebastian climbed on a gate and sat facing the east. The injury to his back hurt now; he had danced too much and drunk too much as well. He thought about Anne. Where had she been during the raid? The searchlights were extinguished one by one and the guns were quiet. For a little while there was complete silence and then a bird began to twitter and a cock crowed from nearby. Another answered immediately and soon there was a chorus from all round. The sky grew light and more birds sang. Over in front of him, a great rounded thundercloud rolled up in the clear sky. The rising sun pointed one side of it a delicate mother-o'-pearl. He looked at it again and saw that it was not a thundercloud but a dome of smoke rising up from the fire.

Chapter Nine
ANNE FORGETS TO BE
FRIGHTENED

ANNE WAS VERY TIRED and went early to bed. Agnes had gone to the theatre with Joe because it was her birthday and had left Anne a cold dinner on a tray and as soon as Anne had finished she had got into bed and fallen asleep almost immediately.

She wakened to the sound of aeroplane engines and gunfire and then a long whining scream and a boom. She sat up in bed. Her heart was beating fast. "That must have been one of those screaming bombs; but a long way off," she thought. There was another immediately and certainly much nearer and then a third and a fourth, nearer still. Anne trembled all over and her heart beat wildly. How cold it has got and yet it was such a hot evening, she thought. There was a terrifying scream. Anne flung herself into the bed and pulled the clothes over her head, certain that the bomb was coming directly at her. There was a deafening explosion and the house seemed to rock backwards and forwards and there was a tinkle of falling glass as the windows gave in the houses nearby. The irregular beat of the German aeroplane engine could be heard distinctly and as if it were cruising round directly over the house. Another bomb fell, a little farther away, but near enough to shake the house again and a shower of broken glass fell on the balcony outside her window. Anne got out of bed and pulled jumper and slacks over her pyjamas. She was trembling all over and hardly knew what she was doing, but she could not bear to be up there alone in her room any longer. She groped for her torch and could not find it. Another bomb fell and she was in a panic and could not even find the light switch. The house rocked again and she was sure it would fall on her and bury her beneath it. It stopped rocking and she found the torch just where she had put it on the table beside her bed. She opened the door and went out on the landing. There was nothing to be heard now but a German engine throbbing in the distance and the tinkle of fire-bells. Anne sniffed and was sure she could smell smoke. The house was quite quiet and dark but the stairs creaked further down. She did not dare to switch on lights in case there were blackout curtains unpulled. Her torch was weak and she was afraid it would not last so she began to grope her way in the darkness. The stairs creaked again and she called out, but no one answered. She flashed her torch, but there was no one there. When she got to the ground floor flat she knocked on the door. There was no answer. She knocked several times and realized that the people must be out and she was alone in the house. The smell of burning was stronger now. It was not imagination. There was a fire somewhere near, but the smell seemed to come from outside. She opened the front door and went out on the steps. The whole eastern sky was lit by a red glow. It was the reflection of a huge fire and the smell of burning, faint at first, was now stronger. Smoke clouds hung overhead and were yellow in the glare of the fire below. All London seemed to be burning. There was no one out in the street. It was quite light with the glow of the fire and Anne could see from end to end, but there was no one at all in the street and no traffic. The glow in the sky grew bright, then dull and then bright again. It seemed very near, but Anne was to learn next day that it was as far away as the Docks, but was such a great fire that its reflection spread all over London. She wanted to go and look at it but she heard the German engines coming nearer. She ran back into the shelter of the house. Another bomb fell at once and the house rocked again. She crouched on the stairs, remembering hazily that this was supposed to be the safest place. This time she knew the house would fall. But it stopped rocking and she was still alive. She sat on the stairs and trembled each time she heard a bomb fall and was terrified.

But after a little she did not feel quite so frightened. The house still stood and she began to reason with herself and repeat all the reassuring things she had read and heard. There are a million houses in London—more—two or three million — it must be several million chances to one that this house will be hit she thought; they say that you don't feel so frightened if you don't own you are frightened. I'm not frightened. . . . A sort of faith cure. . . . I'm not frightened; I'm *not* frightened, I was only startled, I wakened up suddenly. She told herself over and over again that she was not frightened. And she did not feel so frightened. But she was cold and the stairs were hard and uncomfortable and the house was dark and creepy. She thought she would go back to her room. But before she went up she went out again on the steps. The sky was still bright with the fire and the moon was shining and it was suddenly very quiet. In that moment of stillness she heard dogs barking, a chorus of barking, shrill barks as if the dogs were frightened. She stiffened with attention and listened anxiously and then she remembered the veterinary surgeon at the back. Behind her house and the neighbouring houses in the road was a mews, built long ago for the carriages and horses of the owners of these houses. Now the stables were mostly garages but Mr. Bates, a veterinary surgeon, had converted a block into surgery and dogs' hospital and a flat for himself and his daughter. Anne had already made friends with the daughter and the kennel-maid when she had met them out with the dogs at exercise. The noise of barking came from that direction and Anne was terrified at the thought that the hospital, full of sick dogs, might have been hit or perhaps be on fire. She had slammed the door behind her and was running down the street as fast as she could towards the entrance to the mews before she knew what she was doing; it was a quite mechanical action in which her brain seemed to play no part. The guns were roaring again and shrapnel clinked on the pavement round her but she did not notice it; she thought of nothing but the pitiful barking of the dogs and the necessity for reaching them and helping them.

The mews was bright in the light of the moon as she ran down it. She saw wardens knocking at the doors of the flats over the garages, calling if there were anyone within; a pale face looked down from a window and a woman hurried out of a door carrying a baby. A motor-car stood outside Mr. Bates's door, a warden stood by it and he was urging Mr. Bates to hurry, telling him he must go at once while Mr. Bates walked calmly backwards and forwards to his hospital, coming out each time with a dog or two dogs on leads, speaking quietly to them and calming their excitement and packing them into the car. Anne stepped back into the shadow of the wall and came quietly up. The car was full now and the kennel-maid, whom Anne knew, was just driving it off as she arrived.

"How many were in that car?" said Mr. Bates.

"Eight, Father, and there are twelve more," called a girl's voice from inside.

"Four minutes more, Mr, Bates," said the warden, "and then you'll have to go, dogs or no dogs."

Anne slipped into the house and saw Miss Bates on the stairs. "What's happened?" she asked, following her up.

"Unexploded bomb; they've just found it; wanted us to go at once—with twenty sick dogs on our hands! Shut the door behind you and I can turn on the light." Miss Bates seemed to take Anne's presence and help as a matter of course. She hurried down a passage with Anne on her heels. "Let's clear the infectious ward next," she said. "Lucky there are only two distemper cases in it." They were in a small room now. Two puppies whimpered in deep beds of straw. "They must be wrapped in blankets. You'll find some over there." Anne fetched the blankets and Miss Bates filled a hamper with straw. "I'd like to give them hot-water bottles—but it's a warm night and they haven't far to go."

"Where are they going?" asked Anne, lifting up one of the puppies and wrapping it carefully in a blanket. The puppy pushed its hot nose into her hand and tried feebly to play.

"To Robson's—only five minutes away. We made arrangements that if either of us were bombed we'd take the other's dogs." The puppies were warmly packed up in the hamper. Miss Bates quickly washed her hands in disinfectant. "After handling those infectious puppies," she explained and Anne followed her example. Then they each took one end of the hamper and carried it down to the door.

"Now the walking cases," said Miss Bates, hurrying back into the hospital. "Then Eileen can start off with them as soon as she comes back with the car—in that little room on the right down the passage—if you can manage them, I've got two broken legs to carry down." Miss Bates pointed to a door and Anne went in. Two spaniels and a poodle were sitting up in their cages, whining and looking anxious. "Poor darlings," said Anne, stroking their heads. "You can't think what is happening; but you're going for a nice walk now." She looked round for leads and found them hanging on the wall. Luckily the dogs wore their collars in readiness for just such an emergency as this, but they were puzzled and excited and it was with some difficulty that she got the three of them out of the room and down the passage to the door. The car had come back and Mr. Bates and the kennel-maid were packing the hamper with the puppies, into the boot. An anxious-looking warden was helping, urging them all the time to be quick. Anne handed over the three dogs with Miss Bates's message and the kennel-maid set off with them at once, the dogs gambolling beside her as she ran up the mews in the bright moonlight. Miss Bates appeared at the door carrying two small dogs with bandaged legs. "Only five more now," she said, "but they'll all have to be carried." She laid the two dogs down gently into baskets which had been put ready on the floor of the car. A policeman had arrived now. "I'll give you one more minute, sir," he said. Mr. Bates nodded absentmindedly and followed the two girls into the hospital. Anne picked up a little Pekinese. "I can manage another small one if you put it into my arms." Miss Bates gave her a small Sealyham with a bandaged head and Anne carried them out to the car and made them as comfortable as she could. Mr. Bates and his daughter appeared with three more. "Peter! Where's Peter?" cried Anne. Peter was a Dalmatian, the Bates's own dog and it was while stopping in the street to talk to him that Anne had first made the acquaintance of the kennels.

"Up in the flat," said Miss Bates. "I'll get him next."

"I'll fetch him," said Anne. "Poor old chap, he'll think he's being left behind."

"The door's open—if you would fetch him," called the other girl to Anne who was already on the stairs. She found Peter sitting up in his basket in the dining-room, quiet, but clearly worried and alarmed. For a second he looked at her doubtfully then smelt her hand and recognized her. All animals loved and trusted Anne. "Darling! They wouldn't go without you!" she said to him. "I wonder if there's a cat." She ran into the kitchen and there was a cat asleep in a chair. She took it up in her arms and looked quickly through the other rooms to satisfy herself that there were no more animals left behind, and then, hooking a lead on Peter's collar, ran downstairs. She met Mr. Bates on the way. "All finished now," he said. "I'm just taking a last look round. I'm extraordinarily obliged to you for helping—though I don't know how you got here." He patted Anne hastily on the shoulder and she smiled and hurried on downstairs. Miss Bates was in the car and Peter climbed up into the seat beside her. Mr. Bates came out. "That's the lot now. I'll just put a few clothes in a bag and we'll go." But a regular force of wardens had arrived and a policeman took his stand before the door. "No, sir," he said firmly. "I've let you get the dogs out but you're none of you going back into that place till the bomb's removed. Move along, now, please." Wardens and police made a cordon behind them. Anne jumped on the step of the car and it moved slowly along, up the mews and down Cromwell Road till it reached her own front door. Then she dropped off and ran into her own house. As she closed the door behind her she was almost surprised to hear a bomb scream in the distance. She had forgotten about the raid while she was with the others, helping with the dogs. She was tired with her exertions and sat down on the stairs to recover. Funny how you forgot to be frightened when there was something to do; she felt much more jumpy now that she was back alone in this silent creepy house. As soon as she got her breath back she went up to her own room and put on the light and lit the gas fire and made herself some tea. She drank it and began to feel sleepy. What was the good of sitting about like this? It would be better to go to bed. There was the office in the morning to think of; she'd be a wet rag if she didn't get some sleep. She got into bed and put the pillow over her head to shut out the noise of the raid and pulled the bedclothes over that. In a minute she was fast asleep. She wakened again later and it was quiet, but she was very hot with all the things piled on top of her. She threw them off and listened, but she could hear nothing but the fire-bells in the distance. She hoped the dogs were happy in their new quarters. She fell asleep and slept till she was wakened by the All Clear.

It was daylight then and she got up and opened the windows wide and looked out thinking she would see all the houses around her in ruins. But everything looked just as usual. The early morning sun was shining straight down the street, the pigeons were cooing in the roadway and the sun made long shadows behind them; she could hear a milkman clinking his bottles while the road sweeper placidly clattered his shovel and broom; from the distance rose the usual hum of traffic. Then Agnes hurried into the room: "Miss Anne, how worried I've been about you! I shall never forgive myself! I came upstairs as soon as I got in, but you were asleep so I didn't wake you. Were you very frightened, all alone in the house like that?"

"Not at all," said Anne, not quite truthfully, as she got back into bed. "What happened to you? Tell me all about it." Agnes began a long story; they had been told to stay in their seats at the theatre till it was safe to go home—the actors and actresses had come back on the stage when the play ended and entertained them and cups of tea and cakes had been sent round to everyone; if she hadn't been so dreadfully worried, it would have been quite a pleasant evening—but the police and wardens wouldn't let her out of the theatre though she tried several times—when it was a little quieter they got away and had to walk all the way home—"and words couldn't say what I felt when I come up and see you sleeping there in your bed so peaceful like a baby!" she ended. "You're an old angel, Agnes," said Anne. "But you mustn't worry about me. I'm not a baby and I can perfectly well take care of myself." She yawned and before Agnes was out of the room she was fast asleep again.

CHAPTER TEN

MISS PURBECK HOPES FOR THE WORST

ELSIE AND ANNE both arrived punctually at the Ministry next day. And indeed hardly anyone was late, and no one, high or low or old or young, had made the night's happenings an excuse to stay away. But everyone was tired and sleepy for hardly anyone had slept, and everyone was anxious to relate the story of "my" bomb and to point out that they had only been startled and not at all frightened once the first shock and astonishment was past.

"What a night!" said Miss Purbeck. "But it's nothing to what's coming to us."

"Well, it was quite enough to go on with as far as I'm concerned," said Mrs. Jolly. "A bomb fell right in the street behind us and the whole house rocked. I flung myself on the ground and—"

Miss Younge interrupted her. "I was standing on my doorstep," she said, "and the blast nearly blew me off my feet." Everyone began to talk at once. Everyone had felt the blast and everyone's house had rocked and everyone's bomb was bigger and nearer than anyone else's. They were all telling their stories and interrupting each other and no one was listening to what anyone else was saying, when old Mrs. Doweson said, "What has happened to Miss Jones? Shouldn't she be here to-day?" Everyone stopped talking and looked vaguely round for Miss Jones. "Perhaps she has been bombed. It's awful to think that there are nine of us here to-day at this table and in six months' time we may all be dead," said Miss Purbeck. "There were thousands killed last night, so the bus conductor told me."

"You certainly are our little ray of sunshine," said Elsie scornfully. "Why should Miss Jones have been bombed?"

"All right," said Miss Younge who had just come back to the table and sat down in her seat. "I went up to speak to Mrs. Just and Miss S. was on the phone to her."

When Miss Jones arrived an hour later she looked woebegone and exhausted and very unlike the usual neat ex-governess. She was wearing a miscellaneous collection of clothes obviously borrowed from friends and her hair was damp and streaked with dirt. A bomb had exploded on touching the roof of a nearby house and had damaged the roof of her own house. A large cistern had been dislodged, and had crashed through the floors below emptying its contents on to Miss Jones in bed, as it came to rest in the corner of her room. With the water came plaster from the ceiling and at the same time the blast drove the soot from the chimney in a black cloud across her bed. The soot and the plaster and the water had covered her and all her belongings in a horrible mixture, a black, dank filth which lay on the floor several inches thick, on her clothes, in her shoes, on the brushes on her dressing-table, on all the furniture and on her face and hair.

Kind neighbours, whom she had never seen before, had taken her in and fed and warmed her and lent her the clothes in which she now appeared. She had struggled along to the office, prepared, in spite of her night's experiences, to do her ordinary day's work, and she would have stayed if Miss Saltman had not sent her off.

Anne was with the others in a little group standing round Miss Jones, sympathizing with her and listening to her story that for the moment made all the other tales seem flat, when she saw the swing doors open and Sebastian came in and walked up to Miss Saltman's desk. Anne heard him ask politely for leave to speak to Miss Shepley-Rice and she saw Miss Saltman's gracious smile of assent and Mrs. Just's quick glance of interest from him to her. Then he came over in her direction and pleasure and resentment fought within her and resentment won. For a whole week, she thought indignantly, he has shown no signs of wanting to see me; he might have done something about taking me out to lunch but day after day has gone by and there has been no sign of him. It was true, she admitted, that she had forbidden him to wait for her, but still, if he had sent a message as agreed, she would have forgiven him. And now here he was in her own department, doing just what she had told him he was not to do. Sebastian reached her and saw the anger in her eyes. "Good morning," he said. "I came to see if you were still alive."

"Yes, thank you," replied Anne eerily.

"No adventures last night?" asked Seb rather lamely.

"None at all, thank you," said Anne determined not to help him out. Then Sebastian had an inspiration. "Commander Birchenough wants someone to help with some Portuguese. Would your supervisor spare you for a few minutes; it's a quite short thing but not supposed to leave his room."

"It's for Miss Saltman to say," replied Anne. "We must ask her."

"Why didn't you telephone to Miss Saltman?" said Anne, angrily, once they were outside the door. "You promised that you would not speak to me at all in the office."

"I couldn't telephone Birchenough's message because, you know, I only just that moment thought of it!"

"What!" said Anne still more angrily. "You mean to say you made it up!"

"Yes," said Seb, grinning at her. "Don't you think it was a bright idea?"

"I think it was monstrous," said Anne and then she began to laugh too.

"It was, I admit, a lie," said Seb. "But a lie in a good cause. I'm awfully relieved to see that nothing has happened to you. I worried about you quite a lot last night."

"That was very nice of you," said Anne. "I'm quite surprised that you remembered me! How goes your flirtation with the glamorous Mary Shephard?" It was a shot in the dark but Anne saw at once, to her horror, that it had found its mark. For Seb was blushing, there was no doubt about it; he was blushing and uncomfortable and at a loss for something to say and when he thought of something to say it only made matters worse. "Oh! Don't let's bother about Mary," he said in an elaborately casual voice. "Will you dine with me to-night?"

They had reached the lift and Anne put her finger on the bell. "I'm rather tired after last night," she said in a casual voice intended to match his. "I don't think I want to go anywhere this evening. I shall go home and go straight to bed." The lift doors opened and she stepped in and looked back at Seb. "Good-bye," she said and then, as the lift rose and she looked again at him and thought his expression was disconsolate and rather touching, she called back in a much kinder voice, "One day next week, if you'll send me down a note."

Now why did I do that, she thought, as the lift rose to the top floor where she got out and began to walk down the six flights of stairs, very slowly, to give Seb time to vanish. It would be much better if I never saw him again.

When Anne returned to her seat, Elsie was sitting, biting her nails, scowling down at her work. Neither of them spoke for a moment. Then, "Who's your Air Force boy?" began Elsie.

"Why do you say *my* Air Force boy?" said Anne, on her guard at once. "He's nothing to do with me. He came to ask me to do some work in his section."

"Don't tell fibs, Anne. It's not like you and they don't deceive me in the least. You can't pull wool over *my* eyes," said Elsie. "He knew your name for I heard him ask Miss S. if he could speak to you. Come on, out with it! Who is he?"

Reluctantly Anne told his name and his position in the Ministry.

"But you knew him before, didn't you? You never told me anything about him. I asked you if you had a boy friend and you said you hadn't." Elsie spoke sullenly in a voice full of resentment.

"But, my dear Elsie," said Anne, "You can't expect me to give you a catalogue of every man I've ever met in case one of them comes in and asks me to do a translation."

"From the way he looked at you it strikes me he had a good deal more to say to you than that!" said Elsie who was too jealous to attempt to hide it.

"Well that's just where you're wrong," replied Anne. "I don't believe we said more than a dozen words to each other and I don't suppose I'll see him again for months and months." I don't suppose I shall, she thought dismally; why on earth did I refuse to go out with him to-night?

"Was it an interesting translation?" asked Elsie a moment later.

Anne looked up with a blank face. "Which? What do you mean?"

"The one you had to do for Birchenough. It didn't take you long, did it?"

"Oh! Don't be so absurd, Elsie," said Anne, half laughing, half resentful. "Kimble is just a man who lived near us in the country. You were going to tell me just now about what happened to you last night. That's much more interesting. Do go on with it."

Elsie was pleased. So far everyone had been far too intent on their own stories to pay attention to hers and she willingly gave Anne a detailed recital of all the happenings of the night. And as she talked Anne reflected that she must write to Sebastian and tell him that never, never, never must he come and speak to her again in the office because it was quite unbearable to be cross-questioned in this way by Elsie.

When Elsie had finished her story the two of them fell silent and began to work. I wonder if she's telling the truth, thought Elsie. She doesn't *sound* as if she thought much of him—he's a good-looking chap—I believe I've seen him before. And then she remembered. She had met him at the door of the Ministry a few days ago—on Anne's first day—and he had reminded her of Benno. She felt a double pang of jealousy—jealousy of the young man hovering in the background trying to snatch Anne away from her—jealousy of Anne's youth and Anne's lover who was like Benno, her own lover of so many years ago, who was gone now and would never come back.

About twelve o'clock there was an air raid warning and everyone trailed down wearily to the shelter and sat there and yawned and told their bomb stories all over again to anyone who would listen. Then when the All Clear went, they all trailed wearily back to their places. It was a very long day; everyone got sleepier and sleepier as they tried to concentrate on work. To keep awake, they began to talk and then started work again and nodded over their desks and drank as many cups of strong coffee and tea as could be obtained. As long as the sun shone, everyone spoke in a cool and detached way of air raids and bombs and all the things that had happened in the night. But when the sun's rays lengthened and evening was near, faces grew quiet and the talk more sober, and everyone began to think of what was before them all. Everyone asked everyone else what she was going to do and everyone said, "As soon as I get home I shall go straight to bed."

So from the Ministry and from everywhere else where work was done on that Sunday, the workers poured into Tubes and buses and went to their homes to meet what lay before them in the second night of the great attack upon London. They were taking part in a great page of history; but they did not know it; they only knew that danger and discomfort, boredom and hard work were their portion day and night and they just wondered how long it would all last.

The sirens sounded that night as soon as it was dark, just as the blackout curtains were being drawn—but this time no one was taken by surprise; everyone expected it and took to the nearest basement or cellar or garden Anderson.

That night Elsie was just finishing her supper when the warning came, a deafening howl, because the siren was quite near and the wind blowing from that direction. She forced herself to eat quietly and when her plate was empty, deliberately lighted one of the cigarettes that she smoked so rarely and stood up and cleared away the dishes and took them into her kitchenette and washed them and put them tidily into the cupboard. But she rattled the plates a good deal and she noticed that her hands were trembling—entirely of their own volition, for, she assured herself, she was not in the least frightened. It was a curious thing which she had noticed last night already that, though at a moment of danger you might feel perfectly calm and collected, your body might play all sorts of pranks on you. She had often heard the expression "cold with fright"; well, she was cold enough now, suddenly, shivering as if it had been the middle of winter instead of a warm night in September; and yet she was not frightened. She told herself that several times, just as Anne had done last night and as a good many other women in London were doing at the same time.

However, now that the washing up was finished and her room was tidy, she decided she had better go down to her landlady's Anderson shelter. Elsie had promised to go and the woman would be glad of her company. The guns were barking now and something sounded unpleasantly like a bomb in the distance. Elsie put on her warm coat, took a pillow and a rug and her torch and groped her way down the stairs, through the stuffy smelly kitchen and out through the dark garden.

Mrs. Evans, the landlady, with her girl and boy and baby were already inside. The shelter was very small. Two camp-beds, one on each side, took up most of the space. One bed was for Elsie, who was to share it with the girl, the other for Mrs. Evans and the baby and the boy. The girl sat reading quietly by the light of the hurricane lamp, the baby whimpered in its mother's arms and the little boy talked continuously of guns and bombs and aeroplanes; "That's a Jerry, Mum. Listen, do listen. And that's one of our Spitfires, can't you hear the difference in the engine's beat, Mum?" He pulled at his mother's sleeve and she shook him off impatiently. Elsie sat by the girl on the camp-bed, her feet tucked under her to keep them off the floor which was wet even in the dry summer weather, and tried to read a paper which she found in her coat pocket. This shelter is pretty awful, she thought, the crying baby and the tiresome little boy. "Mum, can I go outside for just a minute to look at the search-lights? Mum! Do you think that's a Blenheim bomber? Mum! That's one of our naval guns up at the recreation ground—that big one that's just gone off. Coo! Don't it half make a row!"

Elsie stood up. "I think it's quieter now, I'm going back to the house," she said. Mrs. Evans looked wearily at her.

"I wouldn't if I was you—Oh! That child—" The boy had made a dash for the entrance as Elsie went towards it. She caught him outside in the garden as a bomb came down with a whistle and the windows rattled in the house and she dragged him back into the shelter. His mother cuffed him heartily and while he and the baby wailed in chorus, she pleaded with Elsie. "I wouldn't go back to the house, miss, if I was you; it's better, safer like, if we're all together. Baby will be quiet in a minute; he's over excited like, after last night." And in a few minutes, indeed, the baby stopped crying and fell asleep and his mother laid it in an improvised cradle beside the camp-bed and took the little boy on her lap till he fell asleep, too, in her arms. The girl had already put away her book and, curled in a ball like a kitten, was asleep at the foot of the bed. Elsie stretched out her long legs cautiously so as not to wake the child, laid her head on the pillow and in a few minutes, was fast asleep.

Anne had just finished her dinner when the sirens sounded that evening; Agnes was in the room clearing the table, and she at once issued a peremptory invitation to come down to her own shelter, making it quite clear that she did not expect Anne to disobey. She plainly had it on her conscience that she had been out and left her the night before. Then she bustled round the room and helped Anne to change into slacks and a sweater in which she could sleep comfortably and found her book and her torch and a coat and hurried her downstairs.

The shelter was a big cellar reached from the area and built under the pavement. It had been freshly whitewashed and was lighted by electric light and looked very clean and comfortable. There were bits of carpet and linoleum on the floor, the radio was installed in one corner and a kettle was singing on a small portable stove. It was furnished with odd chairs and upturned boxes and some makeshift beds were laid out in two alcoves which had evidently once been used as wine cellars and had shelves round them and round arched roofs.

The other occupants of the cellar stood up as Anne came in and Agnes introduced them—an elderly butler and his wife from next door where they were acting as caretakers, and their daughter, Doris, a munitions worker. "I hope you don't mind them being here, Miss Anne," whispered Agnes. "Don't be such a dear old snob!" Anne whispered back, "I hope they don't mind me."

For an hour they sat around and read the evening papers in turns and talked and listened to the radio. Then everyone began to yawn. "If you wouldn't mind sharing that corner with Doris, Miss Anne," said Agnes pointing to one of the alcoves, "you'll find it more comfortable than it looks."

In a short time they were all rolled up in blankets on their mattresses, Anne lay beside Doris and by the light of a shaded nightlight looked up at the comfortingly strong-looking roof above her. Down here the noise of the raid was much less intense and although the earth trembled from time to time there was none of that sickening swaying of the house that she had felt upstairs. She was soon sound asleep.

Later she wakened and went out into the main cellar to fetch a drink of water. Agnes was asleep in two chairs, her dog on a cushion near her feet. He thumped his tail sleepily on the ground as Anne stooped to pat him. From the other alcove she could hear the regular breathing of the old butler and his wife. Overhead, the guns barked and rumbled, but down here it felt peaceful and safe. She got into bed and was asleep again in a few minutes and did not wake till she heard the tinkle of teacups.

"It's half-past six, Miss Anne," said Agnes bringing a cup over to her. "The All Clear went nearly an hour ago." Anne sat up and looked round in bewilderment before she realized where she was. The others had left the cellar and the door was now wide open and the daylight and fresh air streamed in. She drank her tea and ran upstairs to the bathroom. It was another glorious day and the sunlight poured in. As she bathed she sang happily. She felt completely refreshed after her good night's rest. It was a lovely day and she was still alive to enjoy it.

It was slow work getting to the office. Diversions were more usual than a straight road and the buses wandered through narrow streets hardly large enough to hold them, where from the seats on the top you could see right into the front floor rooms of the houses on either side. The roads were strewn with broken glass which was being swept up into great piles like heaps of snow waiting to be taken away. Glass was everywhere except in the windows, the tyres of the cars rolled over it, the shoes of the passers-by crunched it to smaller pieces. Bombed houses were already too much of a commonplace to be noticed; they lay in depressing heaps half across the roadway and the traffic squeezed past in the space that was left or went by another route. One house attracted Anne's attention as she passed it. It was a big house from which the entire front had been ripped away and it looked like a giant doll's house, In the rooms thus exposed, the furniture stood, hardly disturbed; there were pictures still in their places, clocks on the mantelpieces, a bookcase by the wall with all the books still neatly arranged; the drawer in a hand-some mahogany chest was half open. Whoever that belonged to must want the things out of that drawer, thought Anne; but perhaps all the people who lived there were dead. There were many groups of people that morning who had been bombed out the night before, waiting for some conveyance to take them away. A crowd of them from a tenement building which had been destroyed were waiting to get on to Anne's bus. They all carried bundles and bags of the few belongings they had been able to save. They looked tired and bewildered; here and there women were crying a little for their lost homes, but they cried quietly for they were all quiet and resigned.

CHAPTER ELEVEN
TABLE TWO CARRIES ON

AFTER THAT SECOND night Londoners began the curious cellar and basement life which was to be their lot for the next months.

When the translators reached the office, everyone had tales to tell of the unusual places and circumstances in which she had spent the night. Miss Saltman had slept on a mattress beneath a grand piano. Perhaps because she was an enthusiastic amateur musician, she had complete faith in the piano as a protection from bombs and had slept excellently. Miss Dunkerley had been staying in a big West End hotel which had been hit. With the rest of the guests and the staff she had been bundled out quickly into the adjoining Tube station; there lying on the platform she had slept soundly for the rest of the night on a mattress which she shared with a chamber-maid from the hotel. Miss Jones had slept in still stranger company; her own flat bombed, she had gone to stay with a friend, but the friend was called out on night duty and the flat was high up in the building, and when the raid started, seemed very noisy and insecure, so Miss Jones was glad to accept the invitation of Monsieur François, the owner of the French delicatessen shop below, to take refuge in his basement. When she went down with Monsieur François, she found there Fred, his waiter son and Fred's friend Ernie, who was someone on the railway, and Madame Marchand, a stern woman with a tightly upholstered black satin bosom and a little pork-pie hat set squarely on her head. Miss Jones sat and talked French brightly and drank a glass of M. François's excellent wine, till the bombs began to fall most uncomfortably near and pieces of the ceiling crashed down. Abandoning the conventions, the company took the best cover they could find; Madame March-and hung her hat carefully on a peg and then, seizing a large tin pail, put that on her head and retired under the kitchen dresser, where she crouched and cursed the "sales Boches" in a steady mutter. Fred, Ernie, and M. François dived under the kitchen table and when a louder and nearer crash came, pulled Miss Jones in with them. They stayed there, hunched up together and finally fell asleep, and Miss Jones, prim retired school-mistress, awakened in the dawn to find herself more or less in the arms of a perfectly strange young railwayman.

One of the others had slept in a broom cupboard and some-one else in the hall and somehow or other, everyone had had a tolerable night's rest. Only the indomitable Mrs. Doweson had slept serenely in her bedroom on the upper floor of a high London house, "It's quite right for you young people to look for safe places, you've your life before you. But at my age, a year or so more or less, doesn't matter. And my own bed is so comfortable. I enjoy it so much—I refuse to leave it."

Bobbie was absent to-day and no news had yet come from her. Miss Purbeck speculated happily upon her probable fate. "Bombed quite certainly. I heard her neighbourhood was almost destroyed," she said brightly. "You know it's like the ten little nigger boys although we are only nine! Two of us have been bombed. I *wonder* who'll be the next—to-night, I expect. Three hospitals were bombed last night and did you read about the girl who was trapped under tons of masonry? It's in the papers to-day; just fancy, she's lying there now almost crushed to—"

"Oh! Do shut up!" said Elsie angrily. "You get on one's nerves with your everlasting defeatism. You know quite well that everyone is a bit jumpy wondering what may happen to them next and you just make everything worse! Really you behave like someone in German pay. That's what the Germans do—pay someone like you to go round spreading rumours and telling horrible stories."

"Miss Pearne!" gasped poor Miss Purbeck, scarlet with horror and almost in tears. "How can you say such a dreadful thing!"

Elsie did not condescend to reply, but went on with her work. The rest of the table were silent too and bent their heads over their desks and did not look up. They did not care to associate themselves with the rudeness and violence of Elsie's words but they agreed with it in substance. Miss Purbeck in peacetime would always have been a bore; in wartime she was almost a danger. All the morning she had been dropping into their ears gruesome stories of the terrible dock fires which were still alight. With the smell of burning in their nostrils all through the day, her tales of burning flesh were unendurable. She couldn't be a German agent, thought Anne. Or could she? I suppose that's what fifth columnists are like. Just ordinary-looking people going round, spreading rumours.

For the next week the guns were seldom silent. Sometimes they seemed to go on without stopping for the whole twenty-four hours. Soon their sound became the background to ordinary life—that ordinary life which was so extraordinary but which Londoners had to pretend was ordinary because only in that way was it possible to live at all. For the extraordinary had to be tamed and ignored and overcome, it had to be reduced to the ordinary as quickly as could be done; conditions were chaotic but chaos had to be conquered. The first thing everywhere and all the time was to get small things straight. There was no time to stand and stare, there were too many practical problems to solve. True, a country cousin up for the day to look at London's ruins might gape and gaze at the great craters in the streets; these immense fantastic holes only astonished Cockneys on Monday—by Friday they were just a familiar and tiresome obstruction to the traffic; there were too many other things to think of—how to get to work and how to get home again, how to cook the breakfast on the faint glimmer of gas that was all most people could coax from their burners, how to make the tea, let alone how to wash or bath, when there was no water at all in the taps. Scrambling over the broken houses, through the dust and the rubble, picking their way through the broken glass and the broken pavement stones, few people had time to look up at the battle which went on overhead by day and by night.

Sunday, September 15th, was another gloriously fine day. Under a deep blue sky through the early morning sunlight, the staff of the Ministry made its difficult way to the office, and as the last arrivals entered the door, the first warning of the day yowled out and everyone was sent down to the shelters. They stayed there an hour. Table Two sat in its usual corner of M.4 and gossiped and knitted and read and reread the newspapers to the last word of the last small advertisement and yawned in desperate boredom. "Well, it took me nearly an hour to boil a kettle on a methylated stove this morning," said Mrs. Jolly. "The gas was cut right off though we did have a little last night, and if I'd have known we were going to be kept down here like this I would have waited and cooked myself a proper breakfast—" "I'd have stayed another hour in bed," said Miss Younge. "I'd have had a proper bath," said Anne. "There was such a tiny trickle of water—" Miss Younge interrupted her, "Mrs. Just is the wise one, she has stopped in bed or had a bath or a proper breakfast— she isn't here anyhow." Everyone looked round for Mrs. Just but she was clearly nowhere in the shelter. "*She* wouldn't stop in bed; she's much too virtuous," said Miss Purbeck. "Perhaps," and her face brightened, "perhaps she's been—" "Now you shut up," interrupted Elsie with quite a gay laugh. "We all know just exactly what you're going to say—a nice little piece about how she's been bombed and is probably now writhing in agony and just what's going to happen to all the rest of us. Consider it said! We've heard it already. Eh?" She looked round at the others for approval and there was a general titter of laughter in which Miss Purbeck joined, though with a reddening face. A few minutes later the All Clear sounded and they all stood up and pushed towards the door. "Miss Pearne is very cheerful nowa-days, did you hear her *laugh*," whispered Mrs. Jolly to Miss Purbeck as they began to climb the stairs. "Air raids seem to agree with her, that's twice I've heard her laugh in the last fort-night. I don't believe I ever saw her even *smile* before." There was a block on the stairs ahead of them and the two plump little women stopped thankfully and leant against the wall, panting and fanning themselves with a folded newspaper. "Oh! These stairs! They'll be the death of me but it's no use waiting for the lift with a crowd of us like this," moaned Mrs. Jolly. "I wonder why Miss Pearne is so pleased with herself. Do you think she's had good news?" "If she has it's bad news for someone else," grunted Miss Purbeck. "Now, we're off again. They say the first ten years are the worst!"

Elsie continued to look cheerful when they were back in the department and her spirits rose as the minutes went by and Mrs. Just still did not appear. Presently the telephone rang and Miss Saltman answered it. After a few minutes' conversation she put back the receiver and sat with a gloomy face, fiddling with the papers on her desk. Then she looked up and beckoned to Elsie.

Elsie, who had been watching her intently, rose quickly to her feet and strode up to the desk. Miss Saltman greeted her with a worried smile and waved her towards Mrs. Just's vacant chair. For a few minutes they talked together and then Elsie came back with a beaming face just as Bobbie appeared with the big white enamel jug full of steaming coffee. Anne groped under her desk and took out their two Woolworth mugs and together they went over to Bobbie to have them filled. "Come over to the other side of the room. I've got some news for you," said Elsie as soon as they had wriggled themselves out of the crowd round Bobbie, holding their mugs stiffly in front of them so as not to spill any of the precious contents. "I've got some news," she went on, "and I don't want anyone else to hear it yet—the others will all be pretty fed up when they do hear it so we may as well have a little peace till then."

They crossed over to a quieter corner of the room. Elsie opened a packet of biscuits, gave some to Anne and they both began to munch. "Well, what is the news?" said Anne. "You look quite pleased—out with it. Don't keep me in suspense."

"I am pleased," said Elsie complacently. "I'm pretty sure that I'm going to get something I want quite badly. That telephone ring just now was from Mrs. Just. There's a time-bomb in her front garden, she says, and she and her old mother who lives with her have had to turn out at five minutes' notice. Now she's got to take the aged parent up to Cambridge and park her with some aunt or someone so she isn't coming in to-morrow. Saltman is in an awful flap and she wants me to take Just's place. Once I get a chance to show Saltman what I can do I'll get the Deputy job all right when Just leaves—I know how to manage her—and that, my dear Anne, is why I'm feeling pleased!"

"Oh! I am pleased too, Elsie," said Anne. "Congratulations! So you are going to be our new Deputy. Isn't that fun! Do the others know?"

"Not on your life, and don't you tell them a word. They're not going to know till I'm actually appointed. I'm not going up to the desk till to-morrow. We're so behind with our work with all these warnings and hours down in the shelter that Saltman wants me to go on translating to-day, but to-morrow morning you'll see me up there sitting in state and then the balloon will go up—the others will just be frantic with jealousy—but we'll keep them guessing, I shan't say a word——Oh *damnation*," she cried angrily, stopping short. "Oh! *Curse!* Isn't that *sickening*," cried Anne, "off we go again to that wretched shelter!" The sirens were howling again and grumbling and muttering, the translators hastily drained their mugs of coffee and reluctantly allowed themselves to be herded to the shelters once more. Downstairs, seated on the cold hard cement bench, leaning wearily against the cold hard wall behind her, Anne thought about the news Elsie had just told her. Anne felt very pleased that Elsie was going to become Deputy when Mrs. Just left, Elsie wanted the job very badly so it was nice that she should get it. But mixed with Anne's unselfish pleasure at the news was a feeling that it was satisfactory from her own point of view. It would mean, Anne hoped, that she and Elsie would not be *quite* so much together; they would no longer sit side by side and perhaps she would not have to go out to lunch *every* day with Elsie. Of course Elsie was an awfully good sort and it was jolly nice of her to look after a new girl like Anne the way she did—Anne did appreciate it—but she did find the weight of all this affection a little oppressive—Elsie seemed to hang over her, there was no other word for it, so much that sometimes Anne wanted to push her away. Now Elsie would be thinking about her new job and not bother so much about her. Anne straightened herself up and smiled unconsciously. And beside her sat Elsie, smiling too, at the remembrance of her talk with Miss Saltman.

"Well, what the hell you two have got to grin at, I don't know!" said Miss Younge staring at them suspiciously. "Personally, I can see nothing delightful about being in this blasted shelter—"

They were kept in the shelter for the rest of the morning. About one o'clock, after discussion among the wardens, Mrs. Doweson made an announcement. "The All Clear has not yet been sounded," she said, "but the Head Warden says that those who wish may go out to lunch at their own risk. At your own risk, mind, and I advise you to be as quick as you can."

Elsie stood up at once and stretched her cramped limbs. "Come along, Anne, let's go out," she said, "I'm sick to death of this beastly hole."

"Yes," agreed Anne eagerly. "Let's go out and get a breath of fresh air; we might as well die of a bomb as of suffocation. I'll go up and get my things. Shall I bring yours?"

"We're not allowed to go upstairs," said Miss Jones who was standing near them as they were waiting to file out of the doorway. "Mrs. Doweson has just told me. We may go out of doors at our own risk and if we're killed the Ministry is not responsible, but if we go upstairs and are bombed, it is responsible."

"We'll just have to go as we are, then, lucky it's so fine," said Anne as they slowly followed the crowd up the flight of stairs which led to the entrance hall.

At the front door stood the Head Warden. "Remember you go out at your own risk," he called at intervals. "The raid is not yet over." But no one paid any attention; they all pushed out eagerly into the fresh air and the sunshine, everyone bare-headed and most of the women in their gay chintz office overalls.

"My word! It's good to be out! Pouf!" Anne took in great gulps of the air. "Where are we going? It's Sunday, you know. Not many places are open and with all of us coming out together like this—"

"The little dairy in the lane," said Elsie. "We can get a sandwich there. We shan't have time for much more."

Miss Dunkerley and Mrs. Doweson, standing on the doorstep, watched them hurrying down the street, Elsie, tall and gaunt in her sensible mannish clothes, leaning over Anne, holding her possessively by the arm, Anne with her golden head and gay dress, pattering along in her high-heeled shoes, trying to keep up with Elsie's long rapid strides. "That's a strange friendship," said Miss Dunkerley, "a very strange friendship; I know if I were that child's mother I should greatly object to her association with that awful woman!" Mrs. Doweson laughed. "My dear Cecilia!" she said, "parents nowadays are not allowed to choose their daughters' friends. In any case I think it will do Anne good to find out that there are people in the world outside her own small circle. Miss Pearne is the one who is more likely to suffer from the association. She doesn't understand Anne and Anne doesn't understand her, Anne listens to all that Miss Pearne says as if it were the most interesting conversation she had ever heard and as if she had been waiting all her life to meet Miss Pearne, Miss Pearne takes that at its face value and believes it; she doesn't understand that Anne is a kind-hearted well brought up little girl on her best behaviour for the moment. Miss Pearne's idea of good manners is extremely elementary; it would never occur to her that Anne is just giving a display of extra good party manners. Anne is rather impressed with Miss Pearne, rather flattered because she has been taken up by some-one much older and more experienced than herself—perhaps she is rather sorry for her—and so—as my grandson would say—she is ladling out charm by the bucketful. And, of course, she doesn't understand the effect that charm is having on an emotionally starved middle-aged woman like Miss Pearne—nor will she understand how much pain she is giving when presently she turns her charm on someone else—as she will do—if she hasn't a young man already, she certainly will have one soon. I am sorry for the unhappy Miss Pearne."

"Unhappy!" said Miss Dunkerley. "Really if anyone deserved to be unhappy she does—with such objectionable manners!"

"Perhaps, unlike Anne, she had no one to teach her good manners when she was young; I agree that if she had, she was very badly taught," said Mrs. Doweson smiling. Miss Dunkerley looked up at the sky as if she were wondering whether to take an umbrella. "I don't see any German aeroplanes about. I think I must try and get something to eat. You're not coming?" "I can't leave here till the All Clear is sounded. Don't go too far!" Mrs, Doweson stepped back into the doorway and Miss Dunkerley went down the street.

Anne wanted to buy a newspaper and she stopped Elsie by the newspaper seller's pitch at the corner. A little crowd stood round him. On the wall behind was chalked, "Lunch-time Score. Nine-teen Germans down for one British." "Dozens of them down," he told Anne as she bought a paper. "One down in Victoria station yard, 'eard it coming down meself, didn't 'alf make a row."

They ran on to the little dairy and found it crowded already with the Ministry staff all hungry and thirsty after their long morning in the shelters. Behind the counter, the proprietor and his wife and all the helpers that he could muster, stood hacking off rough sandwiches and pushing them into the eager hands outstretched towards them. After many minutes of waiting and of pushing and being pushed, Anne and Elsie were able to secure a hunk of bread and meat each and a bottle of milk with a straw. It was out of the question to sit down in the dairy, impossible even to eat standing up, and clutching their food, they edged their way out again through the narrow doorway while still more of their colleagues pushed past them to get in, fearful that nothing at all would be left by the time they, the latecomers, at last reached the counter.

"Where are we going to eat these?" said Anne, when they got out on the pavement again. "Mine's beginning to disintegrate already and I know I shall drop this bottle!"

"I'm going to eat mine here," said Elsie. "There's nowhere else to go." "A picnic in the gutter," said Anne. "Rather fun though I wish there wasn't quite so much broken glass about—and that nasty smell of burning—The wind's blowing it this way; it's from that block of workmen's flats; it burned all night and they worked all night getting the people out and at eight o'clock this morning a time bomb went off. A lot of A.R.P. people were killed, I'm afraid. One of the charwomen told me, her son was one of the demolition squad and he went off duty a few minutes before the bomb went off," said Elsie. Anne shivered a little and looked up at the strip of blue sky over the narrow lane. Down at the far end she could see the great trees of Lincoln's Inn Fields, waving in the sunlight and the pigeons cooing and lazily hunting for food. "It seems so extraordinarily peaceful here in the City on Sunday like this—one can't believe—" She pushed the straw through the cap of her milk bottle and drank, leaning up against the lamppost. Mrs. Jolly joined them. "You are lucky, getting milk," she said. "They only had this dreadful fizzy ginger beer left by the time I got to the counter." She took a drink through her straw and then began to giggle. "Do look at poor Miss Dunkerley," she whispered to Anne, "I feel I ought to go and hold a coat in front of her; she looks so unhappy." Anne turned cautiously and looked at Miss Dunkerley. She had been squeezed out of the dairy by the crowd and was now standing on the pavement, half turned towards the wall, shamefacedly eating and drinking in the public street. But no one was paying any attention to her; the air was full of rumour and there was excited talk all round. Hundreds of German bombers, it was said, had been over London that morning, flying up the Thames Estuary in wave after wave, and the R.A.F. was attacking them and every few minutes came the news of another and yet another German brought down in the dogfights which were raging overhead. But the Germans were on the run now, it was said, and in fact the All Clear was sounded a few minutes later. Miss Saltman bustled up. "I think we ought to go in quickly now," she said. "We've had such a wasted morning, we must try and get something done now."

"It's not our fault, Miss Saltman," said Elsie indignantly. "We don't want to go down to the shelters. Why don't they let us go on working?" Miss Saltman shrugged her shoulders. "I'm afraid I can't do anything about it, but I think we shan't have many more days like this. I've heard that we're going to have a roof spotter almost at once, then we'll only go down when enemy planes are overhead." "About time, too," answered Elsie. "Come on Anne, if you're ready."

They hurried back up the lane to the Ministry and were admitted through a narrow crack in the door while every pass was examined with more than ordinary care. "The German army might get in disguised like you and me!" said Elsie with elaborate sarcasm, as they stood waiting their turn to get in. "The watchmen only look at us four times a day so they can't be expected to know us by sight!" "Well, I suppose they have to keep to the rules and do as they're told," said Anne placably. "What's going on over there in the hall?" As they came nearer to the entrance they saw inside the hall, a watchman shaking a money-box, a miniature Spitfire: "Twenty-seven Germans down, official," he shouted, rattling the coins in the box. "Show your gratitude and help us to buy the Ministry Spitfires." The women emptied their purses of small change as they passed him, the men searched their pockets. Soon his money-box was full and another had to be found. Even as Anne and Elsie were passing through the hall, news came that another German was down and the watchman changed his chant to, "Another wicket down! Twenty-eight Germans down."

As quickly as they could, the translators hurried to their tables, settled at their desks and got out their work and were soon absorbed. There was a most unusual silence; even Mrs. Jolly was silent. Everyone was anxious to make up for lost time, shocked at the wasted morning they had spent in the shelters. For some minutes there was nothing to be heard but the scratching of pens and the rustle of paper and the click of the clock hands jerking slowly forward. And then came the howl of the sirens, faint and distant at first, then near and loud, loud enough to drown the howl of indignation from the outraged translators, as they slammed down their desks, collected their belongings and wearily stood up and set off once more on the journey downstairs to the shelters.

They were downstairs for the rest of the afternoon, while the battle raged overhead and hundreds more of the enemy swept over the Home Counties to the attack upon London. On that day the Germans could claim that they had successfully interfered with essential war work, for almost the whole of the working hours had been spent in the shelters. But they paid dearly for it. When the day's total bag was counted up, it was found that one hundred and eighty-five German planes had been destroyed. For the translators it had seemed just one tiresome day like any other tiresome day and it was only later that they learned that it had been one of the "great" days for the R.A.F.

CHAPTER TWELVE

ELSIE MUFFS IT

WHEN MRS. DOWESON reached the office next day, she found that exceptionally she was not the first to arrive. Elsie was there already, seated at Miss Saltman's desk in Mrs. Just's chair, hard at work, rapidly, calmly and competently sorting and reducing to order the untidy mountain of papers which had accumulated during the one day that Mrs. Just had been absent. And while Elsie was sorting the papers she was making good resolutions. I must do everything to avoid any quarrels, she was thinking. Fusspot Saltman hates quarrels. Of course Just butters up everyone and they all adore her. I know they'll never adore me. But I must try to get on with them somehow. She looked up as Mrs. Doweson was taking off her gas mask and haversack and all the various objects she carried about her person. Bet this is a shock to her, she thought, I must be civil and polite. So she said brightly, "Good morning. I've come early as I've got to be up here to-day." "Oh, indeed!" said Mrs. Doweson and reflected: Mrs. Just is away and this awful woman is being tried out as Deputy; they ought not to appoint her; she's too common—no manners at all. But then she recollected her own manners and said, "Isn't it a lovely day, Miss Pearne?" "Yes, it is," said Elsie. "You see I've left the windows open," and she waved her hand towards the side windows through which a rather chilly early morning breeze blew down on to Table Two. "As I shall be sitting here the draught won't worry me so I opened them to please you."

"Er—thank you," said Mrs. Doweson surprised by this unexpected politeness and rather annoyed to be obliged to accept. "I certainly think some fresh air will do us good after all those hours we spent yesterday downstairs."

"Well, we shan't be doing that any more," said Elsie. "The roof spotters have arrived already, I've just been hearing about them from another D.L.S. who came in with me." *Another* D.L.S., thought Mrs. Doweson. She regards herself as already appointed as Deputy. I wonder if that's correct? Elsie went on, "The roof spotters are going to be stationed on the roof and we shall go on working after a warning is sounded until the spotter signals that enemy planes are approaching and then we shall go down to the shelters till the danger is past. That's going to mean that we shall probably be downstairs for a few minutes only instead of hours and hours like yesterday." Proud of her inside knowledge she went on to explain how during a warning, junior staff would take turns to stand by the lift shaft on each floor and when danger threatened the spotters would whistle down the lift shaft and the watchers would take up and pass on the warning and so on. And Mrs. Doweson listened patiently, and with apparent interest, and did not allow Elsie to guess that more than a week ago she had been told all about the plan when she dined with her very old friend, the D.D., Colonel Hilles.

All the time she was talking, Elsie was working and soon the desk before her was covered with neat little piles of papers, returns to be filled up here, memoranda there, translations completed in one tray and documents for translation in another. By the time Miss Saltman arrived, everything was in order and all the papers and the returns forms were laid out ready in the same way that Mrs. Just always arranged them. Miss Saltman, as always, soon lost her way among the papers but Elsie quietly put her right again. The first hour passed as smoothly for Miss Saltman as if Mrs. Just had been there. Miss Saltman was pleased and Elsie reflected that life was "not so dusty" after all.

When Anne came in she greeted Elsie with a wink and a grin and went quietly to her place. On her way to the Ministry she had wondered how the others would take it and she found as she had expected that they were taking it extremely hard. Elsie Pearne as a possible Deputy was a bitter pill to swallow, so bitter that it soon displaced bombs and air raids in the conversation at Table Two.

"Why is Miss Pearne sitting up there?" said Mrs. Jolly sharply as soon as she came in.

"Why indeed," said Miss Younge gloomily. "That's what we all want to know. Mrs, Just's away of course but Miss S. has never had anyone to take her place when she's been away before. Myself, I think it means the worst."

"Not that she's going to be Deputy?" said Mrs. Jolly, tossing her yellow curls. "You don't think that, do you? What an awful idea! Oh dear! Just when we've got such a lot to put up with, what with these tiresome raids and the gas and water cut off at home and the noisy nights and queueing up for the buses and standing the whole way—Yes, Miss Jones, you may well stare! That's Miss Pearne in Mrs. Just's place, our new Deputy, if you please!" Miss Jones, who was short-sighted, took a pair of old-fashioned folding pince-nez from the breast-pocket of her coat and polished them on her large dazzlingly white linen pocket handkerchief. Then she adjusted them on her nose and looked towards Miss Saltman's desk. There was no possible doubt of it. There sat Elsie hard at work beside Miss Saltman. Miss Jones flushed a little. "Dear me! How very surprising!" she murmured, and then she pursed her lips tightly and sat down and opened her desk. "Of course! That's why our Elsie was looking so pleased with herself all day yesterday," said Miss Younge. "You remember we all noticed it." "Yes, and didn't I say that if it was good news for her it was bad news for someone else," cried Miss Purbeck. "I wasn't so far wrong!" "I just couldn't bear working under her; I shall resign," said Mrs. Jolly. "I *can't* resign," said Miss Younge. "The miserable salary they pay me here is all I've got to live on. We'll have to try and find some way of keeping her out; better wait and see if she is really going to be appointed. And if she is— we must *do something*."

"I don't see what we can do," said Mrs. Jolly, "and I really couldn't resign either. I mean to say, you don't throw up a good job because someone is put over you whom you don't like."

They sat and grumbled and groaned and thought about doing something all through the morning. Even Miss Dunkerley, who spoke so seldom to her colleagues, let fall some comments on what she called, "a very unfortunate selection". Anne was silent and soon grew rather uncomfortable and began to feel that she ought to try and defend Elsie as her neighbour and friend. But just as she was telling herself that she would stand up for Elsie the very next time one of the others said a word against her, to her great relief a telephone message came and Miss Saltman beckoned to her and sent her off to learn to be a watcher beside the lift shaft under the new system of roof spotters that was being put into force that morning and which Elsie had described to Mrs. Doweson.

"That's better," said Miss Younge as soon as Anne had left the table. "It's going to be bad enough to have Pearne as Deputy without having someone spying for her, sitting at the table with us."

"The child is all right," said Mrs. Jolly. "I expect she is as sick of Miss Pearne as all the rest of us. If you notice it's Miss Pearne who makes all the running—'Come out to lunch, Anne'; 'sit here by me, Anne'; 'do this, Anne'—I don't suppose Anne would bother much about her if she got a chance to get away."

"What worries me so much is the idea of taking my translations to Pearne to check," wailed Miss Purbeck. There was a general chorus of approval. With Elsie Pearne to check their translations they all felt—and began to behave—like schoolchildren with a schoolmistress whom they disliked and feared. Everyone delayed taking their translations to the checking tray, till in the end, Miss Saltman noticed that the tray was still empty and sent Elsie to find out the cause of the delay. Elsie strode down the room and Table Two sullenly watched her approach. To Elsie the moment was delicious. With authority behind her she could administer reproof.

But remembering her resolve to "try and get on with them somehow" she thought she would reprove them with a joke. Her joke—like all her jokes—was a lamentably poor one. "Dear me!" she said. "I suppose it's because I'm not working with you that the tray is empty. I always knew I was the only translator who did any work!" Table Two kept blank unsmiling faces. They slowly took the translations that were ready and pinned them together and threw them into the tray that Elsie carried without looking up at her or speaking. Elsie saw that she had failed;

and in her disappointment she reverted inevitably to type. "It's after twelve," she said. "Some people don't seem to remember that there's a war on." Then she began to stalk back to Miss Salt-man's desk.

Anne, who had come back from the lift shaft, came running after her. "Here's mine," she said. "I've only just finished it. Sorry I've been so long but I've been on watch at the lift." "O.K. Kid," said Elsie, smiling gratefully at Anne and then she whis-pered, "My ears ought to be burning, eh? I bet they've been saying some pretty things about me this morning; you're the only human being in this collection of stuffed owls."

Lunchtime came and Mrs. Doweson said to Anne, "I've found a new place for luncheon. Would you like to try it? It's quite near." Anne hesitated—Elsie would certainly be offended if she did not go with her at the usual time—but it would be rather rude to refuse Mrs. Doweson who was old enough to be her grandmother and it was the first time she had asked her and anyhow it would be awfully nice. So Anne said, "Thank you very much; I'll be ready in two minutes," and she went up to tell Elsie that she was lunching with Mrs. Doweson who had asked her and whom she could not very well refuse. The smile with which Elsie had welcomed her, faded quickly. With an irritable shrug of her shoulders, Elsie said, "Oh, I quite expected it," and dropping her head she pretended to be deeply occupied revis-ing a translation. Anne walked away from the desk. Now she's offended, she thought. I'm sorry. But after all she hasn't bought me. I can lunch with whom I like.

Mrs. Doweson's discovery was a small Italian restaurant where the food was cheap and good. Outside it looked uninter-esting; but the notice "The Proprietor is a British Subject" that hung on a crooked card in the window was effective in attracting custom for it plainly said, "My business is ruined if you treat me as an enemy and if my business is ruined, I am ruined and my wife is ruined and my bambini are ruined so please come in." Inside, the walls were hung with mirrors with views of Naples and Palermo painted in the corners and a painted trellis with grapes and ivy leaves across the rest of the glass; and on each table there was water in a fiasco which had once held Chianti and still had the label on the basket bulge. Anne found that Mrs. Doweson had already made herself a favourite with the Italo-British padrone and his wife, and still more with their small boy and his mongrel puppy, who sat for ages on his haunches, and with two cats who purred and prowled. The two cats took immediate possession of the table and the puppy bounded boldly forward; the little boy followed on pretence of catching the puppy and then lingered round the table, talking shyly and putting the puppy through his tricks till he and all the livestock were driven off by the indignant waiter. Anne thought it was a delightful restaurant with its atmosphere of "being abroad" and she thoroughly enjoyed the gnocchi in tomato sauce which Mrs. Doweson recommended and which was very good and even the coffee that followed which was very bad. Anne had pinned into her frock two carnations which Mrs. Jolly had given her out of a bunch that she had brought to decorate the table. "I never knew anyone so generous as Mrs. Jolly," said Anne. "You know what she always says about herself—'I'm not very clever so I have to make up for it by being nice'—she *is* very nice though she's a funny silly old thing!" "No," said Mrs. Doweson. "I don't agree with you or her! I don't think she is at all silly and I do think she's quite clever—not what one could call intellectual perhaps—but she has sound common sense; she has a silly way of talking—she says everything that comes into her head—but if you have the patience to disentangle the meaning of all her chatter, there is generally good sense behind it."

"Yes, I suppose there is," said Anne rather doubtfully, "But Elsie Pearne is the one who I think is so clever." She went on to praise Elsie as a relief to her conscience for not having defended her when all the rest of the Table were abusing her—she was so efficient, so good at languages, the others were too hard on her and it was really beastly of them to refuse to take up their translations, because she was a good sort. "A good sort," said Mrs. Doweson. "But the wrong sort." Anne cocked her head a little. "Why, Mrs. Doweson?" she asked. "Because for that post we need someone who is first of all a lady and secondly has no nerves. Your Miss Pearne is not a lady and she's a mass of nerves. She'll throw her weight about when things are easy and when there's a crisis, she will crack." "I suppose you are right, Mrs. Doweson," said Anne, "but all the same, she is intelligent and I do think the others should give her a fair chance." "They won't," said Mrs. Doweson. "And if they do, she'll muff it. However we mustn't sit here gossiping—there's a war on. We must get back."

Mrs. Doweson stopped at the post office and Anne hurried on alone. As she turned from the sunlit road into the dark doorway of the Ministry she bumped into a R.A.F. uniform and an arm shot out to stop her from falling and held her very much longer than was needful. "You're running in the wrong direction," said Sebastian, slowly letting her go. "Turn round and come out to lunch with me. At last I've caught you and for a wonder alone! How are you! You know I worry about you so much. Do you notice the premature greyness all brought on by worry about you and what's happening to you during these infernal raids every night? Come on, let's get a taxi." "I'm just coming back from lunch," said Anne trying not to sound as disappointed as she felt. "I went with Mrs. Doweson from my table." Seb did not attempt to hide his disappointment. "I've been trying to meet you every day this week," he said. "The only time I caught a glimpse of you, you were being marched off by that old dragon who sits next you and she was holding you by the arm as if she were a policeman who had just arrested you and I didn't dare speak to you in case you were annoyed!" Anne smiled rather feebly. "I suppose you mean Elsie Pearne by the old dragon—she isn't as fierce as she looks. But why didn't you send me down a note in the morning as we arranged?" "My dear, I couldn't—absolutely impossible. I've been practically alone in the office and have never known when I could get off. But to-morrow is my day off so I insist on your lunching with me. Now no excuses. I shall be here at half-past one, if that suits you, and that's a date! All right?" "All right, Seb, I promise. And here is Mrs. Doweson." Mrs. Doweson came into the hall and Anne introduced Sebastian to her—and then remembered that they already knew each other—Mrs. Doweson's grandson was in Sebastian's unit and when he was on sick leave Sebastian had visited him at her cottage. "I still have the cottage," she said. "I carried Anne off to lunch—an old woman's privilege—I like talking to young people and I didn't know I was robbing you. You must let me make up for it. Will you both come down to the cottage for a weekend or any part of it when you are both free? Fix it up between you and Anne can tell me later what you have agreed." Before either of them could answer, she stumped across the hall and was waving to them from the lift. "What a perfectly marvellous idea," said Seb. "We'll settle the date at lunch to-morrow. Now don't you forget, Anne." "I shan't forget," said Anne and raced off to the lift. As it went up she reflected: I suppose I ought to have refused him. I wish I weren't so miserably weak.

Elsie had gone out to lunch when Anne got in, Anne sat down in her own chair and Mrs. Jolly moved up beside her. "I don't see why I shouldn't sit next you," she said. "As I always say it's an ill wind that blows no one any good and as Miss Pearne has left her chair, at least I don't have to sit next to her. Have a chocolate." Anne took a chocolate and offered Mrs. Jolly some butterscotch from her own bag. "I hear they're going to ration chocolates on account of the Sugar shortage," said Mrs. Jolly. "I don't care if they do," said Miss Younge. "What's worrying me is a rumour I've heard that there'll be a shortage of cigarettes." "I'm told that the Germans are sinking convoys by the dozen," said Miss Purbeck, "and there isn't enough meat in the country to last us for three weeks!" Everyone at the table roared with laughter.

"We've always got our Purbeck to really cheer us up," said Mrs. Jolly. "As a matter of fact we're in clover in this war," said Mrs. Doweson, "We've still got tons of everything compared with the sticky period of the last war. If it weren't for the air raids that spoil one's beauty sleep, we wouldn't know this time that there was a war on at all." "Oh I don't agree with you," said Mrs. Jolly. "I think one feels the war much more this time. It's so gloomy in London. I was about Anne's age in the last war and working in the City. It's true there was a blackout and air raids but we used to dance such a lot. Of course the war was terrible but London was full of men home on leave and we tried to give them a good time to make them forget all the horrors they had to go back to. But there's nothing for young people to do in this war. It must be rotten for you," she said, turning to Anne. "At your age you ought to be out every night dancing and flirting and enjoying yourself." "Don't worry," said Mrs, Doweson. "Youth will be served. From what I see of the young people they're finding ways and means." Anne found herself blushing. As that was the last thing she wanted to do she clenched her teeth and told herself not to be so perfectly idiotic and blushed still more. But Mrs. Jolly did not notice her blushing; she was thinking of the good times she had in the last war. "I don't mind confessing it," she said, "I had lots of fun last time. And I'm glad I did for that's something you've had and that nobody can take away from you and if you don't have it when you're young it isn't likely you'll ever have it." As she said this, Elsie, coming back from lunch, passed behind her chair. "Don't you agree with me, Miss Pearne?" she said, "Agree with what?" said Elsie. "That it is a good thing to have some fun when you're young." "When I was young," said Elsie, "I worked very hard for my living. And I studied in my spare time. Perhaps it would have been better if I'd worked less hard and had some fun. But beggars can't be choosers in this life." And she strode off to her seat at Miss Saltman's desk. "Snubbed!" said Mrs. Jolly cheerfully. "Isn't she a prig? I don't believe she ever was young. She'll come and ask us if *we're* supposed to be working for our livings in a minute so I suppose I'd better stop talking." Mrs. Jolly bent down over her work and was silent, but her jaw still moved up and down as she talked away to herself.

For a little while everyone was quiet and the hands of the big clocks could be heard in the silence as they jerked their way round. Anne was trying to summarise a Portuguese company report. Suddenly she remembered that she had not read through the text of the last translation which she had handed to Elsie just before lunch. "You know," she said to Mrs. Jolly, "I did that long French speech this morning in a frightful rush; I've just been thinking about it. I hope I've not made any howlers." "That's just what you have done," said Miss Younge who had come up behind them on her silent rubber soles. "But Pearne has corrected it. I saw her do it as I passed her desk just now. Of course she would correct it for you and say nothing about it because you're her sweet pet lamb. But if she finds a mistake in any of our things she'll raise such a stink about it that we'll probably be sacked." As though in fulfilment of Miss Younge's prediction, Elsie at that moment came quickly down the room, and stopping in front of Miss Purbeck, she said in a tone that could be heard by everyone: "Miss Purbeck, you've made a bad mistake. You've translated 'eventuellement' by 'eventually' instead of 'should the case arise'. I thought you'd like to know about it so as not to do it again." Miss Purbeck grew scarlet as she took her text from Elsie and looked at the correction. "Thank you," she said. "I'm sorry," and handing the text back, her face still scarlet, she began to work again; when Elsie had left the table she snatched a dictionary and began to look through it. "I know my French is not very good," she said miserably. "I do sometimes make mistakes. And I don't mind when Mrs. Just corrects them because she does it so nicely. But I really can't stand being spoken to in that way." "What did I tell you?" said Miss Younge. "One by one she'll get us all the sack." "Of course she had to shout like that so that the whole room could hear!" said Mrs. Jolly, looking sympathetically at Miss Purbeck, "After all everyone makes a slip sometimes. It's too bad!"

Anne, for her part, felt very cross and disappointed. Elsie had doubly let her down; first by covering up Anne's own mistake (she didn't want to be favoured and she would tell her so!) and secondly by being so brutal with poor old Purbeck. The absurd thing is, she thought, that Elsie really has been trying to be nice. But she has just made a mess of it. It is curious, she's so clever—much cleverer really than any of us when it comes to understanding something difficult—and yet she's just a fool. Even when she tries to be civil she can't help doing the wrong thing. She speaks and acts unkindly and yet she's really not unkind—she just blurts out these awful remarks without thinking how they'll seem to the persons she's talking to. Why couldn't she have had the sense not to criticize poor Purbeck in front of everyone else. She might have known that everyone would then take Purbeck's part against her. She is always complaining that everyone is against her—plotting against her, she calls it—but she always does the one thing that will *put* everyone against her. Miss Dunkerley calls her underbred—but it isn't that at all— you might say the same thing of Mrs. Jolly but nobody could be kinder or more tactful than she is—she babbles a lot but she babbles out kind and tactful things while Elsie cannot open her mouth without offending someone. She's made them all furious now just when she wants to please them; this is her chance and she is muffing it; just as Mrs. Doweson said at lunch she would; they'll never put up with her as Deputy and she'll be dreadfully disappointed. It's a shame. I'd like her to have some luck. But it's her own fault. Why didn't she point out my mistake as she did the other?

The more Anne thought about it the crosser she became. She must really begin to see less of Elsie, she decided. Of course she had been awfully nice to her at the beginning when she was quite new to everything but Anne had never really meant to become such bosom friends with her. It all seemed just to have happened. Elsie had somehow taken hold of her and now it was hard to break away—especially now when the others were all so down on her and she was making such a mess of the Deputy job. But really she was so very possessive and jealous and always up in the air about something, either gloomy and talking about her old age which bored her to tears (because Anne's old age was something so incredibly far away that it meant nothing at all to her) or else she was excited and laughing and making the most awful jokes which Anne didn't think at all funny and never laughed at in time so that Elsie told her one day that she had obviously no sense of humour to which Anne had meekly agreed. And Elsie was worst of all, Anne thought now, when she was affectionate. I really can't stand being yearned over, she said to herself, and I certainly won't allow her to pass over my mistake while she is publicly rude to the others.

And then Anne looked over at Elsie sitting at Miss Saltman's table, She was resting her head on her hand as she always did at work and the light fell full on her head and high forehead. And Anne saw that she was dreadfully pale and had black circles under her eyes. She looks really ghastly and as if she had had no sleep for days, thought Anne. Anne herself slept pretty well but she heard the guns through her sleep and they made her dream and frequently wakened her and she generally felt rather tired and irritable these days when she arrived in the morning. Elsie, she knew, slept very badly. The neighbourhood where she lived was bombed continuously and Elsie had to sleep every night in an uncomfortable shelter with her landlady and the landlady's noisy children which was quite enough to make anyone jumpy and irritable. Of course Elsie was old, too, nearly fifty, frightfully old, it seemed to Anne, and it must be harder for anyone of that age to put up with these tiring days and nights. The best thing to do would be to have it out with her about covering up that mistake and do it nicely without quarrelling with her and then gradually to cool off.

So at tea-time when everyone stopped work for ten minutes and Anne saw that Miss Saltman had left her desk, she braced herself and went up to have it out with Elsie. "Hallo Elsie," she said. "I've a bone to pick with you. The Younge tells me you corrected some howler I made without cursing at me as you did at Purbeck. I hope you won't do that sort of thing again. It's not fair to the others." Elsie looked hard at Anne for a moment and then bowed her head over her work and said very softly, "I thought you were my friend," and then she looked up again and Anne saw to her horror that her eyes were full of tears. "Oh Elsie! How dreadfully seriously you take things," said Anne. And Elsie said fiercely, "You will much oblige me by going to your place. I've got twenty translations to check before five." When Anne had gone, Elsie's brain began to whirl. She was overcome with rage and shame. She had cried in the office; Anne had seen her and the others had probably seen her too; she had behaved like

the ridiculous Purbeck who blubbed every time she was criti-
cized, sniffing loudly and openly dabbing with her handkerchief
at her red and streaming eyes while Mrs. Jolly patted her and
tried to console her. And now she was the cry-baby; she could
never remember such a thing happening to her before in her
life. All the same it was too bad of Anne. It is quite clear, she
thought, that she wants to break away from me—lunch with
Mrs. Doweson—that R.A.F. boy I saw her talking to in the hall
when I went out to lunch, the same one that she went off with
that day and told me a cock-and-bull story about a translation
afterwards—I bet they both spend their time abusing me to her.
I thought I had one friend, I only wanted one. I was content with
that—while others have dozens. And now they are taking my
one. It's too bad. Then jerking herself back to the work in hand,
she jammed her mind on to a Spanish railway report, and half
an hour later, like a criminal returning to the scene of his crime,
she was steeled to go and find out if any of the others had seen
her crying and to defy them if they had. She walked down to the
table on the pretext of fetching a dictionary from her own desk
and Mrs. Jolly gave her the opening she wanted by offering her a
chocolate. "Thanks," said Elsie. "I don't mind if I do; sweets are
good for one in wartime," and she went on to say that the food
shortage was bad for the health—the scarcity of butter affected
the nerves—everyone must feel that—and of course the air raids
deprived them all of sleep, which made it much worse and so
on. She spoke loudly and volubly, trying to make her colleagues
listen to what she was saying so that they might understand
that her breakdown was just a matter of illness, of temporarily
over-wrought nerves which might happen even to the strongest.
"Well, of course, I'm not a bit a nervous person," said Mrs. Jolly,
"It takes a good deal to upset me. But, of course, you're very
highly-strung and excitable, Miss Pearne, anyone can see that. I
expect you always have been, haven't you?"

Mrs. Jolly's reply was a blow to Elsie, In fact, neither Mrs.
Jolly nor anyone but Anne had seen Elsie's tears and Anne had of
course not spoken of them to the others. Now it seemed to Elsie
that, as she had feared, they had all seen what had happened

and that they were laughing at her and calling her hysterical. It was a wretched end to the day that had begun so grandly, the day when at last she had been given a great chance.

Anne saw the horror and misery in Elsie's face. And when Elsie went back to the seat beside the throne, the seat that had become a mockery, she found Anne behind her. "I say," said Anne. "Sorry I was such an ass just now. Of course I know you were only being kind about that howler of mine. Do bury the hatchet. Look here, the new rota is up, and I see that we've both got the same day off next week—Wednesday—will you come to my flat and have lunch with me there—it will make a change—from all this."

Elsie's face was transformed in an instant. She took out her diary and wrote down the engagement. "Right you are, Kid. I'd love it. I'm afraid things haven't gone too well to-day. But I'm tired out. There are moments when I think I'm going mad."

Chapter Thirteen
THINGS HAPPEN TO ANNE

As ANNE STOOD on the step of the bus next morning, and waiting for it to slow down, she heard an aeroplane overhead, a German plane, it seemed by the beat of the engine. The morning spotter, she thought, come to see what the weather is like or to look at the damage they did last night. Goodness! How late I am! And she jumped off the bus and began to hurry in the direction of the office, for she had missed her usual bus that morning and was several minutes late. Then she heard a familiar but still alarming sound—the scream of a bomb. The noise grew louder and louder, like a train coming nearer and she had time to notice that and to remember that if a bomb was falling some way off the noise was loud but did not increase, but if it was going to fall very near the noise grew louder and louder as this noise was doing. And then she saw everyone in the street throwing themselves flat on the ground or dashing into the shops for shelter and she herself jumped into a doorway just as the bomb exploded with the most terrible and terrifying noise she had ever heard in her life. A great blast of wind threw her off her feet and everything seemed to be falling all round her and something hit her on the back of the head. She lay still for some minutes, stupefied, deafened by the noise and half choked by the dust that filled her nose and mouth. Then she sat up and realized with some surprise that she was still alive and not even badly injured. She had been blown into the building and she was now at the bottom of a staircase leading from a small passage way to the floor above. Part of the ceiling had fallen near her and it was a big piece of plaster which had hit her on the head. That piece of plaster was now lying on her best hat beside her on the ground. She looked at the hat which she had put on in honour of the coming luncheon with Sebastian. It was now crushed and grey with the dirty plaster. She lifted it up and listlessly shook it and tried to restore it to shape and groped round under the rubbish for her bag. She found it undamaged and took out her handkerchief and comb; the first thing, she felt, was to rub the dust from her face and comb it out of her hair. Then she shook the plaster from her clothes, took off her shoes and emptied them, for they too were full of dirt; then with an effort, she stood up. Her head was throbbing and she came out of the doorway, rather shakily, and supporting herself against the wall. In the roadway a bus lay on its side; it was, in fact, the bus she had missed that morning because she had been late. Police and stretcher bearers were lifting people out through the windows of the bus, carefully protecting them from the jagged edges of glass still sticking in the frames. A cloud of dust was darkening the sunshine; it was rising from a hillock of bricks and rubble which lay across the pavement; Anne looked at it and saw that this hillock of bricks and rubble was all that now remained of the little Italian restaurant where she had lunched with Mrs. Doweson the day before. A man with blackened face and torn clothes went past her carrying the limp body of a boy—the Anglo-Italian little boy who had put the puppy through its tricks. Anne wondered if anyone would remember to look for that puppy and the cats. The blood from the little boy's head was smeared all over the coat of the man who was carrying him. Anne staggered back to her doorway and was violently sick.

When the spasm had passed she began to try and reach a small side turning that would take her to the office. A policeman hurrying past stopped and looked at her. "Are you all right, Miss?" he asked kindly. "Not hurt are you?"

"I'm all right, thank you. I'm not hurt, only a bit upset for a minute or two. I saw—" she indicated with a gesture what lay behind her.

"Not a pretty sight—especially when you're not used to it. Where do you want to go?" She told him. She felt better now and urged him not to waste time on her. "If you're sure you're all right, miss, I'll go. There's plenty for me to do—but you don't look very grand." He took her as far as the police cordon which had already closed the area to all traffic, passed her through and left her and she walked on as quickly as she could to the office. As she went through the doorway she felt something wet at the back of her head. She put up her hand and when she looked at it, it was covered with blood. She showed her pass to the man at the door and collapsed in a heap at his feet.

When she came properly to her senses again, she was on a couch in the First Aid room of the Ministry, with her head bandaged. There were several other people lying on couches and others were being bandaged and treated at a table. She moved and a nurse came over to her. "That's better," she said. "Drink this and go to sleep and you'll be all right soon." Anne obeyed and when she wakened again it was several hours later. Her head was sore and aching but she felt better and sat up. The nurse came to her again and felt her pulse. "I think you're nearly all right. How does your head feel? It was only a small cut but you got a nasty bang. The best thing now is to get you home and to bed for a good rest. There is a gentleman waiting here for you with a car. I'll tell him you're nearly ready. He's been here for a long time."

*   *   *   *   *

Anne stood up and began to tidy herself wondering vaguely who on earth the gentleman could be. She heard the nurse telephoning to the head porter to send the gentleman along. She had just decided that she was being sent home in one of the Ministry's official cars when she heard a knock at the door. The nurse called her over and Anne looked outside the door and saw Sebastian.

"She's all ready," said the nurse in the impersonal cheerful voice that all nurses acquire. "And she's nearly quite well. She'll have to go quietly for a day or so and then she'll be as right as rain." She took Anne's arm and walked with her to the doorway and helped her into a large comfortable-looking car which was standing outside.

"Thank God you're all right, Anne. I thought you were dead. I came and looked at you when you were asleep and you looked so white," said Seb as soon as they were alone. His voice was full of relief and more emotional than Anne had ever known it. He took her hand and pressed it gently and then let in the gear lever and the car rolled quietly off.

"How did you find out what had happened?" asked Anne.

"I was off to-day but I had to ring the department about something. They told me a bomb had fallen near the Ministry and some of the staff had been hurt—they couldn't tell me the names. So I rushed down here at once and found out what had happened. They told me you were asleep and could go when you wakened. I had a look at you and you looked ghastly, you poor little darling. So I went away and did a bit of telephoning and made some arrangements and got hold of this car to take you away in and I've been waiting for you to awaken ever since."

"Arrangements?" said Anne rather weakly. "Er—do I come into the arrangements and where are we going now?"

"Of course you come into the arrangements. And we're going now to Mrs. Doweson's cottage. You're going to stay there for a couple of days and you're not going back to work till you're fit—till I'm satisfied that you're fit," said Sebastian. He spoke very firmly.

"To Mrs. Doweson's cottage?" said Anne in astonishment. "How does she come into it? When did she ask me? I don't understand at all."

"Mrs. Doweson was giving you all first aid when I arrived. Didn't you know she was a trained nurse? She was some sort of tremendous swell in the Red Cross in the last war. We agreed that you ought to have a couple of quiet nights in the country and she suggested I should bring you straight down to the cottage. She's there herself now. It's her half day so she went down early to prepare for us."

"It all sounds lovely," said Anne contentedly. "But clothes! We'll have to go back to Cromwell Road and fetch some—I haven't even a toothbrush," and she sat up and looked very alarmed.

"Oh yes you have, my dear," said Sebastian complacently. "Just look behind at that suitcase!" Anne looked and saw one of her suitcases on the back seat beside one of Sebastian's. "Father has arranged everything for you—you just leave it all to him. Mrs. Doweson phoned your Agnes and explained and told her to pack it and I fetched it—I had the greatest difficulty in preventing Agnes from coming with us to look after you—had to assure her that you were in the best of hands and so on—she's in an awful flap. I've promised to phone her this evening and tell her how you are."

"Poor Agnes! She would be in a dither! She's like an old hen with me."

"Well, I don't think she looked after you very well on the night of that first raid. She confessed to me—letting you run off like that—rescuing dogs, you might have been killed. It's high time I began to look after you. Why you can't even go to the office without knocking a bomb with your head. You must give up those tricks, Anne, and marry me."

As he finished speaking the siren began to sound. They were halted by a red light, outside a police station where the siren was obviously being operated. It was a loud siren and it was meant to be heard a long way. From so near it was an incredibly loud noise. The car was full of noise, of the hideous wailing and moaning, rising and falling. Anne could hardly hear Sebastian's last words clearly. She began to giggle. It seemed so comic that the words she had so longed to hear should be half drowned by the ridiculous howl of the siren. Then she thought it was not so comic but rather sinister. Her giggle turned into laughter and then into rather tearful laughter and then into something which was very near to tears.

"Oh Anne, don't!" said Seb. "I've never seen you cry even when you were a little girl." He took his hand from the wheel and laid it over hers and tried to look at her. The siren had finished now and the lights had gone green. Behind him half a dozen angry drivers were sounding their horns because he had not moved on but was blocking their way. Anne stopped her tears and said, "Drive on, Seb, and please say all that again. I don't quite understand you—I'm not quite normal yet."

And then Seb proposed more normally and Anne accepted normally and Seb drove down the quietest road he could find and they sealed the bargain in the normal way. "Darling, I oughtn't to worry you so soon," said Seb looking at Anne with concern because she still looked so ill. "But I just couldn't wait. You're looking so white and tired. We must stop somewhere for something to eat and you must rest a little."

They drove on and soon reached the by-pass out of London and then came to an hotel which looked fairly quiet and peace-ful. There was a dining-room looking on to the garden and they took a table by the window and sat without talking much and looked out at the flowerbeds, still gay with autumn flowers. Sebastian ordered wine and made Anne drink some and soon a little colour came back into her cheeks. As he looked at her he thought what a darling she was and how fragile and pathetic she seemed with the bandage round her head but in spite of it she was prettier than ever. And he could have kicked himself for being such a fool as not to have made her marry him a year ago. Presently, to his great relief, she sat up in her chair and began to look more like her usual self.

"I feel much better now. In fact I really feel almost quite well. But Seb—you know you did surprise me so much—I thought you wanted to marry Mary—"

Seb stared at her with quite genuine surprise. "Mary? Marry Mary! Darling Anne I know I'm not very intelligent—I'm only a sort of country bumpkin—but I'm not quite such a fool as that. Don't let's waste time talking about her. We've wasted so much time already. Why on earth didn't we marry when you came back from Portugal—then we should have had some time together before this war started."

"Well! My dear Seb! For one reason because you didn't ask me!"

"I know," he said gloomily. "I was a fool. But somehow everything went wrong. It never occurred to me that I should marry anyone but you. As soon as you went away I wished I had asked you before you left—but we were both really rather young then—everyone would have laughed at us—and I hadn't a bean till Mother died and left me a little money—no possible means of supporting you. And then I decided all the same to ask you as soon as you came back; and then as I say, everything went wrong. I was so certain this war was coming that it didn't seem worth doing anything while one was waiting for it. And you didn't seem to care for me any more when you came back. You know, darling, you weren't like the same person."

"I didn't feel as if I were—everything had changed so completely. It was like a different world. You seemed different too, you seemed so rich and I was so beastly poor—you were still living in a proper house with cars and horses and everything else and we were in that poky little house at the end of the village; that was a beastly summer for me."

"It was pretty dismal for me though I liked being in the R.A.F. I was depressed at the thought that there was going to be, a war and yet terrified that there might not be one—if you know what I mean—that Chamberlain and his lot were going to let Hitler get away with it again—that Munich business was pretty awful. Everything seemed such a muddle. I couldn't settle to anything—even to marrying you, darling! Now everything seems quite clear. I've had a talk with my father. You know we've been farming a good deal of the land ourselves. I'm going to take over that work from him, learn how to do it and how to manage the place. Anne, I do hope you'll like living at the Hall and being the 'young squire's' wife? You'll have to do lots of dull things I'm afraid. Am I talking too much? Sure I'm not tiring you?" He looked at her anxiously but she smiled and reassured him.

"I'm all right now, really I am. Tell me, what are the dull things I shall have to do when I marry you? I had better know the worst before I decide."

"Well, you know the sort of things—all the things Mother used to do when she was alive—opening flower shows and bazaars and sitting on committees and fussing about Women's Institutes—you'll have to see quite a lot of the new vicar's wife. You haven't met her yet which is lucky for me or you would probably back out. Darling, it will be fun to see you looking very solemn and wearing rather a dowdy hat—you'll have to keep a few just for these occasions—and holding a bouquet of rather wilted looking flowers that one of the village children has just presented to you—and having pleasure in declaring this bazaar open, to the cheers of the crowd. But if you can bear that sort of thing, there are others to make up, animals, the horses, the dogs. You can have dozens of dogs, just as many as ever you like. Anne, you've got a sweet expression on your face just now—I suppose it is because you are thinking of the dogs?"

Anne smiled at him very tenderly and put her hand in his. "No," she said. "I was not thinking about the dogs."

Mrs. Doweson's cottage was a small eighteenth-century house, long and low, painted white and with big french windows opening on to the garden. As they came up the drive they saw her. She had changed her office clothes for a white linen coat and skirt and wore comfortable white tennis shoes instead of her usual sturdy boots. She had a big gardening apron tied round her waist and was vigorously hoeing one of the flower beds; a large basket, nearly full of weeds and bits of grass, proved the energy with which she had been working. Playing on the lawn behind her were two large white bulldogs and a very small Yorkshire terrier who all began to bark loudly when they heard the car. Mrs. Doweson left her work and came to greet them followed by the dogs.

"My gardener has been called up and this old man I've got is absolutely no use at all. So I have to do just everything myself," she said, and then, "How are you my dear?" taking Anne's hand. "Much better, I can see. In fact you look radiant and if it weren't for that bandage, I wouldn't know you had had an accident. Down Robert! Down Caroline!" she said to the bulldogs who were capering round Anne, wildly wagging their absurd little tails and wriggling in ecstasies of delight.

"Do you really think she looks all right?" said Sebastian after he had greeted his hostess. He spoke rather anxiously and put his arm across Anne's shoulders. "I've rather a conscience about her because I've been behaving like a brute all the way down and taking advantage of her weak state to bully her into promising to marry me."

"I certainly don't think it has done her any harm nor does she look very unhappy about it! My dears! I do congratulate you both and wish you all the luck in the world." She kissed Anne affectionately and squeezed Sebastian's hand. "This makes it all the nicer for me to have you both here! And now come along and have some tea."

She led the way into a big light sitting-room. It was rather a surprising room because it was so unlike what would be expected of the drawing-room of an old lady of Mrs. Doweson's age. There were none of the knick-knacks which old ladies usually cherish because they were fashionable when they were young, the many photographs in silver or leather frames, the bits of china, the ornaments, the souvenirs of the places they once lived in, all carefully arranged on little tables which have always to be treated with a good deal of care lest they topple over and send their precious contents flying. Mrs. Doweson's sitting-room was quite different. It was furnished with an immense settee and big deep arm-chairs in which long-legged males could sprawl at ease and which were covered in a washable material which would withstand the attacks of muddy paws and children's feet. The few tables about the room were substantial and solid and their purpose was obviously to provide a resting place for books and cigarettes and drinks and an adequate number of large solid ashtrays into which a man could knock out his pipe. Two sides of the walls were lined by bookcases and one wall was broken by the three large french windows—all open, of course—which led into the garden.

The three dogs followed them in and at a severe glance from their mistress, retired to their baskets, two very large and one very small, which stood against the wall.

Anne was at once made to rest comfortably in one of the big armchairs with a cushion behind her head and her feet on a stool. Mrs. Doweson began to pour out tea and Sebastian roamed about the room and pulled out a book here and there from the shelves and looked completely happy.

"I call this the Doweson Home of Rest!" said their hostess. "All the children and the grandchildren come down here when-ever they get a day or two off. They just turn up when they like and generally there are one or two of them here all the time. And I come whenever I can get away from Grover Street."

"It is a perfect place," said Anne enthusiastically. "And as for the dogs—" The bulldogs had sneaked quietly out of their baskets and now sat one on each side of Anne, Caroline with her chin firmly pressed down on Anne's knees and Robert, with one paw outstretched for her to hold. "What do you do with them when you are in London?" she asked, stroking Caroline's head with one hand and with the other, shaking hands with Robert to his infinite delight.

"The bulldogs stay with the gardener's wife; she adores them and they are company for her when her husband is away and they are really rather large for our tiny flat in London. But I couldn't live without a dog of some kind so I bought Lou-Lou; she doesn't take up any room and she comes up and down with me." At the sound of her name the little Yorkshire looked up. She had a long heavy coat and the hair on the top of her head was, said Mrs. Doweson, always carefully combed out and plaited and tied with a ribbon, but Caroline had just pulled off and eaten the ribbon and that was why Lou-Lou was so untidy. But Anne thought she looked sweet with her hair hanging over her forehead in a thick mane under which her little bright eyes peeped out. Hopping out of her basket she ran across the room and jumped lightly on her mistress's knee. Robert at once looked intensely offended and lumbering across in his turn, tried to climb up beside Lou-Lou. "Go down, you great silly," said Mrs. Doweson, pushing him away. "All bulldogs want to be lap dogs and the bigger they are the more they want to curl up on your knee. Robert weighs well over a half hundredweight and he has never yet found a knee which can support him but he never becomes discouraged. Now go to your baskets, all of you, you know you are not allowed to do this at mealtimes!" Lou-Lou and Caroline obeyed at once, Caroline trying to look as if she were very frightened and wagging her minute tail all the time to show that it was a game. Robert flung himself on his back and lay with his four paws in the air pretending that he was unable to move. His mistress prodded him with her foot and he gave a broad smile and flopping on to his side began to snore loudly with one eye half open to see if she were noticing that he was now fast asleep. "He's just a clown," said Anne in delight. "After the war, Seb, we must have some bulldogs."

"If you once start, you'll always have to have one. No one who has once owned—or been owned by—a bulldog is ever happy without one. They're quite different from other dogs."

Very soon after tea Anne was sent to bed. She went protesting that she was perfectly well, but when she had stretched her limbs between the cool linen sheets she realised that she was extremely glad to be there. She lay watching through the window the tops of the high old trees, waving in the sunlight, green and then gold and at last black against the darkening sky. Her dinner came up and soon afterwards, she fell asleep.

She awakened next morning feeling quite well. A lazy happy couple of days went fast, much too fast; soon they had to get ready to go back to London. The bulldogs had a last romp on the lawn and then went off sadly to the gardener's cottage. Lou-Lou, when they were no longer there to steal the picture, became very important and barked a great deal and tried to make every-one look at her. When the car came to the door and the luggage appeared, she became terrified that she would be forgotten and followed her mistress so closely that it was almost impossible not to tread on her. Finally, when she became too much of a nuisance, Mrs. Doweson picked her up and stuffed her into the huge side pocket of her overcoat where she sat quietly with her head and tiny front paws peeping out, watching the proceedings with her bright intelligent little eyes.

Later that evening Anne and Seb met for dinner. Over it they discussed plans for their wedding. The sirens had sounded and guns barked and boomed in the distance. Somehow they would have to get home through the raid, but that was a problem that could wait till the time came.

"You have to give three weeks' notice," said Seb. "I've found out all about how to get married. How about three weeks to-morrow?"

Anne took out her diary. "They're very sticky about leave at the Ministry just now. I suppose getting married would count as an 'urgent private affair'—they might give me a day off. But it's my long weekend a month next Friday. Of course we *could* get married in the lunch hour, but I think it would be nicer to have a little longer. We'll get four days if we wait till then—that is if you can get leave too?"

Seb thought he could, so they booked the date. He suggested, though without much hope that Anne would agree, that she might leave the Ministry as soon as they were married and go and live somewhere in the country which would be safer than London and where he might join her for weekends. But she flatly refused. She wanted to stay at the Ministry where she believed her work was of some use. "As long as you're in London, I'm staying there," she said firmly. "If you are transferred, I shall try and get a transfer too. Government offices are everywhere now and I shall surely be able to get a job somewhere near you. Do you think you are likely to be moved?" Seb looked very serious. "I was just going to talk to you about that, Anne, there's something I must tell you. I had a medical the day before yesterday." Anne's heart sank. Of course he was better now and he was going to be returned to his unit and would have to fly again. She took out a cigarette and lighted it carefully, looking down so that he could not see her unhappy expression. He went on. "The doctor says my cursed back is still not right and he doesn't hold out much hope of my being any use for anything but a ground job for the duration at least. Probably I'll be left at the Ministry. I'm afraid you're marrying a bit of a crock. I'll never be an ace now, Anne. Do you mind?"

Anne smiled and tried to hide her immense relief. "Not a bit, Seb. In fact you know, it's really rather nicer for me, though, of course, it's bad luck for you. Still everyone can't fly after all and you'll be very useful in your present job. They're rather pleased with you, aren't they?" To herself she thought: great man, that doctor! I should like to hug him.

"Who are we going to ask to the wedding? We'd better make a list right away," she said, taking out a pencil, and the back of an envelope from her handbag. "Granny and Mrs. Doweson—what's the matter? What have you lost?" Sebastian was slapping his pockets, one after the other. "Wedding! Ring! It just reminded me. Good Lord! What have I done with it?" At last he discovered a small jeweller's case and gave it to Anne. "I hope you'll like it, I bought it just now in rather a hurry. If you hate it we'll change it." Anne opened the case. Inside was a beautiful sapphire, a single magnificent stone plainly set in platinum.

When Anne's excitement over his gift had subsided a little, they returned to the wedding plans. They added a few more names to the list but they both wished the wedding should be quiet and without fuss.

"I should have liked to ask O'Connor but he will be gone back to Ireland by then. We were at the House together and I've seen a lot of him lately and I want you both to meet before he goes away. Shall we all lunch together one day next week? What about Wednesday? That would suit me best and it's a good day for him. I'll try and get him on the phone right away." Anne agreed and Seb went off to the telephone. A sudden idea struck her and she took out her diary. Wednesday was the day for which she had invited Elsie Pearne to lunch; she had completely forgotten it. Seb came back from the phone having secured O'Connor. "That's all right," he said when she told him of the earlier arrangement with Elsie. "Ask her to come too. That will make a four. O'Connor is a very amusing fellow. She'll like him. Where shall we go? Somewhere quiet where the food is good or somewhere noisy with a band and people to look at?" Anne knew from experience of their dismal lunches that Elsie took very little interest in her food. "Somewhere noisy with a band. Do you think we shall be able to find a flat in time?" She settled down to a discussion of this exciting problem. The office seemed very far away and Elsie just one of the collection of dim figures with whom it was peopled.

Chapter Fourteen
LUNCHEON AT THE PARK-LUCULLUS

As WEDNESDAY approached Elsie began to look forward more and more to the luncheon with Anne. Anne was not coming back to the office till Thursday and Elsie was missing her terribly. She was bitterly jealous when she discovered Anne had been staying with Mrs. Doweson though a little appeased when the tactful old lady made it seem that the visit had been part of the cure, to give the child a couple of days of peace and quiet in the country away from the noise of the guns in London. She had not mentioned Anne's engagement. Nor had Anne herself though she had sent a nice message by Mrs. Doweson telling Elsie that she had recovered and would expect her on Wednesday as arranged, so Elsie knew nothing of it. It was sweet of Anne to have sent that message, thought Elsie. It showed that she too was looking forward to the date. Elsie was longing to see Anne's flat and be among her belongings and pass a few hours of complete intimacy with her. It would mark a new stage in their friendship. And then she would ask Anne in return to her own digs. Before then she must smarten up her room a little. There was that old blue divan cover. It didn't go with anything. She had been meaning to buy a new one for some time. In the lunch hour she went down to John Lewis's and bought a divan cover; it was artificial silk and yellow ochre in colour to match the other things in her room. She also bought a little bedside lamp and a matchbox with a golden tassel. On the way back she felt pleased and excited. Would it be possible, she wondered, to persuade Anne to share a flat with her. She had once or twice tried sharing a flat with other women, and, it was true, it had not been a success—but Anne was quite different from those women, so much easier to get on with, so good-tempered and such nice manners, not a bit selfish like they had been; Anne always gave in and let one have one's own way. They ought to get on splendidly. If they clubbed together they could have quite a nice little place—one of those new flats which had just been built in Brondesbury, near her own place, perhaps. When she got the Deputy job she could afford a bit more for rent. Of course, young Anne had rather grand ideas and might want to live further up West; they might get something in Maida Vale; that was a nice district and very convenient for the office. But of course they must not be too ambitious; there was the future to think of. At Anne's place on Wednesday she would have a chance to sound her and see what she thought of the idea. It would be nice to live with Anne and hear her laugh—and watch her pretty, silly, amusing young ways. It would wake one up a bit, one was letting oneself get old and panicky, giving way too much to moods.

Elsie spent all Tuesday in this mood of happy anticipation. And then when she got home after work on Tuesday evening she found a telegram from Anne waiting for her. As soon as she opened the front door, her landlady shouted up from the basement, "A telegram for you, Miss Pearne, I pushed it under the door." Elsie's spirits sank at once. She found the orange envelope on the floor and for the moment let it lie there. She threw the bulky parcel with the divan cover and the lamp—that she had carried home all the way from the shop to the office and from the office home because she was in such a hurry to see their effect—on to the bed and her hat and gloves after them; she felt suddenly hollow inside and her mouth set in its habitual hard line. Of course Anne had put her off. At last she picked up the envelope and opened it with a hand that shook a little and read the telegram. It was not as bad as she expected. Anne asked her to meet at the Park-Lucullus instead of at Anne's own flat. But why on earth the Park-Lucullus? Had the child come into a fortune? How could Anne afford to give her lunch in a place like that?

Elsie dived into the revolving door of the Park-Lucullus under the embroidered arm of the Park-Lucullus commissionaire; she felt like a child playing oranges and lemons for the first time; when she escaped on the other side she saw Anne with the two young men. They were waiting for her, sitting over cocktails, chattering and laughing. Anne had changed her usual blue linen work frock for a smart little black dress; she was wearing one of her ridiculous little hats perched on one side of her head and on the other side her hair shone pale gold. One of the young men wore an Air Force uniform. Elsie recognized him at once. She had seen him in the Ministry hovering round Anne; he was the young man who had reminded her of Benno.

Elsie stood hesitating a moment in the crowd round the door. She felt a little bewildered by these surroundings. For the Park-Lucullus is constructed to impress. It caters for the more prosperous middle classes and specializes in providing an up-West atmosphere for suburban people. It is big, noisy, extremely respectable and very gilded. It gives excellent value for money—in good wholesome food, a nice square of floor for dancing and an orchestra that croons and moans. As most of its visitors are there to celebrate some occasion they have for the most part a dressed-up-for-the-occasion appearance and the place is always full of men in new suits and women in new dresses with hair that is too fashionable and nails that are too red. Elsie felt that she looked like a bedraggled London sparrow among this highly coloured crowd. She caught sight of herself in a mirror—no make-up to soften the lines of her rather sallow face, her hair brushed flat under her mannish felt hat, her tall angular form covered with her usual office outfit, dark coat and skirt, tidy and well-brushed, but by no means new-looking, and grey blouse and collar and black tie. She had an impulse to dive back into the revolving cage and go somewhere and telephone to Anne that she could not meet her; but Anne had already seen her and was waving. Reluctantly Elsie crossed the room towards her, striding along through the crowd, her head lowered as if to resist an attack and her mouth set hard.

Anne and the two young men stood up as Elsie approached; then Anne came forward quickly to meet her, greeted her warmly and introduced her to the others. The young man in the R.A.F. uniform as Elsie had already guessed, was Sebastian Kimble; the other man was called O'Connor. Elsie barely noticed O'Connor but she stared hard and suspiciously at Sebastian as she shook hands coldly with all three and sat down awkwardly, unsmiling and embarrassed. She drank off the cocktail, which Sebastian offered her, with a brief "Thanks". Anne who had already had two cocktails said rather unfortunately, "Miss Pearne you know, is a colleague of mine. We grow in beauty side by side, we fill our home with glee!" "There's not much beauty about me," snapped Elsie. "Have another cocktail," said Sebastian wildly. Elsie took it and there was a silence. As she sipped her drink she thought, what an idiot I was to come. They don't want me and that little bitch Anne has just got me here to make a fool of me and pull my leg. But now Sebastian was saying, "Let's go inside and have some food," and as they all stood up to go, Anne took Elsie's arm and began to apologize for the change of plans. "No need to make excuses," Elsie answered. "I shouldn't expect you to refuse anything better just for me." "You old silly," said Anne. "I thought it would amuse you to come here."

At the table Elsie looked round with conscious superiority at the business men and their wives who thronged the huge room. So these, she thought, are the idle rich—men with fat incomes and parasite women with nothing to do but buy these loud clothes and have their hair done and their nails made red. The waiter handed menu cards to Elsie and Anne; Sebastian asked them if they would like the set lunch or something different. "I don't mind," said Elsie speaking indifferently to emphasize that she was quite at ease. The lunch came; hors d'oeuvres, soup, fish, chicken. Sebastian and O'Connor were talking about the war—the Germans this—the Italians that—Elsie did not listen; she was thinking about the knives and forks. She must not use the wrong one for the wrong thing—no, the wrong one for the right thing—she would look an idiot and everyone was watching her. She looked at Anne's tiny hands, moving so surely and with such calm assurance. Anne knew the right fork and spoon to use. Elsie looked down at her own hands—they seemed enormous. How could one do anything with such huge hands. She dropped her fork and stooped to pick it up. O'Connor, who had not seen it was only a fork, half jumped from his seat to retrieve whatever it was that she had dropped and at the same time a waiter darted forward with another fork and they all knocked into one another. Anne and Sebastian roared with laughter. Elsie turned crimson. Now she had done it! Of course at the Park-Lucullus one did not use again a fork which had fallen to the floor; one left it for a servant to pick up.

When O'Connor was reseated, Sebastian signed to the waiter to fill up the glasses. They had drunk hock with the fish. Now champagne was being served with the chicken. Elsie emptied her glass at once. The wine was giving her Dutch courage. Sebastian asked her if she had seen "Gone With the Wind". "It's not come yet to Brondesbury," she answered. "I shall wait till it comes to my own place." Sebastian said politely that local cinemas were so much more convenient than the West End. "That's not the reason," Elsie answered truculently. "I don't go to West-End cinemas because I can't afford it. I've not got any three and sixpences to waste on my pleasures." Anne said desperately, "Nobody has these days." And there was silence. And Elsie caught Anne and Sebastian exchanging glances from the corner of their eyes. Of course that was it. Those two! She might have known it. All this was just for Anne. Sebastian was making this

Anne's party, and she, Elsie, was just an interloper. But it ought to have been *her* party. It ought to have been *her* party at Anne's flat. These men, both of them, were the interlopers. She would show them. And leaning across the table to Anne she began to talk rapidly of Ministry shop. "Bobbie has been away again and is back—more half-witted than ever. Her father has been ill—I thought she would never stop talking about his wretched symptoms. Miss Younge had a time bomb and, of course, she had to pose as a heroine. Miss Saltman told me she was very pleased with my work and between you and me, I think I'm sure to get the Deputy's job. I ought to, I'm better qualified than anyone else. I say! I told Mrs. Doweson where to get to yesterday—" Elsie talked and talked, pointedly ignoring the two men, who listened at first, looking rather bored, and then began a conversation of their own. Anne sat looking unhappy, and trying to join in the two conversations. At last Elsie saw that Anne was more interested in what the men were saying and she stopped talking abruptly. Anne turned to O'Connor who was talking about his experiences as correspondent for a Dublin paper in Paris. He had gone from Paris to Bordeaux at the time of the French surrender. He was talking wittily of his adventures on the way. Anne and Sebastian were listening with delight. But Elsie sat with a sour expression on her face. She hated O'Connor and she didn't want to hear him talk; he was only talking because he was bored with her. The waiter had filled her glass again and as she sipped the wine, she thought about the last time she had drunk champagne. It was at a wedding when she was living in Geneva. The young man had been under her in the office and she had taught him all he knew; he married the manager's daughter and then a few weeks later, he was made an assistant manager over her head—just because he was a man, of course. It was always the same thing. Men and graft got everything. And now here was this up-stage young man holding the floor while Anne and Sebastian made sheep's eyes at one another and she, Elsie, had to sit dumb and pretend to like it. And anyway he didn't know what he was talking about. She knew more about France than he did! And she would show him here and now. "And what do you think was the cause of the French collapse?" she asked him suddenly in a loud defiant tone. He hesitated and stopped in the middle of his anecdote. "Really, I don't think I'm qualified to say," he replied. "I was only in France at the end. I saw many things that interested me—straws that showed, perhaps, how the wind blew—but I don't think I could sum up such an important matter in a few words."

"Well, *I* can," said Elsie. "In one word; I lived in France for two years and I can tell you this—it was just graft. All the French are corrupt, there isn't an honest man or woman among them— the things that I could tell you—" She drained her glass. She was growing angrier, remembering old grievances. "The Germans just bought them. You can buy anyone in France if you offer them a bribe and if you don't—why you just get nothing—as I know to my cost." She went on to relate a long story of a quarrel she had had with a French landlord; it seemed very interesting to her at that moment and she told it in detail. "Of course he thought he could do what he liked with me because I was a woman and on my own. But I taught him!" She looked angrily at O'Connor, who dropped his eyes to his wrist watch and lit a cigarette. Anne tried to get him restarted with, "Sebastian tells me that you're the only man living who understands Ireland. He says you are going there next week?" But Elsie cut in again. "Ireland! You're going to Ireland! Well, I hope you'll tell them what we think of them here." Anne and Sebastian both wriggled in their chairs. Sebastian said, "Have a brandy, O'Connor." Anne said, "Mr. O'Connor, will you pass me a cigarette." They both emphasized his name very slightly. Afterwards Elsie realized that they were trying to tell her that he was an Irishman, thinking perhaps that she had not heard his name. But her head now was far from clear and she did not understand their hint in time.

"Ireland!" she continued. "Ireland! If I had my way I'd invade it. The Irish are nothing but a lot of miserable cowards, hiding behind the British fleet."

That was the end of the party. Anne rose to her feet. "It's terribly hot in here. Elsie, do you mind if we have coffee in the hall. The men can follow us later." She put her hand under

Elsie's arm and led her away from the table. They sat down in the hall and the coffee came and she and Elsie drank it almost in silence. Elsie was alone with her at last but she did not feel this was a good opportunity to say all the things she had been meaning to tell her. For one thing, Anne seemed in a funny mood. She was very polite but she had the same sort of stony look on her face that Sebastian had had when Elsie was talking to O'Connor about Ireland. Elsie felt that she had again done something wrong but she was too fuddled to know what. She yawned several times and began to feel very sleepy and yet curiously wide awake; her tongue seemed to be talking of its own volition and she could distinctly hear what it was saying and how cleverly it brought out the words and stopped them from running one into another as they were trying to do. The floor was behaving curiously, slanting just a little, sometimes one way and sometimes another. She was a little drunk! That was what it was. Cocktails always upset her. She decided she had better go home at once. Anne made no attempt to delay her but asked her if she would be all right. Elsie, to her own great astonishment, heard herself saying that she would like a taxi. Anne helped her to the revolving door; then it was oranges and lemons again under the porter's arm. When she escaped on the other side, Anne followed her and gave Elsie's address to the taxi-driver. Elsie sank back into the seat feeling very tired and watched Anne walk back into the restaurant. She tried to wave to her but Anne did not seem to see.

When Elsie got home she threw herself on the bed, still in her outdoor clothes and fell instantly to sleep. She wakened up an hour or so later and felt very thirsty and not very well. She took a long drink of water and remembered drowsily, how with brilliant argument she had worsted that odious young man. Then she fell asleep again. When she wakened, she was cramped and stiff and her head ached. It was quite dark and the sirens were sounding. Her window stood uncurtained and open to the night sky. She groped her way across the room and pulled the curtains and then switched on the light and stood blinking in the sudden glare looking down at her crumpled clothes, slowly and painfully remembering the party and what she had said and done. She did not now feel that she had talked so very brilliantly; she began to have a suspicion that she might have seemed rather rude. She remembered how Anne had looked and her stony face and cold politeness when they sat together, at the end, in the hall.

The guns began suddenly; they were loud and the window glass rattled. But Elsie paid no attention. Her mouth was parched and her head was throbbing and she decided to make some tea. As she stood waiting for the kettle to boil, she reviewed the luncheon at the Park-Lucullus. She relived it all while the guns crashed and the house shook as a bomb fell nearby. She had got drunk and insulted everyone. She would have to apologize. But she couldn't do it at the office in front of all the others. Perhaps she could write to Anne—but it was too late now, the letter wouldn't arrive in time. After all, why the hell should she apologize. They were probably all three just laughing themselves sick at the thought of her by this time; they had something better than the choice of spending the night in a cramped leaking Anderson shelter with those noisy brats of her landlady's or being bombed in this rotten rickety house. Wherever they were sheltering it was somewhere Ritzy. Apologies be damned. She would just go to sleep in her own bed and forget it. And forget these horrible people and the air raid too.

CHAPTER FIFTEEN
NERVOUS CONSPIRATORS

WELL, THAT PARTY was a proper flop, thought Anne on her way to work next morning. How badly Elsie behaved. Seb was really angry with her, he thinks she is the most awful woman he ever met. I never realized quite what a queer old thing she is till I saw her sitting at that table with Seb and O'Connor and saying all those awful things. Thank goodness I shan't be seeing so much of her now; she won't be sitting by me much longer and Seb and I will be lunching together most days. I'm rather glad my ring had to go back to the jeweller's to be made smaller. I needn't tell the office about my engagement till it comes back—I know Elsie will be disagreeable about it. She went off into a daydream of all the wonderful things she and Seb were going to do which lasted till, pushing open the swing doors of the Translation Section, she stopped short with a gasp of astonishment. "What on earth has happened?" she cried. Mrs. Doweson was sitting smiling blissfully in a gale of wind. All the windows were smashed or cracked and half a dozen charwomen were busy with brooms, sweeping up the broken glass which lay all over the floor and the desks near the window. For one wild moment Anne thought Mrs. Doweson must have gone mad and broken all the windows in one of her fights with Elsie. Then she realized what had really happened. "A bomb in the night," said Mrs. Doweson. "It has smashed all the windows round this corner of the building. How are you, my dear?"

"How are you?" said Miss Purbeck, who had just come in with Mrs. Jolly. "We didn't expect to see you back so soon. In fact we heard that you had been killed or very seriously injured and it wasn't till Mrs. Doweson told us—I mean we were delighted to hear—that is we were afraid you were going to be disfigured for life even if you recovered—"

"Miss Purbeck! What dreadful things you do say!" cried Mrs. Jolly. "We never thought anything of the sort and we're delighted to see you back safe and sound—"

"I heard there were ever so many more casualties than we were told. Now *do* tell me all about it," interrupted Miss Purbeck, her eyes shining with anticipation. "It is so interesting to hear just what happened from somebody who actually saw it all. Did you really see anyone blown to bits? Was there a lot of blood?" Her voice dropped to a whisper of delighted horror. "I heard some people were buried under the ruins for hours and hours and some of them are still there."

"I'm sorry," said Anne. "I'm afraid I didn't see anything interesting at all. My eyes were so full of dust and plaster that I could hardly see what I was doing and I got away as soon as I could." Miss Purbeck looked disappointed. She's thinking how some people waste their opportunities, thought Anne. I suppose she would have stood for hours and feasted her eyes if she had been in my place. No, I don't think she would. It was too horrible, even for her; and with a little inward shiver, Anne tried to think of something else.

She had no difficulty in finding something nice to think about; the difficulty was to keep her mind at all on what she was doing and not to go off into delicious dreams of Sebastian and the wonderful thing that had happened to her since she last sat in this office. How completely everything had changed for her since then! She switched her mind back to her present surroundings and then she noticed that in the first place, Elsie was most unusually late for every seat at the table was filled now except hers, and in the second, that all the occupants of these seats had stopped chattering about bombs and the broken windows and were whispering together in groups. Anne tried to catch what they were saying. "What's happening?" she said at last. "What's the mystery? Why are you all whispering like this?"

"Oh well, you see while you were away," said Mrs. Jolly, "we all made up our minds—"

"Look out!" said Miss Younge. Mrs. Jolly stopped short as the swing doors burst open and Elsie hurried in. "Hullo, Anne," she said. "I'm late!" She threw her gas mask on her desk and strode over to Miss Saltman's desk to make her apologies. "Fusspot couldn't say much to me. I think it's the first time I've been late since the war started," she said when she came back, and clapping Anne heartily on the back and letting her hand rest there, she asked in an elaborately casual voice, "Well, how are you feeling after yesterday's dissipation?"

"Splendid," said Anne and she moved her shoulder so that Elsie's hand fell away and opened her desk and began to hunt intently in it for some article of lost property without looking again in Elsie's direction. Elsie stared at her crossly and then took off her hat and sat down to her desk and began to work without speaking again. She's going to sulk now, thought Anne. She's offended as usual but really I don't care a hang whether she is or she isn't. If anyone has got a right to be offended it's I—she isn't even going to apologize for the way she behaved yesterday!

Table Two worked in silence for a while. Then a number of workmen arrived and began to deal with the windows and work became rather difficult. The workmen began by smashing out all the glass that was left. It fell in cascades to the floor inside and the pavement outside. Anne laughed with glee as she watched them; it made her feel so irresponsible, she said, she would have loved to have helped, one so seldom had a chance to smash out windows without incurring some penalty. No one could work in this noise and in a few minutes, everyone but Elsie, was laughing and chattering with Anne and watching with amused horror as each piece of glass went flying under the workmen's hammers. Miss Dunkerley and Miss Jones smiled soberly with the rest, leaning back in their chairs and resting for a few minutes from their work; but Elsie did not even look up and though she must have found it difficult to concentrate, she made a pretence of being engrossed in her work.

Suddenly Anne remembered all the mystery and whispering that had been going on round the table earlier in the morning. Mrs. Jolly had been going to tell her the secret but someone had interrupted her. Anne called to her over Elsie's bowed head: "I say, Mrs. Jolly, what was it you were going to tell me; some secret, you know, that you were all whispering about? Has some horrid scandal leaked out while I was away?" There was an awkward silence. Mrs. Jolly grew red and looked embarrassed and Miss Younge made curious grimaces at Anne with sidelong glances at Elsie. Anne grinned and as she did so Elsie looked up and caught Miss Younge's significant glances at herself and Anne's response. Then, looking very hurt and unhappy, she returned to her work. Shall I speak to her, thought Anne, She does look miserable. No, I shan't. Serve her right. She spoilt my party yesterday with her bad manners. Let her sulk.

* * * * *

The workmen departed leaving empty spaces where the window glass had been. Luckily, it was a warm day and the sunlight poured in and except for the fact that the wind blew all papers and light objects off the desk at intervals, it was not disagreeable. Table Two settled down to work and with an effort Anne managed to concentrate on her work sufficiently to finish her translation. Remembering her past mistake, she read it through very carefully and was just going to take it up to be checked when a note arrived by a girl messenger from Sebastian. ". . . . they were lunching together—hoped it would be better fun than yesterday. . . . he had fetched her ring . . . he loved her." Anne started to scribble a reply but the messenger went off without waiting for it. Then she looked up and saw the time, pushed the note unfinished into her bag and took her translation up to Miss Saltman's desk. The telephone bell rang as she reached it and Mrs. Just picked up the receiver. "Colonel Hilles would be glad if you would go to his office as soon as you are free," she said when she had taken the message. "That's lucky," said Miss Saltman, jumping up and dropping her bag and glasses. "I wanted to tell him that I had decided on Miss Pearne's appointment and to ask him to agree. Now where's that list of things I wanted to talk to him about the first chance I had of seeing him—salary increases, Mrs. Jolly's leave—a whole lot of things." She scrabbled about among the papers on her desk. Mrs. Just picked up her bag, put her glasses in their case and handed them to her, took the list from the safe place in which she had laid it and put it into Miss Saltman's hand and watched her bustle down the room and through the swing doors.

"Sounded to me as if he were in a very bad temper," said Mrs. Just holding out her hand for Anne's translation. "But I didn't say so—no use putting the wind up her—she'll know the worst quite soon enough—but something has upset the old boy."

Miss Younge, Miss Purbeck and Mrs. Jolly were standing together in a little group a few yards from the table, their heads close together. On her way back to the table, Anne went up to them and pushed her way into the group. "Now then, you conspirators," she said, "let me into the secret." Miss Younge took no notice; she was whispering excitedly. "Colonel Hilles sent for her; I heard it when I was passing the telephone. Do you think it's about—?" She nodded significantly without completing the sentence. "I shouldn't be surprised. I do wonder what is going to happen and whether we did the right thing," said Miss Purbeck nervously. They all went back to their seats.

Elsie looked up and put her hand on Anne's arm. "Nearly lunchtime, Anne," she said with rather a forced smile. "Where shall we go to-day? Shall we try somewhere new?"

"Sorry," said Anne cheerfully. "I*m going shopping."

Elsie raised her eyebrows. "New clothes in wartime! I should have thought you had plenty already."

"Well, I haven't," snapped Anne. "And really, I think I may buy my clothes without asking your permission."

Elsie stood up with a black face, shut her desk with a bang and went off to the cloakroom to wash. "And a good riddance too!" said Mrs. Jolly. "What a filthy temper she's in to-day."

"Well, we shan't be seeing so much of her when she's Deputy," said Anne. "*If* she becomes Deputy," said Mrs. Jolly mysteriously. "Why I thought it was all fixed," said Anne. "I don't much care what happens anyhow. One o'clock at last and I'm off to lunch!"

Miss Saltman came back into the room at this moment. She had been away a long time and now she looked red and flurried. She went up to Mrs. Just and began to talk to her excitedly and then Mrs. Just came over and stopped them all as they were going out to lunch. "Miss Saltman wants to speak to you at three o'clock, will you all come up to her desk at that hour—all of you, that is, except Miss Pearne."

"What's up?" said Anne flippantly. "She looks very fractious." She put on her hat and looked at it critically and wished there was no war on and that she had lots of new clothes. Elsie came back from the cloakroom, put on her hat and went off to lunch without speaking again to Anne.

But the rest of the table were standing about and looking serious and a little frightened. "Do you think we are all going to be sacked?" wailed Miss Purbeck. "I wish we'd never done it now." "Of course not, they can't sack us all," said Miss Younge stoutly, pulling her coat from the peg and turning to Mrs. Just who was inspecting her hat in a scrap of mirror, she asked, "What's it all about anyhow?"

"You'll know when the time comes. But I'm glad I'm not in your place," added Mrs. Just smiling, with a tinge of malice in her voice. Anne knew that Mrs. Just did not like Miss Younge and her habit of slinking about on silent rubber soles.

Anne ran off gaily to meet Seb at a small restaurant near the Ministry where he usually lunched; soon she saw him waiting for her in the street by the door and she hastened her step for at present they had such a short time to spend together that she did not want to waste a moment of it.

He was waiting for her literally by the door of the restaurant for the door was off its hinges and very splintered and broken and was propped up against the wall. All the windows had gone too and only the ragged remains of window curtains were left flapping in the cool October breeze, for the same bomb which destroyed the Ministry windows had damaged the restaurant. But it was still open and a meal of some sort had been prepared; the tables were full of the regular customers seated at their accustomed tables, waiting patiently to be served; for they did not intend that "that man" should disturb their regular habits.

Seb led her to his usual table and the waiter came to attend to them. He smiled benevolently at the sight of the young lovers and particularly of the young gentleman who always gave such generous tips and picked up the menu which had been blown off the table and handed it to Sebastian. But the menu card and everything that was written on it, the waiter had to explain, was a mere matter of form; in the kitchen—what was left of it—there was no gas, no electricity, no water even for the moment and in fact all that he could offer was cold pork pie and sardines and a nice glass of cold milk.

Anne and Seb roared with laughter; Seb asked Anne if she would like to go somewhere else but Anne refused and said that all the other places in the neighbourhood were in much the same condition and yesterday they had had an enormous meal at the Park-Lucullus and had overeaten and they could do very well with less to-day; after all, there was a war on. So Sebastian told the waiter to bring what he could find. Anne smiled at Seb and Seb smiled at Anne, and each knew that the other was thinking that even dry bread and water would be delicious provided that they ate it together.

The pork pie and the sardines and the milk arrived and they began to eat them with a good appetite. "Quite a picnic, isn't it?" said a complete stranger at the next table. "A long time since I've drunk milk!" said a red-faced man from another table. Everyone was looking mildly amused at the strange conditions and making comments to each other across the tables. It made a change to have a picnic instead of the usual dull and solid lunch and there might have been nothing to eat at all—and they might not have been alive to eat it. Being alive at all gave a zest to everything in those days.

After lunch Anne and Seb had time to walk slowly once round the garden of Lincoln's Inn Fields. Anne loved the great plane trees and they talked together of the time when they would both be able to live again in the country. As they came out through the gate, they met Elsie. She dropped her head and began to read the newspaper she was carrying, pretending she had not seen them.

Anne came in with Seb's engagement ring on her finger. The sharp-eyed Mrs. Jolly noticed it at once. "And how long have you been concealing that from us?" she said. "Let me look at it. Why, I never saw such a lovely ring! And who's the lucky man and when's it to be?" They all clustered round her to look at the ring and tease and chaff her. But Elsie remained in her seat and did not look up or speak.

"I say!" said Anne. "Look at the time! It's getting on for three. Haven't we all got to go up and be scolded by Miss Saltman. I wonder what it's all about. Does she still look cross, do you think?"

"Crosser than ever!" said Miss Purbeck. "We'd better go now and learn the worst." Anne believed that she knew what Miss Saltman was going to tell them—that Elsie had been appointed Deputy—though she did not see why that should make Miss Saltman look so cross.

CHAPTER SIXTEEN
THINGS HAPPEN TO ELSIE

MISS PURBECK had shivers down her back as she sat waiting till it was three o'clock and time to go up to Miss Saltman's desk. It was like waiting to go into the dentist's room. She was very frightened; it was all very well to say that they couldn't all be sacked. That was quite true but one or two might be picked out as examples. And if any were sacked Miss Purbeck would be one of them. She felt sure of that; she knew her work was not really up to standard. She tried dreadfully hard but she just *couldn't* understand the things they had to translate—she knew what the Italian words meant in English but when she wrote down the English words, Mrs. Just said they didn't make sense. The translations were so very technical! After all she hadn't had any experience of technical things and she'd never had much time for reading. She wished she had saved more money; that hundred pounds had just melted away when once she broke into it for the journey home from Italy and it had taken her twenty years to save it. She wasn't good at saving; she spent too much money on sweets and things to eat. It was because she lived in boarding houses all the time. They gave you enough to eat—enough to keep you from being hungry—but if you were only a companion or living with "special terms" in funny little rooms that couldn't be let at the ordinary rates, you didn't get the best cuts from the joint! The waiters knew all about you, especially if you couldn't afford to give them tips and you didn't get much but scraps of fat and gristle! And she'd got into the habit of buying herself little extras and eating them at night up in her bedroom. But she spent a lot that way in the course of the week.

As the hands of the clock jerked to three o'clock her heart beat fast. Table Two stood up and went up to Miss Saltman's desk and stood round it like schoolgirls waiting be scolded by the headmistress and Miss Purbeck tried to hide herself behind Miss Younge and to keep her hands from trembling.

On the desk, in front of Miss Saltman, lay a typewritten paper at the foot of which were a number of signatures written in the form of a circle so that no one signature stood at the top. It looked crumpled and dog-eared and as if it had been retrieved from the wastepaper basket. Mrs Jolly nudged Miss Younge. "There it is, you see, I thought—" Miss Saltman looked at them angrily, hesitating a moment before speaking as if she were trying to find suitable dignified words to express her feelings; but she was too angry and all her thoughts came out in an excited rush.

"Table Two, you've behaved very badly. Colonel Hilles is very annoyed with you and I'm shocked at your ingratitude. I've always done my best to look after you and to make you happy and then you go behind my back and behind Colonel Hilles's back and send in a petition to the Director General. You know this is irregular. You know quite well that in a Government office any complaint must be addressed to your immediate superior— to myself that is—who will present it to the proper quarter. That's in the rules and regulations which you've all read and signed. Why couldn't you come to me and talk to me about it?" She stopped a moment and Anne broke in.

"But Miss Saltman, I don't understand. What petition? I haven't signed a petition."

"I know that, Miss Shepley-Rice. You are guiltless in the matter—whether because you had more sense than to sign a petition—which I hope is the case—or whether because you were away ill—I don't know. But I called you up with the others because you are indirectly concerned and you had better know what is happening. One other at the Table has also had the sense—perhaps I had better say the decency—not to put her name to this ridiculous document, so I need not keep her any longer." Mrs. Doweson left the group and went back to her seat at the table. The others stood round the desk, fidgeting, with red faces and looking embarrassed and rather frightened. Mrs. Jolly began a confused explanation. "We're very sorry, Miss Saltman, if we've done something wrong. You see we didn't mean to go behind your back but we were afraid you wouldn't listen to us and we were so upset—"

"And when have I ever refused to listen to your complaints? I'm sure I spend most of my day listening to them—complaints that the room is too hot or too cold or that you don't get enough money or enough leave or that you're overworked—or something. You cannot say that I don't listen to your *complaints*. But I can't waste the whole day on this nonsensical business. I understand from this paper—" she picked it up and looked at it with disgust. "I understand from this petition which you have had the—" she hesitated for a suitable word and then changed the phrasing—"this petition with which you have been so foolish as to trouble the Director General—the *Director General*, mark you, with all his important duties—asks that Miss Pearne should not be appointed as Deputy. Miss Pearne will not be Deputy. Colonel Hilles has arranged that Table One will lend us an experienced translator for three months and during that time Miss Shepley-Rice will be trained specially and if she is satisfactory, she will then be appointed Deputy." There was a general mutter of surprise and Anne stared in astonishment. "The matter is now settled and I see no useful purpose in further discussion of it. That will do, thank you."

Table Two trooped away in silence and sat down at their desks. Miss Purbeck could breathe easily at last. It was over and it did not seem as if anyone was going to be sacked. "No thank you, Mrs. Jolly," she said, pushing away the box of chocolates which the other woman was offering her. "I'm really going to give up sweets till the war is over. Well, perhaps—just one little one, they do look so delicious—but this is really the last time!"

Miss Saltman, red and ruffled, threw all the papers off the top of her desk in a wild search for something she imagined she had lost. "What an idiotic thing for them to do," said Mrs. Just, picking everything up off the floor and replacing it on the desk as far as possible from Miss Saltman.

"Idiotic from their own point of view because they've all dished their chances of promotion and most unkind to me."

"I'm sure they didn't mean to be unkind to you. You know people get carried away with the idea of petitions. They like to feel they are addressing personally an important person. Younge would love that and she was the ringleader, I fancy. And another thing is that everyone is a little unbalanced just now with the lack of proper sleep. I am sure that Dunkerley and Jones would never have been persuaded to sign that paper otherwise. I suppose Colonel Hilles was furious."

"Absolutely furious—you know—mutiny-in-the-ranks sort of idea—and most of all with me which is very unfair. Luckily the petition didn't get further than the D.G.'s secretary who sent it at once to Hilles for an explanation. He seems to think I've been bullying the Table and forcing on them a deputy whom they all dislike. I explained to him how efficient Miss Pearne is and though she has an unfortunate manner, I thought they would all settle down once she was appointed. But he said no one could be appointed who was as unpopular as she seemed to be, no matter how efficient she might be. And he said none of the others could be appointed because they were obviously a pack of fools to have sent that petition and that left Shepley-Rice—though I will say that he said from the very beginning that she would be the best choice. It seems that the new policy is to appoint promising youngsters as secretaries rather than as deputies—just a little plan to throw *still* more work on the unfortunate supervisors," she concluded bitterly.

"I believe you'll be quite pleased with Shepley-Rice when she has had a little training," said Mrs. Just. "You know I think you did consider her seriously at one time. I rather fancy it was you who suggested her to the D.D." This was quite untrue and Mrs. Just knew it. But she knew Miss Saltman would only accept the appointment with a good grace if she thought she were getting her own way. And Mrs. Just wanted her to accept it both because she thought it was a good appointment and because she wanted to get the matter settled so that her own departure might not be delayed. "I believe you first put the idea into his head," she continued. "Ye-es, now I come to think of it, I believe I did," said Miss Saltman; soon she became a little more cheerful and began to believe that Anne's appointment was entirely her own idea. But then she remembered a disagreeable task and became gloomy again. "Now," she sighed, "I shall have to break the news to Miss Pearne. She'll be very disappointed and it would be rather unkind to let her hear the story from the others—they're not likely to put it nicely! Will you ask her to come up and speak to me. Oh dear! I suppose there are some people who envy me my job!"

Anne ran down the passage on a message for Mrs. Just. She felt very happy and excited—too happy, she told herself, it was unlucky to be too happy in these uncertain days. But all the same, this was a marvellous week—first her engagement and now she was going to be promoted—she was going to be made Deputy! She could hardly believe it. Of course, the thought of the responsibility was frightening but Miss S. had just told her that she would not have quite the same position as Mrs. Just. Apparently there weren't going to be any more deputies like Mrs. Just—Anne hadn't quite understood what Miss S. was saying because she had seemed rather angry about it—all translations would have to be checked by the Language Supervisor only, said Miss S. so Anne, thank goodness! wouldn't have to do that—she was going to be more like a secretary than a Deputy. But even if the job was less important than everyone had thought it was going to be, still it was promotion and Anne was thrilled that she should be promised promotion so soon. She wondered if she could get a word with Sebastian and tell him the news.

And then to Anne's astonishment she met Mary—Mary, in the sacred precincts of the Ministry, walking calmly along and talking to Seb!

Mary was, as usual, wearing a smart and rather remarkable costume—beautifully cut leather breeches, a leather jerkin and a kind of helmet, also of leather, with big goggles pushed up on the top of her head and thick leather gloves and high leather boots. Under the helmet, showed her silvery gold hair, exquisitely dressed, and her face was as perfectly made up as if she were just going to a party. Anne became instantly conscious that her own hair needed setting very badly and that it was a long time since she had had time to make up her face and that her blue linen dress was crumpled and not particularly clean. But she stood her ground; Seb was her lawful property now and she was not going to put up with any nonsense from Mary Shephard and the sooner Mary knew it the better. So Anne greeted her with affectionate friendliness and asked after all her doings and how and why she came to be working in the Ministry and told her how delighted she was to see her. Mary returned her greetings with even more affection and kissed her warmly. "How lovely it is to see you again, Anne, my sweet, and how well you are looking—perhaps just a little tired and pale—but what can one expect with all this dreadful hard work. I heard you were in London and I was wondering how I could get hold of you—we must lunch together one day. No, I'm not actually working here. I've got a new job, Father got it for me, I started yesterday. It's too amusing! I'm a despatch rider and I take despatches regularly between a lot of Government offices on a motor cycle, my dears! At least they call them despatches but they look like a lot of silly old letters to me. I believe I'm not supposed to be experienced enough to take the really important ones. I had to buy the motor cycle myself, they wanted me to use an old push-bike, if you please. Anne, darling, don't you think these clothes are rather nice? Of course I had to get them specially made for me—" The door of an adjacent office opened and an elderly colonel looked out with a very cross face. "Do you realize that people are trying to work in these offices?" he barked. "Will you kindly make a little less noise!" Mary turned on him the full battery of her baby-blue eyes and her pretty pouting mouth. "I beg your pardon," she said sweetly. "I'm so sorry, I didn't realize—do forgive me—" The colonel looked much less angry and his frown began to fade into a fatuous smile. "I'm so sorry, sir," said Sebastian. The colonel bowed graciously and returned to his office and the young people moved hastily away. "Quite an old pet," said Mary coolly, "but we seem rather unpopular. Isn't there any place here where we can talk in peace? It's ages since I last saw you Seb, and I've lots to tell you." Anne decided it was time to administer the knock-out blow. "But Mary," she said in her sweetest voice, "has Seb told you the great news? I don't believe he has. You must con—" "I must catch that lift," said Seb interrupting her. "There's a man waiting for me upstairs. Goodbye, Mary. 'Bye Anne." He dashed away from them towards a lift just coming into sight at the end of the passage. "I must go too," said Mary, darting off in the same direction. But the lift gates were shut long before she got near them. She turned round and walked slowly back towards Anne. "What a hurry he's in," she said discontentedly. "Well, we are supposed to be *working* in this place," said Anne. She was amused at Seb's sudden departure. He had so obviously bolted to avoid the awkward moment when Anne told Mary of their engagement.

"I suppose I shall have to finish my job too," said Mary, taking a bundle of letters from a case slung on her shoulders; "I've got all these letters to deliver. How on earth am I to find my way about this rabbit warren of a place?" Her voice was still sulky.

Anne took the letters from her and looked through them and told her exactly how to find each addressee. "Thanks so much," said Mary when she had finished. "Tell me, my sweet, which—er—which floor does Seb work on?" "The third," said Anne shortly. "His office is very hush-hush. I shouldn't think they would let you into it." "I don't suppose I am likely to want to go into it," said Mary, turning away towards the lift. "I was only just wondering. What were you going to tell me just now when Seb rushed away?" Anne smiled blissfully. "Only to tell you about our engagement. Seb and I are to be married in three weeks' time. Won't you congratulate me?"

It was the knock-out blow all right. Mary was astounded; she gaped at Anne with mouth half open and her make-up showed like paint on a doll's face. She managed to mutter a few words of conventional congratulation and then hurried away.

I don't think those letters will be delivered very carefully, thought Anne. I hope they aren't very important—and I hope she'll get the sack very, very soon. Which floor does Seb work on indeed! What cheek! What's it got to do with her?

While Anne was out of the room, Table Two talked excitedly about her appointment. It was a great surprise; no one had ever thought of her as among the "possibles". Miss Younge muttered and grumbled and talked about influence and tried to work up feeling against her, but Mrs. Doweson defended Anne warmly. In any case, said the old lady, the appointment was made now and the only sensible thing was to accept it. The others, who felt that Miss Younge had already led them into enough trouble, came over to Mrs. Doweson's point of view and Miss Younge found herself in minority. Elsie alone sat perfectly silent and expressed no view for or against the appointment. Presently Miss Younge discovered by her usual method of snooping round Miss Saltman's desk, that Anne was to be "only" a secretary and not a "real" Deputy like Mrs. Just, That, she said, when she came back and told the others, made all the difference in the world and Anne was welcome as far as she was concerned, to a job which was nothing but an errand girl's. "And Miss S. is furious," she added, "They're going to make our Miss S. do some work at last—instead of putting it all on the Deputy."

When Anne came back to the table, everyone except Elsie congratulated her on the appointment; she was very happy that they were all so nice about it but sorry that poor old Elsie seemed so disappointed.

Elsie sat at her desk and stared down at it. Miss Saltman had just told her; she knew now that she was not to be Deputy; she was to be passed over for Anne—a girl half her own age with no experience, with no qualifications at all. For a time she hardly knew what was going on around her—the fools and nitwits were jabbering away as usual, but she did not listen to what they were saying—she did not want to listen—Anne—Anne—Anne, that was all they could talk about. And on top of everything her tooth had suddenly begun to ache, badly, with horrid little jerks of pain. She put her finger into her mouth and rubbed her gum hard. I must get some oil of cloves on the way home, she thought. But it won't do any good really. I suppose it will mean a guinea to a dentist in the end. Miss Younge stared at her and grimaced at Miss Purbeck; "She looks quite queer," whispered Miss Purbeck and Mrs. Jolly nudged her in reply. Elsie saw their signs and grimaces and knew they were talking about her; her tooth throbbed and she was gripped with pain and rage and humiliation. Then her eye fell on her newspaper, *The Times*, and her face lightened a little as she looked at the column headed "Situations Vacant". There, two days before, she had seen an advertisement: "Capable business woman wanted to take charge of buying office. Experience and knowledge of French and Spanish essential. Good salary and prospects." She had answered that advertisement and now she took comfort in hoping for the job.

Thank God, I posted that letter after all, she thought. I nearly didn't because I thought I'd rather stay here and be Deputy. But *now*! What a relief it would be. How sick I am of this place! I ought to get a reply to-morrow or the day after. I believe I shall get it; I've got all the qualifications. They'd be sorry here if they lost me. People as competent as I am don't grow on every tree. She began to look a little happier and soon picked up her pen and went on with her work.

Anne, sitting beside her, sneezed suddenly and pulled her handkerchief quickly out of her bag. Something white fell to the ground.

"Bless you!" said Mrs. Jolly as Anne sneezed again. "You've caught cold. It's pretty parky with all these windows gone, I'm sure I—"

"I haven't caught cold," said Anne. "It's the dust. Just look at it, it's blowing in from the street and my desk is covered. My hands are simply filthy. I must go and wash." She took her towel from the drawer and stood up.

From the corner of her eye Elsie saw something white lying on the floor and she glanced down at a piece of paper lying there. Written in a large bold handwriting, her own name caught her eye. It was impossible not to read further—it was Anne's handwriting. "Old Pearne is, of course, a screaming bore—sorry I inflicted her on you, but I'm choking her off, she really can't behave. . . ." Anne looked down at the same moment; it was part of the letter she had been writing to Sebastian which she had pushed into her bag and forgotten; she bent down hastily, picked up the paper and put it in her bag. Her face, scarlet with embarrassment, she looked at Elsie and Elsie, with a face as white as Anne's was red, stared back at her. Then Anne dropped her eyes and ran out of the room. Elsie watched her as far as the door; her eyes began to glitter and she felt as if she were choking. She wrenched open her drawer, snatched her towel and strode hurriedly after Anne.

She found her standing in the cloakroom, reading again with a horrified face, the letter which Elsie had seen. She turned round as Elsie came into the room. "I'm so sorry, Elsie," she stammered. "Of course, I didn't mean that—it was a joke—"

"A joke! Very likely! You've had plenty of jokes, you and your boy friends—plenty of jokes at my expense, I've no doubt, jeering and laughing at me behind my back. That's all you asked me to lunch for, to make a laughing stock of me. Do you think I didn't know it? I'm a screaming bore, am I? Well, I'll tell you what you are. You're a false-hearted little fool with a pretty face! You've got a pretty face, all right, I'll grant you that. Your sort always have; that's what you catch the men with. And because you've got a pretty face you get round everybody and now you've got my job. That's what you've been working for all the time, I suppose, making a fool of me and pretending to be my friend and making up to Colonel Hilles all the time so that you'd get the job."

"Oh! Don't be such a fool," interrupted Anne. "I've only spoken once in my life to Colonel Hilles, when he interviewed me when I first came here."

"Sez you," sneered Elsie. "I know your sort. I've met them before. Get round the men and get all you want out of them." Her voice grew louder and more hysterical. "If it wasn't the D.D., it was your boy friend got you the job. People like me—we can be efficient and work till we drop—we get nothing—and then a little chit like you comes along and knows what to give the men to get what she wants—"

"What a very unpleasant person you are!" said Anne. She looked Elsie up and down with a stare of cold indifference that made Elsie want to choke her. "Now just listen to me and stop screaming," continued Anne. "I should like never to speak to you again but we're working in the same office and we've got to make the best of it. I'll be civil to you in public because I must, but don't speak to me again out of office hours." With her chin in the air and her face flushed with anger, Anne walked towards the door of the room. As she reached the door, she looked back. "Listeners never hear any good of themselves; neither do people who read other people's letters. Serves you jolly well right!" Elsie made a dash in her direction. Her face was working, her teeth clenched and she raised her hand in an ugly clawing gesture as if she would like to tear at Anne's face. It was a lie! She hadn't read other people's letters—at least the letter was put right under her nose and she couldn't help reading it!

Voices and running footsteps came down the corridor and a noisy group of junior office staff pushed open the door. One of them collided with Elsie as she stood and stared at the door through which Anne had gone out. "Pardon," said the girl, "but if you will block the gangway—"

"Damn you," said Elsie furiously. "Why the hell can't you look where you're going!" The young girl stared at her in surprise. "That's a nice way to talk, I must say," said another indignantly. "And what language! Ireen apologized to you—there's no need to speak to her like that. You ought to be reported, swearing at her and all."

"Get out of my light," said Elsie violently. She pushed her way roughly through the group to the other end of the room. The young girls looked at each other in frightened silence then made for the door. "Come on, Ireen, let's go and wash in the other cloakroom. She looks quite funny, she's crackers if you ask me," Elsie heard one say as they pushed out into the passage.

Crackers! That was their silly slang word for madness.

The word checked Elsie's rising hysteria. I must be careful, she thought. They're in the plot against me too—spies from upstairs. They're all in the plot and Anne's the chief one. They put her up to pretend to be my friend so that she could spy on me. But I'm not going to think of her. That's all finished with now. I've got to back to that room and sit at the desk next to her with all those blasted old bitches staring at me to see how I'm taking it. Thank God, it's half-past four. She's telling them now; they're all jeering and laughing at me—She heard footsteps again in the passage and quickly filling a basin with water, she began to wash her face. The door opened and Mrs. Jolly bustled over to the basins. "Oh! Are you washing too?" she said. "I'm so filthy I'd like to have a bath. No chance of that to-night, worse luck. All the water is cut off round our way since our bomb the night before last and we hardly get enough to fill a kettle. You know I don't think this way of living is really very good for one; I mean one doesn't really get enough sleep, does one really, and you know, if you'll excuse me saying so, Miss Pearne, I think you look dreadfully tired. Do you ever get a comfortable night's rest?" Elsie raised her face out of the water and buried it in the towel. There was so much kindness in Mrs. Jolly's voice as she stood gazing at Elsie with amiability written all over her pink foolish face that Elsie was almost touched. She dried her face carefully before answering. I look so tired, she says; she means crackers too; it's just a different way of putting it. I don't want them to think that. Mrs. Jolly was babbling on. Elsie interrupted her, speaking in a cool, carefully controlled voice. "I daresay I do look tired. I slept very badly last night; in fact I haven't slept properly since the raids began. They have been very bad down my way. I have not been very comfortable. I sleep in my landlady's Anderson when it's too bad to stay in my own room and her children are very noisy." Mrs. Jolly beamed with delight—it wasn't often that Elsie bothered to speak to her—and she was still chattering away when Elsie left the cloakroom and went back to her section and sat down at her desk. Elsie had herself under control now. It's quite true, she thought, I don't get enough sleep and that German doctor told me that I wanted more than most people when I went to him about those dreadful headaches I used to get when I was working hard. If I were to get that job I've applied for I think I should have to move—though I don't know where one could go to get away from the noise of the raids. A week ago I was thinking of sharing a flat with Anne! Well, that dream is finished and done with now—and I'm done with Anne too! False little cat! Purring and playing so prettily and hiding her sharp claws! A dirty little spy like all the rest of them. She clenched her fists under the table. But I'm not going to think of her, *I'm not going to think of her.* Steady now—they're all staring at me, watching me to see how I'm taking it. Thank God it's ten to five. This awful day is nearly over.

CHAPTER SEVENTEEN
FLAT HUNTING

IT WAS Anne's day off. She was going to the hairdresser and the dressmaker and then she was going to meet Sebastian for lunch and they were going to look for a flat. She had a huge pile of letters from house agents. During her sick leave last week she had telephoned to every house agent whose address she could find. As a result of the air raids, empty flats in London were plentiful and the house agents had responded with such a wealth of replies that the letter box at Cromwell Road was filled and emptied again and again during the next few days. Anne had already spent an evening weeding out the pile but there were still dozens of flats that all seemed equally desirable for one reason or the other.

We can't possibly look at all those this afternoon, she thought, and I can't carry that great bundle about with me all the morning. I must pick out a few of the best. All these flats seem perfectly lovely—living in any one of them with Seb will be marvellous. It will be fun having a little kitchen of my own—I shall tell the servant to go out and I shall learn to cook a wonderful dinner for Seb; we'll wait on ourselves and be all alone together. This one has "access to a garden"; now that would be nice for the dogs because we shall have one or two with us of course. It's an upper maisonette—whatever that means—entrance hall, kit., usual offices, three rec., five beds., two bath., sounds rather large for two perhaps but convenient if we want to have people to stay. We'll see that. I like the idea of a garden for the dogs. She added the address to a list she was making, feeling very business-like and practical. By the end of an hour, she had reduced the bundle to a size which would go conveniently into her new handbag without spoiling its shape. Her choice had been mainly influenced by the convenience of the dogs. This one had a garden, that one was close to the park and the rejected pile contained all the flats which seemed to be on busy roads where the dogs might meet with an accident. For herself all that mattered was living with Seb and any sort of flat would suit her equally well.

They lunched at the Dorchester. Seb ordered oysters and a bottle of Chablis and refused to allow Anne even to mention the office. To-day they were going to think only about themselves and their plans. Had she found them a flat?

As soon as they had finished eating, Anne took out her bundle of replies from the house agents and began to go through them with Seb, explaining gravely the good points of each one that she had selected. From thinking in the morning that they might have one or two dogs up in town with them, she had now come to think that if they found a suitable place, they might have them all; it would be such fun to have a few puppies about the place; she did miss them so dreadfully.

Seb listened equally gravely. He well knew that marrying Anne, he was marrying a zoo—a menagerie that would grow and grow and have to be tended from turbulent youth to decrepit old age and whose comfort and well being would be a major preoccupation of their lives. He didn't mind that, of course; dogs and other animals was almost as inevitable a part of his life as of Anne's. But he knew that there would be occasions which would call for the exercise of tact—and this, he thought, was one of them—half a dozen dogs romping on someone else's furniture— puppies on the carpets—that was going to complicate things a little too much! The air raids, he suggested, would be bad for the puppies' nerves, much better to let them grow up in the country, in fact the noise of the guns might upset the older dogs, and there might be difficulties if they had to be evacuated suddenly, and so forth. Reluctantly Anne agreed that it would be better perhaps to have only one small easily portable dog with them for the present—she might have them all up in turns.

That point settled, the selection of a flat became quite easy and they picked out a few that seemed particularly attractive and set off to look at them. A taxi from outside the Dorchester took them to the first address in Bayswater. This had sounded attractive because it faced the park; they found it was a Tudor-style skyscraper with imitation oak beams stuck all over the front and all the rooms in the flat they were offered looked out on to a brick wall; so they turned it down. The second flat, in an imitation renaissance palace, was smelly and grubby. The third flat was very clean but furnished in a mixture of Tottenham Court Road, Jacobean and Chelsea Baroque, and Anne thought the furniture and everything about it was so fussy that she couldn't bear it. It was getting rather late now and Seb told the driver to hurry as quickly as possible to the next address. The driver took Seb at his word and made a short cut through a badly bombed area and they bowled along the edge of huge road craters, plunged up and down miniature mountain ranges and once even darted through a street closed for a time bomb before the wardens were able to stop them; before Anne had finished laughing at the warden's horrified face the cab had drawn up outside a large block of flats in the Campden Hill neighbourhood.

It was a new modern building, white and shining in the sun. They looked at a flat on the first floor and fell in love with it at first sight. It had a large sitting-room with a huge plate glass window all along one side, giving on to a balcony and overlooking a garden (to which they "had access", Anne discovered with joy) which was full of immense trees which in summertime hid entirely the opposite buildings. A plate glass screen cut off the dining recess which was lined with glass-doored cupboards in which stood a lovely collection of modern table glass. There were two bedrooms, a pretty bathroom and an efficiently equipped kitchen full of gadgets. The furniture was modern to suit its surroundings, well padded and comfortable and with no decoration but that of the beautifully grained woods of which it was made and the lovely textiles used for coverings and curtains.

"Do you like it, Anne? Shall we take it?" asked Sebastian. "I adore it but I suppose we can afford it? Isn't it very expensive?" said Anne. "Expensive?" said Sebastian vaguely. "Why no, it's quite cheap." He looked at the house agent's letter and read out the rent. "No, it's not expensive," he repeated and read out the amount of the rent. It was more than twice the whole of Anne's salary on which she had been attempting to live. She realized with some surprise that in a few weeks' time she would be a comparatively rich woman.

She was interrupted in her thoughts by the housekeeper who was showing the flat to them and who wanted to demonstrate to Anne some of the superior features of the kitchen arrangements. She called Anne "Madam" instead of "Miss" which made Anne feel very grown up and married already and Anne followed her round and looked at hot water cupboards and the refrigerator and the stove and a great many other things of which she had very little idea of the meaning although she tried to look and sound very wise and knowing. "You'll find it a very easy flat to manage, Madam," said the housekeeper. "There's surprisingly little work in it."

"I've got an idea about that," said Sebastian. "I thought we'd get my old nurse to come and look after the housekeeping. She's eating her head off with boredom and would love to come and look after us. How would that suit you, Anne? You won't have much time for domesticity if you're going to keep on your job till the war ends."

Anne said that that would suit her perfectly and that it was very clever of Seb to have thought of it. She remembered old Nannie very well; in fact she had stood in considerable awe of her in the days when she was a little girl going to tea with the little boy Sebastian in the nursery at the Hall. What fun everything was and how marvellous it was going to be to live in this perfect flat with Sebastian who was really perfect too although she thought it wiser not to tell him so too often. They laughed together and ragged each other and rushed about the flat opening doors and making new discoveries and shouting to each other about them till suddenly they discovered how late it was and tore downstairs to the waiting taxi and told the man to drive as quickly as possible to the house agent so that they could secure the flat before anyone else took it.

"Well, that's settled," said Seb when they came out of the agent's office and they had taken the flat. "He is sending me the agreement to-morrow and I'll wire to old Nannie and tell her to come up next week and get the place ready for us. Now is there any reason why we should wait three weeks to be married. I've discovered you can get a special licence and be married as quickly as you like."

"Seb! All the things I've got to do! I've got no clothes at all!"

"What's the matter with the dress you're wearing? It looks charming to me. I was just thinking how sweet you were looking."

"Seb, you old ass! It's last year's frock; it looks simply awful." She squeezed his arm. "Be patient a little longer; it's only three weeks on Friday—not so very long."

They would have liked to finish their day with dinner and a theatre but at this time all the London theatres were closed on account of the raids; so they chose a local cinema. Even the flicks closed down at nine o'clock so they went before instead of after dinner and returned to Cromwell Road to Anne's place for the evening meal.

This was at the suggestion of Agnes who daily implored Anne not to stay out of doors after a raid warning and rated Sebastian soundly for keeping her out. One of the ground floor rooms had now fallen vacant and she had arranged it as a dining-room. She cooked dinner for them and served it there.

"Good night, Seb darling," said Anne afterwards when she was seeing him off at the front door. "Be careful going home and if you hear any bombs falling near, mind you take shelter at once. It's been a lovely day."

CHAPTER EIGHTEEN
A DOCUMENT LOST

THE SUMMER seemed to have come to a sudden end and it was a dismal morning, dark and raining, with a cold wind that blew the first dead leaves along the pavements. It was dismal outside and it was still more dismal in the Translation Section of the Ministry; when the first arrivals came in, shaking the rain from their wet umbrellas and coats and grumbling at the sudden change in the weather, they found their room in almost complete darkness—the windows were boarded up and the electric light was cut off. The windows had been boarded up by the workmen who had knocked out the broken glass; they had done their work thoroughly and while the rain and some of the wind were shut out, so too was all the light; only faint gleams came through the cracks and it was just possible to grope one's way between the desks. A broken water main was responsible for the failure of the electric light; an electrician, hammering and cheerfully whistling as he waited for his mates, foretold that it would be a long job.

Work was quite impossible in the darkness and Table Two sat and gossiped and complained of the piercing cold draughts which blew through the cracks in the window boards and fluttered the papers on their desks, while Miss Saltman telephoned wildly for candles. "Would you believe it!" she said, angrily slamming down the receiver. "They have no candles in stock!"

"Can't someone be sent out to buy some?" asked Mrs. Just. "Oh dear me, no!" replied Miss Saltman bitterly. "This is a Government office! To procure candles, they must be requisitioned on the correct form and obtained from the correct department—probably a special Treasury grant will have to be earmarked for the purpose! And in the meantime we can lose a whole morning's work! These civil servants drive me mad!"

A few minutes later, however, some candles did arrive and were distributed among the translators who stuck them on saucers and the lids of sweet tins and settled down at last to work.

All this time Elsie's seat had been vacant. She was late again—nearly an hour late to-day—but when she came in at last and hurried to make her apologies, Miss Saltman looked at her white face and the circles under her tired-looking eyes and made no comment on her late arrival.

But though Elsie looked ill, she was feeling much better and much calmer than she had been feeling for the last few days. Last night she had gone early to bed in a state of complete exhaustion and had taken the last dose left in the bottle of a sleeping draught which her German doctor had once prescribed for her. There had been no alarms in the night and she had slept heavily for twelve hours, awakening only at eight o'clock when her landlady came upstairs and banged on her door. Her toothache, too, was better. But she bought oil of cloves on the way to the office in case it began again.

As Elsie went back now to her own desk, Anne, whose head was full of her own interests and who had almost forgotten their quarrel, looked up with a half smile ready to greet her.

But Elsie looked back at her, coldly and unsmiling and merely gave a casual nod as if Anne were almost a complete stranger. That was what she meant Anne to be for the future, as far as she was concerned. She had made up her mind about it yesterday. She was going to forget Anne, to ignore her, to go back to the time before she had met Anne; Anne was eating away her strength, making her weak, hysterical and emotional. Of course it was part of the plot; they had sent this pretty child to break down her hardness, to soften her so that they could get at her. It was quite clear now; she had thought it all out yesterday and she felt calm and rested and her old strong self again.

Anne had given a little shrug of the shoulders at Elsie's rebuff and then returned to her work. Elsie now sat down beside her and began to force herself to concentrate on a translation that Mrs. Just had given her.

But it was not at all easy to concentrate on work in the conditions prevailing that morning. The candles flickered wildly in the draught and were almost extinguished each time a door was opened; they were too few in number and had to be shared by several people and as the light they gave was quite inadequate, every one tried surreptitiously to move the candle nearer to herself. The electricians had now arrived in full force and were pulling up the floorboards, while at the other end of the room, some workmen were hammering in a few finishing touches to the boards over the windows.

In the middle of the morning, when the confusion was at its height, a girl messenger came in with an important and confidential translation, so confidential that she had been instructed to obtain Miss Saltman's signature for it before she gave it up. Mrs. Just opened the sealed envelope and took out a sheet of foolscap paper covered with writing in rather faint blue ink. "Not even typed and in an impossible handwriting!" she exclaimed. "Of course we would get something important and difficult like this on the day that the lights fail!"

"What's the language?" asked Miss Saltman. "Portuguese. Pearne knows it but not nearly as well as Shepley-Rice. Which shall I give it to?"

"Give it to Shepley-Rice and impress on her that it's confidential. If she doesn't finish it by lunchtime, it must be locked in her desk while she is out. Explain it all to her."

Mrs. Just did so as she handed the paper to Anne. "It's not typed, I'm afraid; it's in a most curious handwriting, all loops and flourishes, not very easy to read," she added. Anne looked at it in dismay—a perfect horror, she thought, and very difficult to read by the light of the candle she shared with Elsie. She pushed up close to the candle and then had to twist round awkwardly so that the translation she was writing was not directly under her neighbour's eyes.

"You needn't squirm about like that," said Elsie at last. "I don't want to look at your precious document!"

"You couldn't read it if you did!" said Anne. "It's impossible to read. I never saw such a fist!"

Elsie glanced at the paper which lay on the further side of Anne's desk. She turned her eyes away and then looked again at it with interest. She knew that handwriting! She had recognized it at once! She was sure it was Benno's hand-writing; it must be; she knew it only too well; for years she had kept a couple of notes that he had written her. Was he in Portugal now? When she last heard of him he had been in Italy. What was he doing? How maddening not to be able to read that wretched paper and find out! Confidential my foot! It had only gone to Anne because it was her special language—otherwise Elsie would have got it for certain. How tantalizing, it was just too far away for her to read.

By lunchtime, when the lights came on, Anne was halfway through. She went out to lunch with Sebastian at her usual time but came back early and worked without stopping till half-past three when she was within a few sentences of the end. An alert sounded and once again it was her turn for duty at the lift-shaft to take the signal from the roof spotter.

She put all the papers on which she was working into her drawer, laying the Portuguese text carefully on the top, locked the drawer and put the key into her bag and ran off to the lift. A little later she got the alarm from the roof—enemy planes approaching—and had to blow her whistle and give the general alarm. That meant that everyone in the building had to go down to the shelters.

Table Two rose grumbling and set off for the door. Gun-fire sounded near and hastened their progress a little. At the door-way, Mrs. Just looked back. "I suppose Shepley-Rice did remember to put that Portuguese report away and to lock her drawer. Could you look, Miss Pearne?" Elsie was at the end of the queue and the only one who could turn back without block-ing the way of the others. She went back to the table and tried the drawer. It was firmly locked. She hesitated and glanced round. The room was empty now and the others were half-way down the passage with their backs towards her. She took the key of her own desk drawer and tried it in Anne's lock. As she expected, the key turned in the lock with only a little difficulty. The report with the translation lay, as Anne had placed it, on the top of a pile of miscellaneous oddments, tins of sweets, newspa-pers, stationery, books and so forth. Elsie took the report and looked at it. She saw in a moment that it was of no interest to her—a report on some complicated invention—the writing was not really much like Benno's when she looked at it closely—and anyhow it was signed by someone quite different. Of course when she came to think of it, it was most unlikely that this report which had come from Portugal could have been written by Benno! It was just that he had been in her mind lately—she had dreamed of him once or twice during her troubled nights. She pushed the sheet of paper hastily back into the drawer as she heard the Home Guards tramping down the passage to take up their station at the doors as was the custom during an alert. The drawer was so untidy that there was hardly room to get it in. She pushed it roughly to the back as a voice from the doorway bade her hurry down to the shelter, jerked the drawer till it shut, locked it and ran quickly after the others.

For the last week it had been unusual to be kept more than a few minutes in the shelters although the warnings often came several times in the day. But this time the alarm was a long one, and Table Two was more bored than usual for there was nothing interesting to talk about. There was really nothing more to say about air raids; there was one nearly every night and that was that; if the bombs fell far away, you felt brave, if they fell near, you quaked. Stories of "my" bomb were taboo, no one would listen and no one wanted even to tell them any more. And there was nothing more to say about the appointment of the new Deputy; that was all settled—there was really nothing to say at all.

Mrs. Jolly changed her position on the hard bench and gave a huge yawn, putting her hand politely in front of her mouth. "Isn't this just one of those days when everything goes wrong?" she said wearily. "So dark this morning—and the draughts in our room—"

"They'll have to do something about the draughts!" said Elsie angrily. "We shall all get pneumonia and there's no one to look after me if I get ill—I've just got to get better the best way—"

"I've got a stiff neck already," said Miss Younge. "The draughts aren't so bad your side of the table as they are on ours," said Mrs. Jolly, "and it's worse now than it was earlier to-day. I'm sure I'm not one to fuss much about feeling cold but really the blotting paper actually blew off my desk just before we came down here. Oh dear! Just look at the time—nearly five and we shall have to clear up our desks when we do get upstairs and by the time we get home we shall hardly have time to swallow a mouthful of food before the sirens go again and the raids start for the rest of the night!"

"How do you spell centenary?" said Bobbie. She was squatting on the floor busy with paper and pencil on a corner of the bench which she was using as a table. Anne told her. "What do you want to know for and what on earth are you doing?"

"Drafting a notice to announce the week's total amount collected for the Spitfire Fund," said Bobbie importantly. Bobbie was one of the collectors for the Spitfire which was being bought by the Ministry Staff. "We've done so well and I'm going to say that the fund on this floor has reached its centenary. We've collected a hundred pounds altogether."

"That's not the way to use the word," said Elsie scornfully. "What an ignoramus you are. Didn't you ever go to school?"

"Not very often," said Bobbie cheerfully. "I used to have headaches and they let me stay at home. I didn't get quite all this on our floor. I got ninety-nine pounds and two shillings and then I met Colonel Hilles outside his office and he gave me another eighteen shillings to make it a hundred. Isn't he ever such a nice man?"

"He's the nicest man in the world as long as you behave yourself," said Mrs. Just. "But you look out Bobbie; if you get reported to him he can give you such a dressing down that you'll wish you'd never been born." The All Clear went at last and there was a wild dash upstairs. Everyone left the shelters far more quickly than he or she came down to them but each person had to leave in proper order. Table Two came very near the end of the queue and it was nearly half-past five before the translators at last reached their own room—nearly half an hour after the usual time for going home.

Miss Saltman had gone already. "What shall I do about that Portuguese translation?" Anne asked Mrs. Just. "It's almost finished but not revised; I'm afraid it will take me at least another hour."

"You can't possibly stay to finish it to-night. You might be caught by a raid and not be able to get home at all. The D.D. has ruled that no one is to work overtime just now for that reason— no one is allowed to stay except firewatchers or Home Guards or people of that kind—you'll have to take it upstairs and have it locked in the safe. Mind you get a signature for it from whoever has the safe key."

Anne went over to her desk. On top of it lay a little note; she recognized the big sprawling handwriting. It was from Mary; she must have brought it in while they were all out of the room. Anne opened it. "Anne my sweet," she read. "Afraid I didn't tell you properly when we met how very very happy I am about your engagement but I was so worried about all those wretched letters I had to deliver. I send you both my lovingest wishes for your happiness. What will you have for a present and when's it to be and what are you going to wear? Satin and orange blossom or just going-away things? Do tell me all about it—I'm so thrilled." Nice of her to have written, thought Anne and then she started clearing up. Nearly everyone had gone now. Bobbie was standing in front of the notice board, gazing up at it. Mrs. Just was putting on her hat. "Hurry up, Bobbie," she said. "You can put up your notice in the morning."

"I've done it and it looks lovely. Good night," cried Bobbie and scampered towards the door. "I should hurry and take that report up to the safe if I were you, or you'll find everyone has gone home," Mrs. Just called to Anne, as she switched off all the lights but the one over Anne's desk. "Put out that light, won't you. I must rush now or I shall lose my train. Good night." The swing doors closed behind her. Strictly speaking, she should have waited to see Anne out, she thought, as she hurried down the passage. But it was so late now and so difficult to get home these days; her trains were so few and so crowded and after all Anne wasn't like one of the others—she would take her place as Deputy before long; she was a responsible person.

Anne was tired. She yawned several times and then unlocked her desk to get out the report so that she could run upstairs with it. The lock stuck a little but she got it open at last. Funny! She thought she had left the report right on top under her pen and blotting paper. Where was the beastly thing! She rummaged about a little. What a tiresome day it had been and now it was so late and if she wasn't lucky she wouldn't get home before the siren went again. Agnes would be in an awful flap. It was some minutes before she realized that the report wasn't there at all. She couldn't believe it and turned all the contents of her drawer out on her desk. But the report just wasn't there.

Anne looked behind the drawer to see if the sheet of paper had caught in the ledges; she looked under the desk and under everyone else's desk and all over the floor. Then she turned out the wastepaper baskets—a dozen scrunched-up sticky paper bags that had contained sweets and biscuits; several lots of dead flowers with smelly wet stalks; Miss Jones's correspondence neatly torn up in small squares; several sheets of paper in Miss Purbeck's writing, begun and torn across because she had made a mistake, and so on—but no report. It was not there nor anywhere else; it had simply vanished. She wondered what she ought to do; it was nearly half-past six and it was unlikely that there would be anyone left in the offices upstairs to which she could report the loss.

She went out of the room. The night watchmen were taking up their posts and looked at her curiously; the stairs and passages were in darkness but for a shaded light here and there. She went down the passage leading to Colonel Hilles's office, determined that if she could find no one else about, she would screw up her courage and tell him what had happened. But his office was in darkness and the door was locked. At the far end of the passage she saw a crack of light under a door and went and opened it. It was the firewatchers' mess-room and a group of girls in dungarees sat round a stove cooking their supper before going on duty. "Hullo Shepley-Rice!" said one. "What are you doing here so late? You'll get caught and kept for the night if you aren't careful." "I'm looking for the D.D.'s secretary but I suppose she has gone," said Anne. "Good night," and she shut the door and went back to her section. A night watchman was standing by the door. "Will you be going soon, Miss?" he asked. "I'm just going to bolt the door. You'll have to ring for me after that if you want to get out." "All right, thank you. I'm going at once," said Anne wearily. There was nothing to stay for. She had looked in every possible place.

Chapter Nineteen
"DISCIPLINARY SANCTIONS"

It was barely half-past eight when Anne reached the Ministry next morning. The night before she had wanted to tell Sebastian all about it and ask him what could have become of that wretched Portuguese report and what she ought to do and what an "Offence against the Defence Regulations" really meant, but Sebastian had been out when she telephoned and she had remembered that he was dining with one of the men in his office and when she telephoned later he was still out and then it was nearly eleven o'clock and she was very tired and had the beginnings of an abominable cold and she had wondered if she were not getting 'flu —and so she had taken some aspirin and gone to bed and slept the sleep of the innocent, for after all she was an innocent even if she were now to be treated as a sinister suspect by the higher powers. She had set her clock at half-past six and when the maddening whirr began she had jumped up at once determined to be first at the office and to look once more through that drawer of hers into which she could swear and would swear till all was blue or any other colour that she had put that report when the siren sounded and they all went downstairs.

And now the drawer was once more out on the table and she had turned out everything—the tins of sweets and the battered old biscuit tin and the three Penguins and her knitting with the ball of tangled wool and all her collection of pens and pencils and clips and rubber and pieces of clean paper that she always forgot to use. But the wretched report was not there, and she put the tins and the wool and the paper and all the rest of the things back again and shut the drawer and sat down looking about the room hoping vaguely that she would see the report somewhere just lying there as if by some miracle to set all right.

She was sitting so when Miss Saltman and Mrs. Just came in together and she rushed up to them and poured out her story. Miss Saltman looked incredulous and made her repeat it again slowly. "Nonsense, child!" she said at the end, "the report can't have disappeared out of your drawer. Go and look for it, will you please, Mrs. Just, it must be there." Mrs. Just and Anne went together and once more took out the drawer from Anne's desk and tipped out all the contents just as Anne herself had done twice last night and again this morning. The paper was quite clearly not there and Mrs. Just said so plainly to Miss Saltman. Other members of Table Two had now arrived and Miss Saltman explained what had happened and they all joined in a comprehensive search of the whole room. It was obvious at once that the report could not be lying on the newly swept floors and the freshly dusted desks, but to show their willingness, they all went on hunting about, moving things aimlessly, lifting up small objects that could hardly have concealed a postage stamp. "Don't be so idiotic! How could it be under that?" said Elsie irritably when Miss Purbeck picked up her inkpot and looked underneath. "It might be—if it was folded small—it was only one sheet—I saw it," said Miss Purbeck. Then Miss Younge said, "I expect she left it lying on the desk and that it's blown behind the radiators or under a cupboard; we had better poke behind them and see."

"I did *not* leave it lying on the desk," Anne said emphatically again and again, but nobody took any notice because everyone was warming up to the hunt and moving everything and making a great deal of dust and getting very dirty themselves. And rather surprisingly, thought Anne, it was Elsie who was leading the hunt. Armed with Mrs. Doweson's umbrella, Elsie was scraping behind the radiators and under the cupboards and in all the inaccessible corners where a paper might have been blown by the draught; and when she rose from her fruitless efforts and finally sat down in her own seat, beating the dust from her hands, her face showed concern and bewilderment; "I'm damned if I know what's become of it," she said. "It absolutely beats me. There's some dirty business somewhere I'll be bound."

Miss Saltman was now getting greatly worried; at first she had repeated over and over again that the report *could* not be lost and that they *must* just *find* it, but now she was coming round to Anne's belief that it had completely disappeared from the room. Then a new idea occurred to her; "I suppose you didn't put it by mistake in someone else's drawer," she said hopefully; and so everyone opened their drawers and Miss Saltman and Mrs, Just bustled round looking inside them. "No, it seems to have gone," said Miss Saltman with a sigh and Elsie said, "It must have been taken while we were down in the shelter." Then Mrs. Just had a brainwave. "Did anyone come into this room while we were away?" she asked and Mrs. Doweson answered; "There were Home Guards on duty at the door all the time we were down; if anyone came into the room they would know. We'll go and ask them. Come along." So Mrs. Just and Mrs. Doweson and Anne went off to question the Guards who were assigned to the doorway of their section. The Guard on duty at the far end of the room was emphatic that no one at all had come through his door; but the Guard at the other end, said that just after the last of the translators had left, a girl in breeches had come to the door and asked for Miss Shepley-Rice. When told that she had gone down to the shelter she asked if she might leave a note on her desk. The girl then walked straight across the room, put the note on the desk, which the Home Guard had pointed out to her and returned—immediately—the Guard was sure. He exchanged a few words with her—she was a very pretty girl, he remarked—and then he had advised her to go down herself to the shelter and she went away. Then Anne remembered the note from Mary that she had found on her desk. "That was Mary Shephard," she explained. "She's a despatch rider and comes to the Ministry with letters; I know her and she left a private note for me. I found it when I came up from the shelter."

"I suppose she couldn't have taken the report," said Mrs. Just. "Have you known her long?"

"A couple of years," answered Anne. "She's the daughter of Sir John Shephard, the tinned food man—everyone knows him, he's so rich. And anyhow how could she have taken it? The desk was locked and the Home Guard would have seen her trying to open it—and why should she take it and how would she have known it was there?"

So Anne and Mrs. Just and Mrs. Doweson went back and reported Mary Shephard's visit to Miss Saltman. But Miss Saltman said that that did not solve the mystery and she broke out: "It's really most annoying! A particularly confidential document! They made me sign for it on a special form! And now it's disappeared! Makes us all look perfectly ridiculous. There's nothing for me to do now but to go and make a clean breast of it to Colonel Hilles. Miss Shepley-Rice, please wait here till I come back."

Miss Saltman left the room. Anne sat down at her desk; she felt completely miserable and looked it. Then a voice behind her said, "Don't worry too much, Anne. It's sure to be all right in the end." The speaker was Elsie and Anne turned round to her with surprise because her voice was kind—but she was speaking quite differently from the way in which she usually spoke to Anne; afterwards Anne thought that she spoke in the detached but kind way in which one might speak to a strange child in the street who was crying. "Oh thank you, Elsie!" said Anne and put her hand on Elsie's arm, "I'm not really worrying, I'm—"

But Elsie shook her hand off with a sharp movement. "That's right," she said and sat down in her own seat.

It was nearly an hour before Miss Saltman came back and she was clearly very much distressed; she stood talking to Mrs. Just and everyone watched them and all noticed that they looked repeatedly at Anne; and then Miss Saltman beckoned Anne and Mrs. Just went away and Anne went up and sat in Mrs. Just's chair and Miss Saltman began to speak to her in a worried embarrassed way, choosing her words and hesitating as she spoke.

"I told Colonel Hilles everything you told me," she said. "He thinks—we think—in fact the matter is really now out of our hands because Colonel Hilles rang up the Director General about it. I don't quite know why they seem to take it so seriously but they do and so we've got to put up with it. I told Colonel Hilles that the thing was simply *bound* to turn up. But he said you were to go to see him now—and I thought perhaps I ought to explain—they are thinking of suspending you until the wretched document is found."

Anne's face was white and her heart was beating fast. "You mean I am—dismissed?" she said.

"No. No. Just what I say—suspended. Just temporarily asked to stay away till it's all put right. Anyway, I'll explain more when you come back. Please go now and see Colonel Hilles. Go to his secretary's room, No. 43. He's expecting you so it will be all right."

As Anne went up in the lift she recalled her earlier interview with Colonel Hilles when she had first applied for the appointment and he had talked about her mother and had been so fatherly and kind; she wondered whether he would be fatherly and kind again or whether, as Mrs. Just had said only yesterday that he sometimes did, he would give her such a dressing down that she would wish she had never been born.

Then she opened the door of his secretary's office and went in. Miss Jackman, his secretary, sat there busy at her typewriter and a fresh-faced junior sat at a big table, sorting papers. There were bowls of flowers about the room which looked attractive and cheerful and most alarmingly tidy; *nothing* could ever be lost here, Anne said to herself, and then Miss Jackman looked up, pleasant and impersonal. "Morning, Shepley-Rice. The D.D. wants to see you; he won't be a moment; the D.A.D.G. is with him. Take a pew over there, will you."

"The D.A.D.G.?" said Anne. She never could learn what all these initials meant. "The Deputy-Assistant-Director-General," said Miss Jackman. "Will he be there when I go in?" asked Anne. "I expect so. Don't look so frightened; he won't eat you," answered Miss Jackman and went into the inner office; she returned a moment later for her notebook and pencil. "He won't keep you a moment," she called to Anne.

But it was twenty long minutes before she came back. Anne sat and waited unhappily. The little junior, who had overheard a few words and had an idea of what was happening, looked at her with pity and offered her the *Daily Mirror* to while away the time and assured her repeatedly that the Colonel would not be long now.

Then the door of the inner office opened and Miss Jackman came out. "Colonel Hilles will see you now," she said and held the door open.

Colonel Hilles was sitting at his own desk; he looked very stern and serious. He signed to Anne to sit down. As she did so she looked from the corner of her eye at the D.A.D.G. who was sitting at another desk, making notes and who looked at her but did not speak.

"Now Miss Shepley-Rice," said the Colonel. "Let me hear, please, the whole story of this extraordinary business." Anne told him her story. He asked her a few questions. "You are certain you locked the drawer when the alert sounded? You were not, perhaps, too excited to remember?" Anne smiled wanly. "I wasn't excited at all. We have far too many warnings to be excited about them. I am quite sure I locked the drawer properly. I tried it carefully before I went down."

"And the key?" he asked. "What did you do with that?"

"I put it in my bag—in my purse. I had the bag in my hand all the time we were downstairs."

"H'm! In any case the Home Guards at the doorways can prove that no one came into the department while you were away—except this girl who left a note on your desk. Who is this girl? What was she doing in the Ministry?"

Anne told him and gave him Mary's name and that of her father. He made a note and then began to turn over some papers on his desk. On top of them Anne recognized the application form, with all particulars of herself and her family, which she had filled in when she applied for the position in the Ministry,

The Colonel put down the papers and looked directly at her. "Among these papers, Miss Shepley-Rice, is the usual form which we require new members of the staff to sign, declaring that they have read and fully understood the rules and regulations governing the procedure and the methods of work here and that they appreciate the confidential nature of the work they are about to undertake and the consequences to themselves if that confidence is betrayed. This form was signed by you. May I take it that you fully understood what you were signing?"

"Ye-es, Colonel Hilles." Anne faltered a little remembering how casually she had written her name at the bottom of the page after one glance at its contents.

"You understood that you would be personally liable for the safekeeping of any confidential documents given into your charge for translation or any other purpose?" Anne gave a small sigh and said yes again.

"A confidential and highly important document given into your charge for the purpose of translation, has disappeared. You have allowed it to be lost. I can only suppose that this was due to gross carelessness." He looked sternly at Anne and her heart beat fast; she could see no trace now of the kind and fatherly man who had interviewed her when she first came to the Ministry. He continued speaking. "I have no alternative but to believe that you are guilty of gross carelessness. We cannot tolerate carelessness; we can show no leniency to this fault, to commit which is to be as blame-worthy as the sentinel who sleeps at his post. If this report is found, Miss Shepley-Rice, I shall be glad to reinstate you: but until it is found, you are suspended." As he spoke the last words, he stood up from his desk, went to the door and held it open for Anne. She went out and he closed the door behind her.

"Thank the Lord that's over," Colonel Hilles said taking out his cigarette case and offering it to the D.A.D.G. "I'd rather sack ten men than one girl. This one at least, didn't burst into tears like most of them do."

"At any rate," said the D.A.D.G., "we now have a satisfactory answer when that Socialist fellow asks his question in the House next week."

"Yes," said Colonel Hilles. "We shall be able to say 'it is a fact that an important confidential document was recently found missing. A serious view has been taken of the occurrence and disciplinary sanctions have been applied.'"

"That's the goods," said the D.A.D.G. "Disciplinary sanctions. That's the stuff. Nothing has been heard, I suppose, of the despatch case that old fool of a general lost from his car?"

"No, his papers have not been found and never will be I'm afraid. They were stolen, I'm convinced. They're in Berlin by now. I wish we could sack *him*. He's the bloke who set all these blasted Socialists on our track."

"What has happened to the report that this girl has lost? You don't think that was stolen, do you?" asked the D.A.D.G. "Not for one moment," said the Colonel. "This girl's all right. Her father was Dick Shepley-Rice. Did some fine work in the last war. I knew his family well and her mother's too. I think she probably tore it up by mistake and threw it into the waste-paper basket—something of that sort—and she's too frightened to say so. Anyway, it doesn't really matter. The Admiralty had a photostat made before parting with it and there's nothing in it the enemy don't know—so it's all a storm in a teacup. But the General's despatch case really had some stuff in it."

While the higher powers were thus putting her crime into perspective, Anne with a white face but with her head held very high, had walked blindly past Miss Jackman and out of her office and back to the Translation Section. Miss Saltman was watching for her and as soon as she saw her pushing open the swing doors, she beckoned to her. Mrs. Just stood up and went away again and Miss Saltman told Anne to sit down in the vacant seat. "I'm sorry, Miss Shepley-Rice, that all this has happened," she said kindly. Anne said, "So indeed am I." And Miss Saltman went on. "For some reason that I don't understand, Colonel Hilles seemed to think that what he called 'disciplinary sanctions' were essential. I spoke up for you but I'm in his bad books over that wretched petition business and he wouldn't listen to anything I said. So now you must give me your pass and all your confidential papers. Don't take it too much to heart. Perhaps after all it's all for the best," she continued in a brisk and pleasant voice. "You've had a lot of worry and now you can have a nice rest till the report is found. I'm quite sure it will be. You have relations in the country, haven't you?" Anne struggled to control her voice. "My grandmother lives in Somerset."

"Yes, well that's splendid," said Miss Saltman brightly. "You go and stay with her and have a nice holiday and you'll soon feel quite differently about things and if we find that report we'll send you a telegram. Now run along and pack up your papers and your belongings and I should try and get off to your grandmother first thing in the morning."

Anne stood up. "Thank you, Miss Saltman. I'll get my pass and papers at once. How soon must I go?"

Miss Saltman gave a forced and nervous laugh. "Don't talk like that, child, as if you were a criminal or infectious. It's nearly lunchtime now. Wait and have some lunch and then pack up quietly and get off home before the trains and buses get crowded."

"Thank you very much," said Anne in a flat voice. "I don't think I want any lunch." She went back to the table and straight to her desk and began to collect her papers. The others looked up with inquiring faces but Anne pretended not to see them. "What's happened? Do t—" Miss Purbeck began to speak and stopped hastily at a savage gesture from Elsie. In a few minutes Anne was ready. She went back to Miss Saltman's desk, took her pass and her key from her bag and handed them over with her papers. Then she went to the hatstand, put on her outdoor clothes and came back to the table.

"Good-bye," she said and walked quickly away before anyone could answer. Elsie jumped to her feet and ran after her. "What's the matter? Where are you going, Anne? What has happened?" she said excitedly, laying a hand on Anne's arm to hold her back.

Anne gently shook it off. "I can't tell you. I'm going for a few days to Somerset. I'll write. I must go now. Good-bye."

Chapter Twenty
TOOTHACHE . . . BUT NOT ONLY THAT

As soon as Anne was out of the room a babble of conversation broke out at Table Two, Miss Younge had been, as usual, hovering round Miss Saltman's desk; she now came back to the table. "She's been sacked!" she said excitedly. "I saw her give back her pass and her confidential papers; I saw her give them to Miss S. Our paragon of all the virtues—our new Deputy—our Anne has been sacked!" Her voice ended on a high note of malicious triumph. Mrs. Jolly looked shocked; "I *am* sorry," she said. "I was afraid something of the sort had happened because she looked simply awful after Miss S. spoke to her just now. I suppose that was when she told her. Poor little thing and she doesn't look a bit well now and I'm sure it's no wonder with everyone badgering her about that wretched paper that's been lost—" "But if she's sacked," said Miss Younge interrupting her, "if she's sacked it must mean that they've found out there's been some funny business over that report. After all she was the last person to see it—she could easily have taken it home with her at night—we've only got her word that she didn't—it was so confidential and that means it was worth something to someone." Mrs. Doweson looked up and was about to speak but Miss Purbeck broke in, "Do you mean she *stole* it? You think she's going to be arrested? Good gracious! She'd be taken to the Tower, wouldn't she? That's where they put spies and traitors. Just fancy one of us—" Mrs. Doweson stopped her, "I never heard such nonsense in all my life," she said in a stern voice, "all we know is that Miss Saltman has let her go home; very likely she's not well."

"But her pass," said Miss Younge impatiently, "they don't take your pass away if you go home ill—only if you are leaving for good." "Well, we don't know anything about her pass," said Miss Dunkerley, looking up from her work. "After all, people who are always trying to see and hear things that they are not intended to see and hear, are often mistaken. We don't know that she did have to give up her pass." Miss Younge reddened. "She did give it up. I saw her give it up." "All we know about Miss Shepley-Rice is that she was not looking well and has now gone home—but there's one other thing that I know," said Mrs. Doweson; she looked meaningly at Miss Younge and Miss Purbeck; "I know that there's such a thing as the law of slander and libel and people who talk wild nonsense about thieves and spies are very likely to find themselves in a very unpleasant position." Miss Purbeck at once looked frightened and began to stammer excuses; Mrs. Doweson, who for the first time that anyone present could remember, had quite plainly lost her temper, thumped her hand on the table; "Now I suggest that we talk about something else," she said, "or even do a little work for a change." She took up her pen and began to write busily and after a few more whispered comments and mutterings, the rest of the table did the same.

Elsie had taken no part in the discussion about Anne. She had seemed to be working throughout particularly hard, only pausing now and again to rub oil of cloves on her gum for her toothache was, as she described it, "giving her the pip again". In fact she hardly saw the text she was pretending to translate; she stared at the paper, and her lips moved as though conning the printed words but her thoughts were through the page and the table and the floor, down deep, plunging to the bottom of her conscience and the foundations of her life. She was a prey to her toothache and her problems—the temptation to throw all in and walk away and forget the whole damn show without a word spoken about opening that cursed drawer—the insistent voice nagging away like the toothache, repeating its rhythm in hideous syncopation, driving her to blare aloud her silly curiosity that had put her in this hole. For Elsie, that morning, had received an answer to her application for the "Situation vacant" in *The Times*. She had written a sensible letter setting out her business experience in Berlin and Paris and elsewhere, claiming quite justly that she had all the qualifications. And the firm—it turned out to be Austen Wedlock's—had invited her to call on Monday of next week and somehow she felt that she had this appointment in her pocket. Now she opened her bag and looked at the envelope with Austen Wedlock's name in the left-hand corner; if she played her cards well she might escape from this circle of enemies at Table Two and be again an independent person, a business woman dealing, not with a parcel of old hens but with men, business men, toughs, men who did things in the world of big affairs. She was wasted here in this collection of back-biting cats. But then the tooth and the voice nagged; she must do something about that miserable Portuguese report. After all, she *had* been the last person to handle it; she had taken it out of Anne's drawer. It was true that she had certainly put it back again. But perhaps her key had not properly locked the drawer. She had not tried it—at least she could not remember having tried the lock again after she had turned the key—and perhaps the thing had been stolen; there was a war on and it might have been code or something. Anyway Anne had been sacked—or suspended which came to the same thing, she supposed. Of course it didn't matter to Anne. She had her boy friend and her grandmother and she was really only a pin-money worker. But still—perhaps—the tooth-voice nagged and nagged.

And then suddenly she decided. She grabbed the bag that held the Austen Wedlock letter, at once a weapon and a shield, and with the bag under her armpit, like a gangster's gun, she strode over to Miss Saltman's desk.

"Is it true, Miss Saltman, that Miss Shepley-Rice has been dismissed for the loss of that report?" she said peremptorily. Miss Saltman looked surprised. "Well, I don't know that I am entitled to tell you anything about Miss Shepley-Rice's affairs," she said stiffly.

"You must tell me; it's important. I want to know," said Elsie. Miss Saltman raised her eyebrows but did not speak; Elsie stared at her and waited; then she went on. "If she has been dismissed, it is grossly unfair and she must be allowed to come back at once!" "I really don't know what right you have to say that it is grossly unfair—after all she was the last person to handle the report—but I don't propose to discuss it with you," said Miss Saltman. "I've every right to say it's unfair," said Elsie roughly. "She wasn't the last person to handle the report. I was."

Mrs. Just laid down the bundle of returns she was checking and stared; Miss Saltman sat back in her chair and looked bewildered. "Are you sure you know what you are talking about?" she said to Elsie. "What do you mean?" "Just what I say," said Elsie truculently. "I was the last to go down to the shelter that afternoon. Mrs. Just asked me to go back and see that Shepley-Rice had put the report away and locked her drawer. I went back to see and in fact I opened the drawer with my own key and took out the report. But I put it back." "And why, pray, did you take it out? What right had you to touch it?" "I just looked at it out of curiosity—I thought I recognised the handwriting—I saw that was a mistake at once and I put it straight back into the drawer and went downstairs." "Did you lock the drawer again?"

asked Miss Saltman. "Yes," said Elsie with a little note of doubt in her voice. "As a matter of fact that's the only thing I'm not sure about. The key didn't fit properly and it was rather difficult to lock it again and I was in a hurry. I'm wondering now if I did lock it properly. But anyhow, Miss Shepley-Rice is not to blame so will they take her back now?" "I really cannot tell you," said Miss Saltman coldly. "That is a matter for Colonel Hilles. Now I suppose I must go to him at once and tell him of this new development and what he will say I simply cannot imagine. I think it was an extraordinary thing for you to have done—and Miss Shepley-Rice getting all the blame for it—" "Well, that's why I've mentioned it," said Elsie impatiently, "so that she won't be blamed any longer. And now I hope they'll let her come back at once."

But Miss Saltman was on her feet, preparing for another interview with Colonel Hilles. "Please sit down here," she said, "and wait till I come back."

Elsie sat at the table opposite Mrs. Just—the table where a few days before she had throned it in Mrs. Just's seat, till she had made so pitiful a mess of it or, as she saw it, till "they" had thrown her out of it with their spite and their petition. Mrs. Just busied herself with Miss Saltman's papers. She did not speak. And Elsie too was silent. Her tooth throbbed and she rubbed her gum. "Toothache?" said Mrs. Just, not unkindly. "Like the devil," answered Elsie. "You must go to the dentist—it's the only way." Elsie grunted something about wasting a guinea; then she took her gun—the Austen Wedlock letter—from its case; when old Fusspot came back she would put her finger on the trigger and then "Bang!"

Miss Saltman came back. Elsie faced her. "Well," she said. "How did he take it? Can Miss Shepley-Rice come back?" Miss Saltman settled herself with some deliberation in her seat. She had thought out what she would say as she came down in the lift and now she said it pat. "I was only able to see Colonel Hilles for a minute. He was just going to the War Office. But I told him the position and he instructs me to say that he takes a most serious view of your behaviour and—"

"I don't care what view he takes of *my* behaviour," Elsie interrupted. "I'm only concerned about Miss Shepley-Rice. For my part (and here she fingered her gun) I'm intending to resign; so Colonel Hilles and anyone else can think what they like of me. If Colonel Hilles is so angry that he has a blue fit I really don't care."

But then Miss Saltman surprisingly revealed that she, too, had her gun. "I suppose it has not occurred to you", she said, "that you may not be *allowed* to resign? In fact, I can tell you, Miss Pearne, that until this matter is cleared up, you will certainly remain a member of the Staff entirely at the Ministry's orders. Colonel Hilles has instructed me to say that you are now under disciplinary suspension in exactly the same way as Miss Shepley-Rice."

Elsie's face went ashen-white. Her chance of escape was torn into strips. That Austen Wedlock interview—which she was going to walk away with and start a new chapter—was now impossible. She could not refer them to the Ministry who would answer, "at present under disciplinary suspension", and she could not conceal the Ministry because she had already referred to her present post there in her letter of application. And even if she took the line that they only required business references, she could not get business references now from Berlin and Paris, there was a war on, communications were cut off. She sat stunned, with her tooth throbbing, while Miss Saltman continued: "Now please, Miss Pearne, be good enough to collect your pass and confidential papers and let me have them when you go home to-night."

"I've a frightful toothache," Elsie said. "I think I must go to the dentist. As I'm suspended, I may as well go there now."

"As you please," said Miss Saltman. "Let me have your pass, then, and your papers now."

Elsie went back to her desk and began to collect her papers and Miss Saltman unburdened her anger to Mrs. Just.

"Really," she said, "the whole business is the most ridiculous muddle. Colonel Hilles was furious and it's bound to reflect on the whole lot of us. Table Two will now be the table where things get lost or stolen and people break open one another's drawers and quiz at things they're not supposed to see." And Mrs. Just said, "Whatever induced the Pearne woman to do it? She's supposed to have brains and yet she always behaves like a ridiculous fool."

Elsie's hands were trembling as she looked out her pass and papers. And the eyes of Table Two upon her drilled holes like gimlets in her head. She slipped the papers inside the Spanish letter she had been translating and shut and locked her drawer and gripped her bag—with the mock gun in it—and faced the eyes which lowered at once like the eyes of the dolls that children put to bed. And then she burst out: "You needn't imagine *I've* got the sack because I'm going home early. To save you wearing your tongues out gossiping, I'll tell you that I'm going to the dentist. I saw you hanging round the desk, Miss Nosy Parker," she said to Miss Younge. "I saw you creeping about on your soft shoes all the time I was talking to Miss Saltman—trying to listen to what we were saying, in your usual fashion." Miss Younge reddened but stood her ground. "No one could help hearing the way you shouted and I heard you say you opened the drawer and took out the report to read it because you were curious, so I'd like to know what right you've got to call me a Nosy Parker! So there!" She looked round the table triumphantly as Elsie strode off to give up her papers at Miss Saltman's desk.

In the hall downstairs Elsie went to the telephone cupboard. The first thing was to stop the aching of this blasted tooth. She must ring up the dentist. The next thing was to tell Anne what she had done and what they had done to her because of what she had done. After all it was as much Anne's fault as hers, or rather it was probably as little the one's as the other's. But Anne had gone to the country—to see her grandmother—a nice comfortable country house with dogs, she remembered what Anne had told her about it. She had no country house to retreat to. Only Brondesbury—Hengistbury Crescent. Oh this damn tooth! There was a dentist in a house two turnings from her lodgings, near the corner of the High Road; she had often read the name "Stephen Ferrier, Dental Surgeon" on the plate. She found the number and asked for an appointment as soon as possible. He would squeeze her in "if possible" if she came down at once—within the next hour. Elsie left the cupboard and found herself facing Sebastian who smiled and said, "Good afternoon," with automatic politeness.

Actually Sebastian when he greeted her had not yet remembered who Elsie was. He knew that he knew her and that "Good afternoon" was called for but it was not till Elsie answered that he remembered her as Anne's queer old colleague who had got tight at luncheon and been so rude to O'Connor. But now Elsie had literally buttonholed him. She wanted Anne's address and here was a chance to get it. "Good afternoon," she said, her hand on his lapel. "I have to write to Anne, I know she's in Somerset. But I want her exact address."

"In Somerset!" said Sebastian dumbfounded. "That's the first I've heard of it. Wasn't she at work to-day? I phoned her early this morning to tell her I'd be out all to-day and they said she wasn't there. I suppose that's why."

And then Elsie remembered that Anne had only gone that morning and that there had hardly been time for her to tell Sebastian anything about her suspension. "Good gracious!" said Elsie. "Then you haven't heard of the schemozzle. Both Anne and I are in disgrace."

She spoke as lightly as she could but he looked at her and saw that she looked little short of ghastly and sensed at once that here was something that for Anne's sake he must know.

They were now at the door of the Ministry and he pushed it open. Instinctively they both shrank quickly back into the porch. The rain was pouring down in torrents and blew slantingly in the wind into the meagre shelter of the doorway and beat upon their faces. Sebastian raised his hand to a taxi waiting on the other side of the road. He turned and looked at Elsie crouching against the door to escape the deluging rain. "We can't stand and talk here. I'm taking a taxi. If you're going anywhere I'll give you a lift." The taxi drew up at the curb and now it was Sebastian who buttonholed Elsie, taking her by the elbow and hurrying her across the pavement through the rain into the taxi, before she was able to reply.

Elsie dropped on the seat and dried her face on her hand-kerchief; "I didn't bring a mack or an umbrella; I didn't think it would rain like this," she said. Sebastian asked her where she was going and she gave the dentist's address. "But you needn't take me all the way to Brondesbury. The Tube station will do quite well." Sebastian called the address through the window to the driver and then turned to her and said. "Now tell me. What have Anne and you been up to? What is the schemozzle?"

Elsie told him the whole story. He leaned back and watched the rain beating on the windows as he listened. He saw the whole thing entirely as it affected himself and Anne. The missing report business was all nonsense. It was bound to turn up—unless some idiot had destroyed it somehow thinking it was wastepaper. But it was a confounded nuisance if Anne had really gone off to Somerset at this moment—three weeks before their wedding. He must go to her flat and find out and if she had gone he must get leave to-morrow and go down to her grandmother and haul her back.

The taxi was heading northwards through one of the sordid small streets off the Euston Road. Most of the miserable little houses on either side of the street had been bombed and black-ened bricks, charred beams and broken remnants of furniture lay mingled in desolate heaps under the rain. "Good job some of this rubbish has been cleared away," he said, indicating with a wave of his hand, the broken houses they were passing. "Yes, I suppose it is a good job," said Elsie absently. "Though I don't know if the people who lived in them would think that. What exactly is Anne's address in Somerset? I must write to her and confess that I opened the drawer and that I'm literally turned out in the rain."

Sebastian gave it to her. She wrote it on the back of the Austen Wedlock envelope. And as she wrote Sebastian looked at her and noticed how hideously tired and white she looked with dark rings round her eyes and he felt suddenly sorry for her. She had a rotten time, so Anne always said, living alone in a poky little room without a penny to bless herself with beyond what she earned. He began to exert himself to talk companionably to her, about Anne and about the Ministry and anything else that he thought might interest her. She looks as if she wants a drink and God knows I do, he thought. "I wonder where we are?" he said. Elsie peered out of the window. "We're in Maida Vale now, just getting to the Kilburn High Road."

"That doesn't convey anything to me," said Sebastian, "but I was wondering if we couldn't stop somewhere and have a cocktail—or tea or something; would you care for that?" Elsie hesitated; it was obvious from her expression that she would like it and Sebastian insisted. "To tell the truth, I would," she said at last. "I could hardly get any lunch to-day, everywhere round the office seems to have been bombed and it's very difficult to get any food. I'm feeling quite faint. And as I'm going to the dentist I want to keep my pecker up. I have a horror of that dreadful drill."

"Then we must certainly have a drink," Sebastian said. "Let's tell the driver to stop at some place."

"There's quite a nice hotel round here," said Elsie. "I've never been into it myself of course but it would be quite all right to go to with a gentleman." She gave the name to the driver and a few minutes later they were in the lounge of a large pretentious public house in the Kilburn High Road.

Sebastian found seats in a comfortable corner and while Elsie sipped a glass of port he quickly swallowed several gins and bitters. Elsie accepted a second glass of port. And then he remembered the last occasion that Elsie had drunk wine in his company. I mustn't let her get blotto he decided and shepherded her back to the cab.

"Thanks awfully," Elsie said when they were once more in the taxi. "That was just what I wanted." And now it was her turn to look sideways at her companion. How handsome the boy was. Anne would certainly enjoy him as her lover. Men always looked their best in blue. Benno had worn blue. Benno—but now from the side of the cab she saw that they were nearly at Brondesbury, nearly at her lodgings, nearly at the dentist where she would have to suffer that infernal drill or gas if he decided, "there's nothing to be done to it; we must have it out."

"Here we are," she said to Sebastian, putting her hand on his knee as she peered across him through the rain-swept window. "The second turning on the left after Hengistbury Crescent." At the dentist's door, she rapped sharply on the window. Sebastian got out and held out his hand to help her. She looked at him, standing handsome and self-possessed with the rain showering down on him, politely waiting for her by the door and suddenly she was overwhelmed by self-consciousness. "Thanks ever so for the lift," she said and to her annoyance she was blushing darkly as she shook his hand.

When she had gone Sebastian looked round him at the rows of monotonous little villas. He had no idea where he was and hoped the taxi-driver knew the way back to civilization. How dismal for anyone to live in such an awful neighbourhood—he wondered why the old bird chose it. He supposed it was cheap. It ought to be. He stepped back into the cab and gave the address of Anne's flat. Silly little goose getting into such a silly old mess or, as the old girl called it, a "schemozzle".

Chapter Twenty-One
THE YOUNG MAN WITH A GLOVE

THE DENTIST GAVE Elsie an anaesthetic and extracted her tooth. While she was under the anaesthetic Elsie dreamed she was in her new job and had done so well in it that the King had sent for her and presented her with a medal in the presence of a cheering crowd which included all the staff of the Ministry—and Benno too. He was wearing a blue Air Force uniform like Sebastian and Anne was beside him and he had his arm round her, but it wasn't really Anne at all but Elsie, the young Elsie of the days when Benno loved her and she was standing, and cheering the older Elsie's success.

She remembered the dream as she walked away from the dentist's down the noisy High Road towards her home. It was the end of the Saturday shopping rush. The rain had stopped and women thronged the pavement, pushing perambulators in front of them; cutting themselves a path through the crowd as a plough cuts its way through the snow. As Elsie dodged between them or round them, heavy shopping bags banged against her knees and she had to stop continually to disentangle herself from the strings of children clinging to the perambulators or their mothers' hands. In the gutter, hawkers shuffled through a litter of faded vegetable leaves and dirty paper and screamed against one another in a last desperate effort to clear the remainder of their wares. It was a dream all right, she thought. And likely to remain a dream. The only bits of luck I ever get are in a dream. I wish to God I could stay in one all the time.

She turned off the High Road and its noise grew fainter as she walked up the hill. She called down to her landlady when she got indoors.

"I'm in, Mrs. Evans. What are you giving me for supper?" The woman came to the foot of the basement stairs and looked up at her. From the open kitchen door came a mingled smell of sour milk and the water in which clothes have been boiled.

"Some Irish stew, Miss. We had some for our dinner and I was going to hot it up."

"Oh! I can't eat that," said Elsie irritably. "I've just come from the dentist and my mouth is sore. Can't I have a boiled egg?"

"Sorry Miss. There isn't one in the house. They haven't any at the dairy I know. You might get one in the High Road but there's no one to send. Gertie and Fred are at the pictures and I can't leave Baby." She spoke indifferently. Miss Pearne was a quiet lodger and she paid regularly but she wasn't one you would put yourself out for—too sarcastic and disagreeable.

"All right," said Elsie with a click of impatience. "If you let me have some milk I'll warm it on the gas ring and have it later."

"Very good, Miss, if you'd rather. I'll send it up by Gertie when she comes in," said Mrs Evans turning back into the kitchen again. "There's a letter for you on the table."

Lazy old cat, thought Elsie as she climbed the stairs wearily. She could easily have found something for me if she'd wanted to. Too much trouble of course. She found the letter on her table—a second letter from Austen Wedlock's confirming the interview on Monday—she had telephoned early that morning to say that she would keep the appointment and they had written by return to confirm it—*that* showed how keen they were on getting her! Of course she wouldn't get the job now that she couldn't give the Ministry as reference; that was the end of it. Was there ever such bad luck!

The window was wide open and the cold east wind blew in. She went across and shut it and pulled the blackout curtains and switched on the light. It was very cold. She looked at the empty grate and wished she could have a fire but she knew better than to ask Mrs. Evans to light one so early in the year and at such short notice. She still felt a little sick and faint after the anaesthetic and she was tired and hungry and shivering with cold, when she began, as always, to change the clothes she wore in the office for an older dress that she wore at home. She put a woolly coat over it and then, as she still felt cold, drew her overcoat round her shoulders. She slumped down on the bed, crushing the new yellow divan cover that she had bought less than a fortnight ago, on the day before that luncheon party, on the day when she had been making happy plans to invite Anne to come and see her digs. She sat staring at the wall opposite her.

God! What a fool I was to tell Saltman I opened that drawer. What made me do it? Anne would have done it. *Anne!* What has Anne to do with me?

Anne in similar circumstances would have confessed at once, Elsie knew quite well. She would have done it automatically, without thinking it would be possible to do anything else—just a sort of reflex action.

Schoolgirl heroics, thought Elsie. The old school tie! *My* old school tie! Mustn't let the old school down. She almost laughed

aloud at the thought of the Highgatebury Board-school tie.
Council schools they call them nowadays, but they were still
board-schools in my time. To think of me filling myself up with
all that sort of rot just because I've been about with those people
for a bit. I don't know what came over me. I just lost my head for
a minute when I went up to Saltman. If I had thought, I would
have seen how different it is for me. Anne can afford heroics.
I can't. She's all right whatever happens to her with a well-off
man waiting to marry her. What does it matter if she did lose
her job? Disappointing perhaps but she'll soon get over that. But
losing my job matters all right to me. It's the end of everything
for me! It isn't fair! It isn't fair. Just for a moment of idiocy I've
lost everything. I'm finished.

The sirens sounded and she heard the Evans children clattering up the path and running noisily downstairs to the kitchen. If
it was a bad raid they would expect Elsie to go out and join them
in the Anderson shelter. But she wouldn't go to-night, however
bad it might be. What do I care, she thought. A bomb would be
the best thing that could happen to me—settle all my problems
the quickest way!

Always she had been unlucky—one disappointment after
another, right back to her schooldays when they had made her
give up her scholarship. She saw in her mind the young Elsie,
fighting grimly, taking one blow after the other, rising always to
fight again, alone with her back against the wall. Always alone,
that had been the worst of it—or the best. She had wanted to
believe that it had been the best, that she gloried in her strength
and independence.

> She cared for nobody, no, not she
> And nobody cared for her.

That was really the only way; if you cared you got hurt. She
had learned that lesson long ago when she had let herself care
and her heart had been nearly broken.

She looked up at the Titian reproduction, "The Young Man
with the Glove", that hung over her fireplace.

*   *   *   *   *

Benno! Benito Braun—Paris in springtime, the chestnuts in bloom and the couples whispering under the trees. She remembered so well the day she had bought the picture.

It was on her first visit to Paris, during the first year she had spent with Todd's Tours. She was young then, not yet twenty-eight and though she was not pretty, she was fresh and her face was unlined, time and disappointment had not yet carved those two deep lines from nose to mouth which now disfigured her face, and her brown hair was bright and abundant.

She had been in Paris about six months when the weather turned suddenly warm and she found she had nothing cool to wear. One of the girls she worked with was rather nice and Elsie asked her advice. The girl took her to the place where she got her own clothes and helped her to choose. Elsie had never seen so many pretty frocks before. Flattered and cajoled by a good saleswoman and urged on by her friend (who was thinking perhaps of the *petit bénéfice* for herself which the dressmaker would certainly give her) Elsie lost her head and bought a dress which cost her almost as much as she had been accustomed to spend on her whole wardrobe in a year. But it fitted her and it suited her and it was a lovely dress. When it came home she was almost frightened to touch it, it was so lovely, but she wore it next day to the office to show her friend the effect.

"But you can't wear it with that hat!" said the other girl at once. "They look ridiculous together. You must buy a new hat."

Elsie explained. Yesterday evening she had tried to buy a new hat but nowhere could she find one to suit her. They were all too small.

"Of course they would be. It's your hair," said her friend. "You'll never find a smart hat to fit over that great bun of yours; long hair has gone quite out of fashion. Why don't you have yours cut? Look here. Get off sharp at *midi* and I'll take you to André, my coiffeur; he's a dear and always does me in the lunch hour."

Elsie pondered a moment. All her life she had been accustomed to wash her hair herself, with soap flakes and plenty of hot water. It seemed very extravagant to have it done for her when it was so easy to do herself. But she liked the idea of having it cut, of getting rid of the heavy bun which was so hot in the summer and made it so difficult to buy a hat. So her friend telephoned to André and Elsie duly delivered herself into the hairdresser's hands. An hour later her mass of hair was being swept off the floor and she was gazing with delight at her reflection, at her shining head, washed, waved and fashionably cut and dressed. But she was not to escape yet.

"Mademoiselle needs just a touch of make-up to bring out her finer points," said André's woman assistant looking at Elsie's honestly washed and shiny-nosed face. "If she would permit me—a touch here and there—a little manicure—"

"Go on Elsie; go the whole hog," said the other girl. "Have a facial and manicure and let Jeanne show you how to make-up; you'll be such a beauty you won't know yourself."

Elsie was too bewildered to resist. The manicurist seized her hands while Jeanne creamed her face and cleaned it and blackened her eyelashes so that they looked quite long and rouged her pale cheeks and reddened her thin lips to more generous proportions and in the end Elsie gazed with astonishment at the strange but almost glamorous young woman who confronted her in the mirror.

After that the hat took a very short time to buy and a transfigured Elsie returned to the office, with an empty purse, but with joy and amazement in her heart.

And there she found Benno sitting at the next desk to her own.

Benito Braun, half English, half Italian, was a clerk from Todd's Milan office, visiting Paris on business for his firm. He gave this elegantly groomed and turned-out young woman a long look of interest and admiration, which no man had ever done before, and he smiled at her and Elsie smiled at him and fell in love at first sight. He continued to look at her till she felt almost uncomfortable and as if she were undressed, but it excited her more and more. He was so handsome, with his dark hair and eyes and pale olive skin. His forehead was broad like her own but while her chin was prominent and determined, his face narrowed down to a small pointed chin which she thought very attractive. And he was so smart, dressed, she supposed, in his best clothes for the visit to the Head Office, wearing a light summer suit of almost a pale blue with tie and socks to tone and a pink shirt and very elegant pointed patent leather shoes. She had never noticed a man's clothes before—but no man had ever noticed hers. Everything about him seemed perfection and she loved the scent of his hair when he leaned over from the next door desk and whispered something in her ear. Excited— almost intoxicated—by his presence and the startling change in her own appearance, all her habitual shyness and moroseness disappeared and she chattered to him and flirted with him and before the afternoon ended he had invited her to dine with him that very evening.

They drank an *apéritif* at the Café Weber and then drove over the river and had an intimate little dinner in a small restaurant in the Boulevard St. Michel and afterwards they went to a big café further along the Boulevard, which was full of artists and other Bohemian people, whom Elsie eyed with interest but some disapproval. They sat outside on the *terrasse* in a dark corner behind one of the big pots of flowering shrubs and watched the crowd moving slowly up and down the pavements. Benno ordered coffee and when she put out her hand to lift her cup, he took it into his own. She let it rest there; she felt proud of her hands to-night with their red and shiny nails. Some of them were bitten to the quick and all of them were too short and square, cut that way deliberately so that they did not get in the way when she was typing. The manicurist had been dissatisfied but Elsie had been delighted. Benno looked at them with a half-smile and then he bent down and gallantly pressed his lips to her fingers. She blushed scarlet with pleasure and again he gave that mysterious half-smile. Under the small table their knees almost touched and presently he slid his foot between her feet so that her foot and ankle were imprisoned between his. She was thrilled and terrified at the contact and sat tongue-tied and shy while Benno talked and told her all about the office in Milan and his unappreciative boss. She listened sympathetically, too full of emotion to talk herself. The time passed quickly and soon, far too soon, they had to think of to-morrow's work. Benno hailed a taxi and in the taxi he drew her close to him and kissed her again and again. At first she was frightened, but soon she was ardently returning his kisses, pressing her tight little lips against his as she sank limply and more deeply into his arms.

"When shall I see you again?" she said eagerly as the taxi drew up outside her *pension*. "Are you coming to the office to-morrow?"

Benno was not coming to the office. "But we'll meet again for dinner, if you like," he said with that indulgent half-smile once more upon his lips.

Next morning she reluctantly washed off the remains of the make-up but she was careful not to touch her eyelashes. She had not time to do her face again before she went to the office and in the evening, unfortunately, she was kept late and had only time for a hasty toilet before she went to keep her appointment with Benno. She did her best with the powder and the rouge and lipstick she had bought but the effect was certainly less satisfactory than when the professional had applied it on the day before, and try as she might, she could not put her hat on at just the same becoming angle as the milliner had placed it. But she did not want to keep Benno waiting and hurried off, but in the end, it was she who was early and had to wait nearly half an hour before he appeared.

She stood, hesitating, outside the café where they were to meet, shy of entering among the men, who, released from the offices, sat about at the tables chatting together or reading their papers, enjoying their *apéritifs*; to Elsie, fresh from the London suburbs, a café seemed very nearly a public house and that, no respectable girl of her class would have dreamed of entering alone.

But at last she plucked up courage and crept into one of the outside seats and waving away the waiter who came for her order, set herself to watch for Benno, full of anxiety and apprehension that he might have forgotten the appointment.

It seemed a very long time before she saw him coming, walking very slowly with a supple grace, like some big cat. He was wearing his blue suit again and a flower in his buttonhole and a grey felt hat set rather on the side of his head. He was certainly walking very slowly indeed considering that he was so late and he stopped frequently and looked into shop windows and straightened his tie and set his hat still more on one side and once her heart beat fast with jealousy when she saw him turn right round and stare after a passing girl. But she began to make excuses for him; he did not hurry because he did not know he was so late and the girl perhaps was a friend of his or he thought she was. Anyhow he had let her go and he was coming to meet her, Elsie. As soon as he saw her he quickened his pace and hurried to meet her and was full of graceful apology that she should have been kept waiting. He sat down beside her and pressed her arm against his side as he explained what had delayed him and then he made her drink an *apéritif* and afterwards, with his arm under hers, they walked along the Boulevard to the same little restaurant where they had dined on the night before.

What with the *apéritif* and the wine at dinner, she became much more talkative than on the preceding evening and forgetting her shyness, chattered away to Benno telling him of her previous jobs and her hopes and ambitions. He had little opportunity to talk himself and though she barely noticed it at the time, afterwards she recalled that his attention had wandered a little. After dinner he suggested that they should go to the 'dancing' next door.

"But I don't know how to dance," said Elsie. Benno stared at her in surprise. Not know how to dance! Impossible! He had never met a young woman who did not know how to dance and he laughed at her objections.

Alas! It was only too true. Elsie had no natural facility for dancing and her only experience had been the valeta and the lancers and the old-fashioned waltz of the Highgatebury "socials" of her adolescence, to which she had occasionally been unwillingly dragged by her family. She floundered like a camel when Benno tried to lead her through a foxtrot and after a few turns they came back again to their table. He looked a little vexed and, she feared, a shade contemptuous. "You don't know how to dance. How is that? I thought every young lady knew how to dance instinctively!"

"I've never had time to learn. I've always been too busy working," said Elsie miserably. How bitterly at that moment she regretted the hours she had spent in study. Of what little value seemed her knowledge of economics and political history compared with the ability to glide, closely held in Benno's arms, gracefully over the floor like all the other couples she saw around her.

He ordered some drinks and they sat rather dismally at their table and looked at the other dancers and made desultory conversation. A young woman came in alone and sat down at the next table. She stared at Elsie, looking her insolently up and down from head to foot and then took out her mirror and powder puff and began to make up her face. Elsie, to whom such aids to beauty were still so much of a novelty, instantly remembered that she had forgotten to do the same thing herself after dinner. Turning, she looked at her reflection in a mirror behind and she saw that her lips were pale, her face red and shining, her smart hat all askew. Her fashionable clothes emphasized her unkempt appearance and she realized angrily what a contrast she must offer to this well-groomed young woman. Muttering something about washing her hands, she went off to the *toilette* where she hoped she might find powder and a comb for she had forgotten to bring any with her. She spent some time tidying herself as best she could and then she went back to the table and found it empty. She looked round for Benno, thinking he too might have gone to the cloakroom, but presently she saw him on the floor, dancing with the young woman from the next table, who had stared at her so contemptuously.

As soon as the music stopped he took the young woman back to her seat and returned to Elsie.

"How beautifully you dance!" she cried. "No wonder you didn't want to dance with me. Is she a friend of yours?"

"Er—yes—an acquaintance," said Benno, turning his wrist to look at his watch. Then he explained that most unfortunately he had to meet a man on business that evening and would have to take her home. She was disappointed that the evening should end so early but excited at the thought of the taxi drive alone with him. She turned to him eagerly, almost as soon as the cab door closed on them, and slipping into his arms, returned his kisses eagerly. Again it was she who asked when they should meet again.

"Funny little thing!" said Benno tenderly, between his kisses, "do you love me so much?" But he had this wretched business friend on his hands for the next two evenings. For Sunday lunch, however, he would be free. How would she like to lunch out in the country?

She accepted of course ecstatically and for the next two days lived in a painful dream of longing and imagined scenes of love. On Sunday she got up early to dress herself for the rendezvous. She looked at herself critically in the mirror. For the first two or three days she had persevered with the make-up. But it wasn't very successful; she hadn't got the knack of it and she was disappointed to find that the curl had gone out of her hair. But she had already spent far too much money on vanities and had no intention of spending more. So by Sunday she had reverted almost to the plain Elsie she had always been. But it couldn't be helped. Her new black dress was, she decided, unsuitable for a day in the country and she routed out an old summer frock she had brought from England. It was unfashionable even in England, both as to length of skirt and general cut, but that also, she thought, couldn't be helped and really didn't matter. She and Benno were, after all, both of them workers earning their own livings and no sensible man in such circumstances would want his future wife to be unreasonably extravagant over dress. For, of course, she confidently expected that Benno would ultimately propose to her. That was the predestined end of a love affair. The novels she had read, the gossip of the girls in the offices at home, had all told her that. First you went out with your boy, then you became engaged to him and when marriage became financially possible, you married and lived happy ever after. Kisses came in the second stage when you were properly engaged. Until then, she knew, you ought to keep your man at a proper distance. Her own affair had gone much faster. Benno had kissed her on the first evening they had met but she put that down to his ardent Latin temperament and the strength of his feelings for her. She was quite sure that he loved her. She had no experience to guide her and she had an immense capacity for self deception. She loved him already so madly that she could not admit the possibility of his not loving her. After all, had she not his kisses, his caresses, his whispered words of sweetness as evidence of his feelings.

At ten o'clock he called for her and they took the train to a little place just outside Paris and lunched at a delightful restaurant on the banks of the Seine, crowded with family parties and couples like themselves who had come out from Paris to enjoy the lovely spring weather. Elsie was a little disconcerted to find that the other young women were so smartly dressed. She thought their clothes and their silk stockings and their high-heeled shoes were quite unsuitable for going on the water in a boat, where they would certainly be spoilt and she pointed this out several times to Benno, laughing at and criticizing unfavourably the costumes of the various girls she saw being handed in and out of boats by their attendant swains. Benno laughed rather wearily and did not talk very much. He had a bad headache, he said, due to overwork and business worries and once more it was she who talked most of the time. When lunch was over he took her on the river and after rowing a little way, he tied up the boat beneath the overhanging branches of a tree and piling up the cushions at one end, he made her lie there by his side.

As Elsie lay beside him she was conscious of the new young green of the trees, the sunlight playing on the water, the music from a gramophone in another boat hidden round the bend.

Benno slipped his arm round underneath her as they lay down and drew her to him and kissed her. She closed her eyes and when she opened them again a few minutes later she saw that he was asleep.

But she lay there contentedly in his arms and watched him. He looked younger when he was asleep and she yearned over him in a passion of tenderness. He did not wake up till nearly five o'clock and then they had to go back to Paris, for even on a Sunday, he had still to think of business.

He stayed in Paris for a week or two more; she saw him frequently at the office where she dared do little more than look at him. He took her once again out to dinner—a hurried meal because he had, as usual, another appointment, afterwards— and once or twice to the cinema and when opportunity offered, he kissed and fondled her. Then he went back to Milan.

It was the day after he went that she bought the Titian reproduction when she saw it in a shop window because it reminded her of Benno as she had seen him in the boat, his shirt open at the throat, his dark hair blown loosely over his head, his little slight moustache and his dark eyes and rather pointed chin, just like the man in the picture. There was a tune too that ran in her head and was associated with her memories of that Sunday afternoon for one of the boats had played it many times as she lay in Benno's arms and listened to it. She bought a record of the tune and a cheap gramophone and played it over and over again.

She had only his office address in Milan so she wrote to him there, almost every day at first and then, as he did not answer, letters rarer in number but passionate, bitter and full of reproaches.

For the first days after he left, she wandered about in a dream, picturing his return and all they would say and do. Then she began to wonder why he did not write and misgivings crept in and soon she was frantic with misery and disappointment, In the evenings she wandered about Paris, Paris in May, so cruel to a frustrated lover, till she could no longer bear the sight of the whispering couples under the trees and shut herself up in her room.

She never saw him or heard of him again. After months of unhappiness, she resigned her position in Todd's Tours and found herself another job, and burying herself in her work, succeeded in allaying the torments of the frustrated passion he had awakened. During her successful years in Berlin she forgot him entirely. But she kept the picture and as she grew older and no other man came into her life, she thought of him more often and gradually came almost to believe that he was Titian's handsome young aristocrat who had stepped down from his frame to adore her.

Benno! In the last weeks he had been often in her thoughts. Anne and Sebastian, the young lovers, they had reminded her. She had put aside for ever, she thought, love and romance and all that nonsense, but lately disturbing memories had come back to her. Sebastian, the dark and handsome young aristocrat in his blue Air Force uniform, with his olive skin and dark eyes and his glowing youth—young like Benno had been and she had been—Anne in her blue frocks, Benno dark and handsome in his blue suit who had stepped down from the picture to love her, they were all becoming entangled in her mind, just as in her dream at the dentist when Benno had worn Sebastian's uniform and had witnessed her success and Anne had changed into the young Elsie. But Sebastian was Anne's lover, not hers, and Anne was going to marry him and he would love Anne and cherish her and when she grew old she would still have him by her side to love and protect her. But Elsie would grow old—was already growing old—in loneliness and ever increasing poverty. In two years she would be fifty and few employers would take on a woman of that age. She had had the one lucky chance of this job with Austen Wedlock's and she had lost that by sheer bad luck. Nothing else could turn up as good as that. It was the chance of a lifetime and you didn't get a chance like that twice. Bad luck, always bad luck, always she had had to work for people who were prejudiced against her because she wasn't pretty and amusing, right from the day when Harbord's had treated her so badly till now when she had lost the position of Deputy and Miss Saltman had made such a ridiculous fuss because she had opened someone else's drawer.

She was growing so cold and hungry that she could bear it no longer and she decided to drink some hot milk and then go to bed. Mrs. Evans had forgotten to bring up the milk—she would, of course—and Elsie trailed wearily downstairs to the head of the basement stairs and up again with a meagre jug of milk which was all her landlady declared she could spare.

She went into her little kitchenette and shut the door behind her to make it warmer. She poured the milk into a saucepan and after putting some pennies into the gas meter, set the milk on the lighted gas ring, put a cup and saucer ready and sat down at the little table to wait for the milk to boil, her elbows on the table, her head resting on her hands. Overcome by dejection and self-pity, she began to sob hysterically. The milk boiled over and extinguished the flame but she did not notice it till the smell of the escaping gas reached her. She was half dazed with misery and emotion and for a moment she thought she was back at the dentist about to take the anaesthetic. She thought again of her dream, the dream from which she wished she had not awakened. She stood up slowly and found her purse. It was full of pennies; she took them and dropped them one by one into the meter, turning the handle, then pushing the coins, till they fell with a click . . . click . . . click.

Chapter Twenty-Two
BOBBIE PLAYS A PART

THE NEXT MORNING Bobbie started on the task she had set herself—to collect a second hundred pounds for the Ministry Spitfire Fund. The notice announcing her first hundred which she still called her "centenary" was on the board and was a great source of satisfaction to her.

After a tour round the Ministry she came back to Table Two rattling her money-box. "It's nearly full," she squeaked, her mouth full of currant bun. "I've got to add it up now; it looks an awful lot." "You've got a hole in your stocking, do you know that, Bobbie?" said Mrs. Jolly. "You do wear your skirts short, anyone would think you were a kid. Why do you do it?" "Dunno, more comfortable," said Bobbie indifferently, looking down at her bony knees protruding beneath the short skirt which barely reached them. There was a dirty mark on the knee of one stocking and her bare skin showed through a hole in the fabric. "I was running and fell down—bruised myself too—must do these figures." She licked the end of her pencil and bent over the table. Mrs. Jolly was dealing with her coiffure. She had set a mirror up on the table and began to comb her little curls of yellow hair and to twist them round a pencil to make them curl more tightly. Miss Dunkerley looked at her with disgust. "Four pounds five and ten makes fifteen and eleven and six —now I've got it wrong," groaned Bobbie. "I never could do sums!" "Here, give it to me," said Mrs. Jolly. "Nine pounds, fifteen," she announced a minute later. "What a pity it isn't ten pounds—I suppose you couldn't—" Bobbie looked round inquiringly at her colleagues. "No, we couldn't," said Miss Younge firmly. "You've been round to us already." "Oh come on," said Bobble pleadingly, "it's only sixpence each all round and we do want to get another two thousand pounds by Christmas." Pretending to groan, they all took out their purses and in another minute Bobbie was exulting over her ten pounds. "Now I want a nice big clean sheet of paper for the notice board," she said. "Well, that we can't give you. We've hardly enough for our own work," said Mrs. Jolly. "Go and ask Mrs. Just for some." Bobbie scampered off to Mrs. Just and came back with a very small sheet of paper. "There look what she's given me! I want a big piece."

"Bobbie, don't talk so much. Don't you know that we've got work to do," said Miss Jones reprovingly, "Can't you use the back of your last notice? Do run away, there's a good girl." Bobbie stood pouting by the side of the table and then, as everyone seemed engrossed in her work, she put a large sweet in her mouth and walked slowly up to the notice board, fetched a chair and climbing on it, reached up and unpinned the notice she had put up on Friday evening. She turned it over in her hand and looked puzzled and then rather startled.

"Oh dear! We are behind! Half-past twelve and all this pile of returns to do," said Miss Saltman. "What are we to do about Pearne and Shepley-Rice? Under which heading do suspensions go? We've never had one before?" said Mrs. Just. "Bobbie, dear, do go away; I'm desperately busy," she added, looking over her shoulder as Bobbie timidly touched her sleeve. "Let me see," said Miss Saltman tapping her desk with her pencil. "Now suspensions—Miss Whyter, *please* don't come bothering us for pieces of paper." Bobbie had come round to her side of the desk and stood, looking rather frightened, first on one foot and then on the other, with one finger in her mouth. "Please, Miss Saltman," she said in a very small voice. "I just want—"

"I've found it," said Mrs. Just. "They go into R column under 'Disciplinary Sanctions, enforced absence as a result of'." Miss Saltman sighed with relief. "That's good," she said, "All these are signed now and ready to go. Well Miss Whyter, what is it? If it's something really important, tell me quickly what it is."

Bobbie held out a sheet of paper covered in big block capitals, her "centenary" notice, the wording of which had been so much derided by Elsie. Miss Saltman glanced at it. "What about it?" she said impatiently. "It's your Spitfire notice isn't it?"

"Yes," said Bobbie slowly, "it's a bit of paper I picked off the floor when we came up from the shelter and no one would give me any clean paper for my notice. It was on the floor so I thought it wasn't any good and I used it."

"Oh, do get on," said Miss Saltman who was hardly listening to what she said. "Can't you see that we are in a hurry?"

"Ye-es," stammered Bobbie. "But, please, I think it may be the piece of paper you were all looking for. It's got something on the back." She pushed the paper into Mrs: Just's hand and ran quickly out of the room. Mrs. Just looked at it with a startled face, handed it to Miss Saltman and burst into a fit of half-hysterical laughter. "It is the Portuguese report!" she cried. "And we've all been hunting for it for hours and hours—just think of it—the Director-General—questions in the House—Scotland Yard—and all the time it has been hanging there in front of our eyes!" She gasped and took out her handkerchief and wiped her eyes, still giggling weakly. "Oh Bobbie! Dear little Bobbie! What it is to have a child playing round our feet with her dear little innocent ways!"

"Child!" said Miss Saltman. "She's forty-five if she's a day— it's arrested development—they ought not to let her stay here." She was laughing too. "I must say there is something comic about it—hanging up there and all of us in such a frightful state because it was lost—but I don't see how it got on to the floor."

"I think that's easily explained," said Mrs. Just, "There's quite a big gap at the back of Shepley-Rice's drawer which was very full and Pearne must have pushed it right through and the wind blew it about the room—you remember how draughty it was when they first boarded up the windows that day—and dear bright little Bobbie picked it up before it was missed and pinned it on the board and there it has been ever since."

Miss Saltman stopped laughing and began to look serious. "It's all very well for you to laugh," she said, "but I've got to go now and tell the D.D. what has happened. We shall become the laughing stock of the Ministry; I hope to goodness the story doesn't get into the papers. I could murder Bobbie; she had better keep out of my way. And poor little Miss Shepley-Rice. Think of the worry she has been through."

"Yes, poor kid," said Mrs. Just. "Can't we send her a telegram? And what about Pearne? She's suspended also. We ought to wire her too."

"Yes, do," said Miss Saltman. "Send each of them a telegram—though I don't think it will hurt Pearne to be kept a little in suspense."

CHAPTER TWENTY-THREE
SEBASTIAN DRINKS A TOAST

IT WAS Friday morning, a week later, nearly eleven o'clock and coffee time—but Table Two had something stronger than coffee to drink to-day. They were drinking sherry for Mrs. Jolly had smuggled in a couple of bottles so that everyone could drink Anne's health because she was going to be married that very afternoon. It was going to be a real war-time wedding, in a registry office with a special licence and only forty-eight hours' leave afterwards for the honeymoon and then back to work again on Monday. Sebastian had taken quite a firm line about it; Anne got into too many hot spots when she was out of his sight, he said, and he was now going to keep her in order and stand for no more delay and the wedding would take place at three o'clock on Friday afternoon when they both of them had their half day off.

So now everyone at Table Two, except Elsie Pearne who was away ill, was standing in a circle round Anne, drinking her health, Sebastian was there too, for he had been lured down to the section on false pretences and caught and surrounded before he could escape and made to join in the celebrations. He stood beside Anne, feeling rather stiff and embarrassed; all these old ladies were terrifying—dear kind old things—but never in his life, he thought, had he tasted anything so revolting as very sweet sherry drunk out of a bright green Woolworth bakelite mug. It had to be drunk out of those mugs, they told him, otherwise Table One would have pretended to be shocked and have started a rumour that the people at Table Two were habitual drunkards and really, after all the things that had happened lately, they had to be rather careful. Even the bottles of sherry had been emptied into the big white enamel jug to make it look as if they were drinking coffee, though Sebastian felt that Bobbie need not have carried the deception so far as to leave what he was quite sure were coffee grounds at the bottom of the jug.

Anne, hot to the back of her neck and so excited that she could hardly bear it, finished a little speech of thanks and they all cheered her as well as they could without raising their voices much above a whisper. "Thank you all so much again," said Anne, laughing and very nearly crying, just a little overcome by sherry so early in the morning. "Now let's drink to absent friends—to poor Elsie—she only came out of hospital on Wednesday—I do wish she were here!"

"Yes," said Mrs. Jolly, "let's drink to poor old Pearne, she's had rotten luck, Bobbie, is there enough sherry left for another round?"

"Oo! Yes!" squeaked Bobbie in a stage whisper. "There's nearly the whole of the second bottle. I'll put it into the jug. Half a tick!" She scampered off. "Now do tell us about poor old Pearne, Anne. When did you hear from her? She had a nasty accident, didn't she?" said Mrs. Jolly. "An accident?" said Miss Purbeck, her face brightening at once. "I'll show you her letter!" said Anne. "I thought she was rather amusing about it." She took out the letter from her bag and opened it and was just about to hand it to Mrs. Jolly. Then she took it quickly back, remembering what, in her excitement, she had forgotten—Elsie's opening sentence: "Thank God!" it ran, "I shall never have to sit again at that lousy table with that collection of mouldy old bitches! I am starting on Monday week in an absolutely first class new job—much the same sort of work that I did in Berlin."

"Er—well," said Anne, "perhaps I had better read it to you. She just says first of all that she is looking forward to being in her new job. Then she says: 'My accident was really comic. I had my tooth out with gas and I suppose it made me a bit dopey. Anyhow I fell asleep when I was waiting for some milk to heat and it boiled over and put out the gas and nearly put me out too because I didn't hear it and didn't wake up! Then it seems that the All Clear went and up comes my landlady to put the kids to bed, smells gas in the landing outside my room, grabs the kids and shoves on their gas masks and puts on her own and goes shrieking down the road to the Wardens' Post and tells them that a gas bomb has fallen in her house! So they all come running round to find it and find me instead, sound asleep and damn near passing out because the gas was escaping a few inches from my head. They carted me off to hospital and said I had carbon monoxide poisoning or something of the sort and I didn't get out till Wednesday. Now I'm staying with my aunt in the country till I start at Austen Wedlock's on Monday week. I am going to manage an office there—looking after their suppliers—just the work I am used to—so you see I've gone up in the world again. I'm sure you'll wish me luck. I shall always remember—" Anne stopped reading abruptly.

Elsie was too sentimental, she thought. "I *do* wish her luck," she said aloud. "And I'm sure you all do too. Let's drink to absent friends." Anne held out her mug to Bobbie who filled it and then went the round of the other mugs, filling Sebastian's up to the top and tipping out with the dregs of the sherry that suspicious brown substance which he had already noticed at the bottom of the jug. Sebastian braced himself and remembered that he was a man and a soldier, and that Mrs. Jolly, beaming with affection and pleasure because she had had the splendid idea of bringing the sherry to drink to dear Anne's health and happiness, was staring straight at him. With a bright, if rather fixed smile, he raised his mug and drained it to the unutterably horrible dregs, murmuring after Anne: "To absent friends—to Elsie Pearne— wishing her luck in her new job!"

THE END

FURROWED MIDDLEBROW

Printed in Great Britain
by Amazon